Call to War

BOOK 3 OF
THE GAVAN MADDOX
CHRONICLES

ALEX POLAK

Published 2020 by Your Book Angel

Copyright © Alex Polak

Printed in the United States

Edited by Keidi Keating

Layout by Rochelle Mensidor

ISBN: 978-1-7356648-8-0

This one is for Tammy and Larry.
You guys are awesome.

Note from the Author

This is a work of fiction, and no comparison is intended with any person, living or dead.

That being said, many people may find parallels with their lives and, ideally, some sense of hope or inspiration in my writing.

If you would like to talk to others about your and their enjoyment, look for my group on Facebook which I've called 'Dinas Affaraon – Followers of the Gavan Maddox Chronicles'. Come and join us, I'd love to hear from you. I once heard another author state that the worst thing a writer can do is not be in contact and listen to his or her readers, and I don't want to make that mistake.

Come and join the family, I'm always about and interacting with the group. The people there are supportive of each other, just like a true family, and we'd love to expand. You'll find out updates about the next release, I do giveaways of signed books with each new release, and I'm always happy to discuss my books.

Hope to see you there soon.

Introduction

Hi there, Gavan Maddox here. I don't know if you remember me. I'm the guy who was sent to find the Veil of Isis. I found it and it transported me to a realm I called Aaru, where I actually *met* Isis. She helped me unlock the magick I had been born with but managed to block from myself as a child, due to my own disbelief. Then I was trained in using my abilities, spending almost a year there before returning to Earth.

I also bonded to a white hawk I named Gauvain (there, you're mentioned. Happy? Now hush up while I'm talking) who became what many magick users call a familiar. When I got back to Earth I found only about ten minutes had passed, and the guy who had been chasing me was still unconscious on the floor.

Then I was forced to deal with the group who had sent me after the Veil in the first place, called The Order of the Nine Seals. They weren't particularly happy when I couldn't give them the Veil, and they didn't believe the tale I passed onto them via their intermediary.

The leader imprisoned and tortured their liaison: a woman named Angelica, in whom I had developed a passing interest. (Shut up Gauvain, I'm telling the story. Stop laughing.) The head of the Order thought she had hidden the truth from him, rather than my simply not telling her the full story. I managed to rescue her, also freeing a set of twins who had been forced to work for the Order.

The twins share one body, only separated from each other at the level of the shoulders. They each have their own neck and head. Both they and Angelica are telepaths, which was why the Order had recruited them in the first place.

Seirina, who had helped me locate the Order, had her own previous issues with them. I therefore took the escapees to her home so we could begin planning how to fight back. She turned out to be a necromancer and an enchantress who was more than three hundred years old. Over those centuries she had developed quite a few links in the magickal community. She contacted some of her acquaintances and we arranged a meeting of interested parties to build a coordinated force for our struggle against the Order, hopefully even destroying them completely in the process.

As we started the meeting another individual decided to attend via speakerphone, alerted to our plans by a unique entity called Iyrin. Iyrin is apparently something called a watcher, who has been linked to Seirina for centuries. It had also recently established a link to me, which I wasn't especially thrilled about. I had decided to ignore it for now and concentrate on the mission at hand, but I was determined to find a way to break the link somehow.

The unannounced attendee had not been fully introduced but Seirina knew him as Mr B, although she said he'd been known to many cultures by many names over the centuries. I had also felt a distinct power from him even though he was only on the phone, so he was clearly someone who wasn't to be trifled with or ignored…

Chapter 1

W hile I recapped the events since Angelica had first walked into Dinas Affaraon, the newcomers exhibited various reactions. Sovereign, the voodoo representative, merely looked politely interested during my recitation though was attentive throughout.

Dominic, the vampire, had merely seemed bored. At least until I mentioned Elrulin switching into a vampire body. *That* got his attention. Then when I mentioned about the vampire consciousness still being present and fighting against the occupation, his eyes went red and his fangs erupted in his fury.

Cheveyo, the Native American shaman, initially appeared to be almost bored. He had, however, looked both alarmed and disgusted at my mention of the windigo. Shortly after that, he seemed to realise the implications. To have a windigo to set against me, there had to be a shaman working for the Order. His eyes focused, his lips thinned in his irritation, at which point he became a lot more attentive to the discussion.

Aurora the Wiccan and Kazemde the were-sphinx, on the other hand, had been utterly captivated from the first mention of the Veil of Isis. They seemed deeply impressed that I had been the Chosen of Isis, destined to retrieve the Veil from its hiding place, and they had almost fallen to their knees in awe when they heard I had actually *spoken* with the goddess herself.

They were fascinated by my description of her, hanging on every word of my recounting of our first meeting. They sat spellbound as I shared the essentials of my time in Aaru, begging for more details each time I mentioned the goddess. They especially enjoyed my portrayal of Roman and Poppy's wedding, when I described how flamboyant Isis had become when she had been drinking.

Mr B laughed over the phone at my recollection of my first encounter with Danu, then simply listened as I went on. The only other time any sound came from the phone was when I mentioned how Atma, the head of the Order, had invaded my mind and I had also been able to access his memories. The phone transmitted a sound like an alarmed gasp, though it was quickly muffled.

There had been no noise from the terrarium behind Seirina's desk, but I could see Iyrin plastering itself against the glass in the lower corner as it heard the voice on the phone. Iyrin was out of sight of most of the room, as it seemed to have picked a spot where only I could see it. The new arrivals had glanced over when the rustling started, but quickly lost interest. They must have thought, as I initially had, that it simply contained some pet lizard or familiar.

When my little tale was done, all the representatives in attendance started arguing. There were differing views over what this new information meant, at least so far as fighting the Order was concerned. Aurora, Cheveyo, and Sovereign, were most excited by my mention of Atma's memory of being cast out of Aaru, giving us his real name. They must have realised, as Seirina and I already had, that knowing someone's true name as a magick user gave you unique ways to attack them.

What interested *me* most of all, though, was what had happened when I said that name out loud. Mr B had actually whispered it *at the same time.* I don't think anyone else had heard, except maybe Seirina, but the implications were staggering.

Had he known Elrulin in Aaru? Had he met and had dealings with him since Elrulin had been cast out? Was he the one who had *trained* Elrulin here on Earth? Why was he interested in helping us?

There was something here I was missing, and it was like a splinter in the back of my mind nagging at me. I needed to have a talk to this Mr B. No, I decided, that was Seirina's name for him. I would use Lucian (from the name 'Lucian Belphegor' Seirina had mentioned when the phone first rang), until such time as I learned any other name for him. If he was from Aaru, I had no reason to treat him with any more reverence or fear than anyone else there.

"Lucian," I began, noting the way that Seirina's eyes widened and her gaze fixed on me at my casual tone and easy use of his name, "I believe you and I need to meet in person and have a little talk. You may not want people knowing too much about you, but I think you'll agree that I am uniquely *aware* of certain things. We need to have a frank and earnest discussion about a few key points. I'll be Frank, you can be Ernest," I quipped at the end, to the further horror of Seirina but to the apparent amusement of Lucian.

"Bold of you to assume I *need* anything from any of you, Mr Maddox," came the sibilant voice from the speakerphone, once the brief chuckle had subsided. "Although you are correct. You are indeed more *enlightened* on various topics. You clearly already have certain suspicions or have made various deductions. It probably would be wiser, then, for us to talk privately."

The speakerphone clicked off and my phone vibrated in my pocket. When I checked, there was a message from an unknown number. I looked over at Seirina, deliberately avoiding the alarmed gaze from Angie, and Seirina nodded once.

"Go," she said. "We can keep discussing the information you've already provided. It's never a good idea to keep him waiting." I stood up, tipping my head to all of the assembled... delegates? That made us sound like the U.N.

More like the U.M.F.: United Magickal Factions. Maybe I should call us the *Integrated* Magickal Factions, then we could be the I.M.F. and I might be able to trick Tom Cruise into helping out! (My brain gets very weird when I'm anxious.)

Iyrin had been almost vibrating with interest across our link while Lucian was speaking. As soon as the phone disconnected, however, it disappeared back into the depths of its leafy home. Its attention shifted to our connection, ready to witness my upcoming discussion with the enigmatic Lucian.

I headed out of the study, dashing up to my room to get Gauvain and my car keys. He woke up as I came in, yawning and stretching, but he quickly focused as I sent him a rapid stream of mental images to update him on the afternoon's occurrences.

He flew to my shoulder as I grabbed my keys and we headed downstairs, ready to get to the car and set off for our rendezvous with the enigmatic Lucian. As I reached the bottom of the stairs, a familiar voice stopped me in my tracks.

"So, you're abandoning me…I mean us…again, huh?" Angelica said bitterly, standing just outside the study door. "Something interesting and potentially powerful crops up and the 'little people' get cast aside?" I could actually *hear* the sarcastic air quotes when she said 'little people', and I have to admit it stung that she thought I was that venal.

Two things stiffened my spine though: First, I hadn't abandoned her for the Veil, she'd sent me after it for the Order. Second, I hadn't abandoned her when I got back. For gods' sake, I'd made a one-man kamikaze assault on the Order's headquarters to *rescue* her when I couldn't get hold of her after my meeting. I couldn't keep apologising forever for something I didn't do.

"Look, I'm sorry again that my misreading of the Order's intentions led to your suffering," I began, wanting to set this straight before I rushed off, "but I *never* abandoned you. You sent me after the Veil in the first place, and I actually *rescued* you from the Order, if you recall. I'm going to meet someone who could potentially be our greatest ally in this fight, or at least a significant source of information. I only started doing any of this because of how the Order treated you in the first place, so if that doesn't tell you anything then I can't help you.

"I'll keep going because of all the other atrocities the Order has committed, but I'm done trying to apologise. Anyone in my position would have done the same thing; you even admitted that when we all talked after getting here that first day. You need to decide if you can separate your feelings for me from your feelings about the Order and what they did. Until then, I have other people to try to help." I was panting for breath at the end of my impassioned diatribe, and something crumbled away in my chest.

"But you left me alone after everything I went through. You never even tried to contact me to see if I was OK!" She was almost in tears at my perceived abandonment.

"Seirina refused to tell me where you were," I replied. "She said if you wanted to talk to me, you would. Otherwise I had to give you time to process what you'd been through. And in case you forgot, the mobile number I have for you doesn't work anymore. You didn't exactly try to contact me either. But fine, if it's easier for you right now, blame me. I do." So saying, my shoulders slumped in self-pity and I turned away.

Gauvain wisely said nothing as I walked down the hallway to the front door, simply gripping my shoulder a little more tightly and rubbing his cheek on the top of my head. I heard a soft sob from behind me before the study door closed but I refused to slow down.

I needed to get to my meeting with Lucian and find out exactly who and what he was, along with where he stood in this mess. I took a deep breath, screwed the lid down hard on my heart, and strode out. I resolved not to even *consider* my own feelings again until either Angelica came to me or the Order was fully defeated.

Until then, this was a war and I was a soldier. I needed to get my head in the game and stop acting like a moony schoolboy.

I unlocked the car with the remote as I approached and got in. Gauvain hopped off my shoulder onto his perch, looking across at me in silent support. I turned on the ignition and put the car into gear, manoeuvring around the two new cars in the driveway that some of our potential allies must have arrived in.

I hoped Seirina would remember to open the gate, and I tapped the horn as a quick reminder. I slowed down, and the gate swung open as I got closer. As I began to go through, a portal flared into existence just beyond the limit of Seirina's wards.

Lucian was clearly using it to bring me to him without letting me actually know where he was. At least I *hoped* that was the case, and not that Elrulin was somehow trying to snatch me up again.

Then again, I reasoned, how would he know exactly when I was leaving? Unless he had someone watching the house? But hadn't the twins and Angelica said that the Order didn't have anyone capable of this level of translocation?

I hated being smart *and* anxious. I know Iyrin had said my anxiety was because of my ability to see the various potential outcomes of any given situation, but that didn't mean I had to like it. A shit sandwich tasted bad, whichever way you sliced it!

My hesitation must have been apparent in my lack of arrival, as my phone buzzed again. I glanced at it (yes, I know, you shouldn't look at your phone while driving. I was stopped, and on private property, so give me a break) and saw a message from an unknown number again. It simply said, "It's safe", so I hoped it was referring to the portal.

I had to move anyway or the gate would close again, so I eased the car forwards. I aimed at the centre of the portal and crept along, speeding up slightly as the gate started to swing shut.

I held my breath and squeezed my eyes almost closed, keeping one eye cracked open enough to keep the car straight, and drove into the magickal gateway. I was immediately glad my eyes were almost shut as I transitioned from night into blazing sunlight. Clearly I wasn't in Yorkshire any more.

Then I saw what was ahead of me and my jaw dropped, my foot slipping off the accelerator. The car crept forwards a few more feet as it was still in gear, until I had the presence of mind to stop it and shut off the engine.

Well now, this *was* gonna be interesting...

Chapter 2

I was struggling to process exactly what I was seeing. The structure in front of me stretched upwards into the sky, making me crane my neck towards the windscreen to see the top since I was so close. It was an amalgamation of different architectural styles, as if this was the original structure from which various ancient cultures took their inspirations.

The main body of the behemoth was a step pyramid, reminiscent of the Pyramid of Kukulkan in Chichen Itza but about three or four times as high. Up the sides and on top were towers that looked like they belonged at Angkor Wat in Cambodia.

The crowns of the towers were flared like a Japanese pagoda, and there was a squarish structure at the pinnacle that was almost Aztecan. There were also stylized lion heads at various ascending intervals on the corners of the levels.

The stone should have been ancient and crumbling if it truly pre-dated those famous sites, but it was bright white with edges as sharp as if they had been quarried yesterday. As wonder dropped my jaw, the heat and humidity penetrated the car like a steam room.

I checked the rear-view mirror and saw the trees formed an almost impenetrable wall. It was clear no one had ever reached here by conventional means. The vines looping between the trunks were so dense that nothing larger than a small- to medium-sized monkey could get through. There were no breaks around the perimeter as far as I could see.

The thing that amazed me was that a structure of this size hadn't been spotted on Google Earth! The top was way above the trees, and the footprint must have been several football pitches long on each side. How the hell had it remained hidden?

Then my astonishment finally relented and allowed my brain to start working again. Clearly this place was being magickally maintained by Lucian. There was no doubt that he must have hidden it in the same way.

I'd be willing to put money on the fact that if he hadn't brought me here, I could have stood within inches of the stones and seen nothing but more trees, or possibly some large natural formation.

I wouldn't have been surprised to learn there was also some kind of psychic repellent on the location that would make people want to stay away from the area, although I must have been immune to it due to my invitation. I looked over at Gauvain and took a deep breath.

"I'm thinking we go on foot from here," I said. "I somehow doubt the car will make it up there." He chuckled in my mind.

Your astute grasp of the obvious is, as ever, remarkable, he responded, making me laugh and at least easing some of the tension. I opened the door, feeling the true extent of the oppressive warmth hit me like a blast furnace.

I held my arm out for G and he stepped on, then walked up to my shoulder. I got out and locked the car, laughing at my automatic reaction. Who on Earth was going to steal it out here? Still, the familiar act gave me a small sense of normality.

I turned to the pyramid and looked for any obvious access point. Nothing at ground level, only a narrow section in front of us with stairs instead of the giant steps that made up the rest of the pyramid's sides.

As I got closer, I saw that the stairs were actually wide enough for about six people to walk up side by side. The mammoth dimensions of the rest of the structure dwarfed them and made me feel like a fly on the side of a skyscraper. This might take a while to get up.

Then I had an idea, thinking magickally for a change.

"Dude, do me a favour and fly up there," I said to Gauvain. "I'll look through your eyes, get an image of the top of the pyramid, and teleport up. Otherwise we'll be here for hours climbing these damned stairs."

Good to see you thinking properly, he said, launching himself and spiralling upwards. *I'm glad you appreciate my superior capabilities in this situation.* I reached out mentally and saw the pyramid with him as he climbed.

His powerful wings rapidly lifted him above the structure, and we circled the area a couple of times to see if there was anything on the other side we needed to be aware of. The other faces of the pyramid were identical to the front except for the stairs. There was only one way up on foot, which made this place a veritable fortress against anyone without an invite.

It was probably an unnecessary precaution, given the magickal security already keeping everyone away, but no doubt it informed the styles of the cultures it influenced. We saw a level area at the top of the stairs, so I withdrew and transported myself there.

This close, I saw that there were Greek and Roman columns and carvings on the structure capping the pyramid. This thing must have either predated all other civilisations, or Lucian may have simply updated it as he saw cultural influences and styles he liked. Magick must make it easy to remodel at the drop of a hat.

I could maybe make some additions to Dinas Affaraon (my shop, not the city in Aaru) that could be useful. I'd have to consider that later.

Meanwhile, there was a nice big opening in front of me. Gauvain finished another circuit of the area and glided down to alight on my shoulder. I braced myself and strode forwards.

As I walked in, I saw engravings on the wall. There were Egyptian hieroglyphics, symbols in squares that I thought might be Aztec or Mayan, something that looked like Arabic script…

I couldn't read any of them, of course, but it was interesting to see how each had their own section. For all I knew, each block could be telling the same story. It would make sense that Lucian would want everyone to have the chance to know what he had to say, but I was going to have to wait to find out what that was. I couldn't see English anywhere, and I was no archaeological linguist.

The walls and ceiling seemed to give off light, as there were no burning torches or electric lighting yet I could still see where I was going. The floor sloped down gradually, then the corridor opened out into a large room.

Thankfully the stone was keeping the sun and heat out, so it was certainly more comfortable in here. The space was a huge square, and on the opposite side from the corridor I'd walked along was a raised dais.

There were two steps up to a single huge chair. Actually, 'chair' was far too prosaic a term for it. The only appropriate name for it was throne. It was a stone monolith, carved all over with various symbols that I couldn't quite make out from where I was standing.

They were accented all over with gold, which also gleamed richly from the walls of the room. My attention was totally arrested by the figure sitting upon the throne, however.

He looked so...normal, I thought in disappointment. I had been expecting someone dramatic, imposing. This guy was a little over average height, maybe five ten or eleven, with sandy coloured hair and wearing a black t-shirt, faded blue jeans with a rip at the left knee, and a pair of scuffed white sneakers.

He looked to be about my age, although my experience with Seirina made me aware that he could be much older. Clearly, if she had known him as long as she said, he must be. If my suspicions were right, he would be much, *much* older.

As if he knew exactly what I was thinking, he cocked his head and lifted the corner of his mouth subtly. I couldn't feel him inside my mind, but that didn't mean he wasn't aware of my thoughts.

"Lucian?" I asked politely, still remembering the power I had felt when he was on the phone. I wasn't prepared to be flippant or worse until I knew precisely who, and what, I was dealing with.

"Indeed, although that is merely one name I have used. As you have no doubt deduced, that is not my original, true name. Cultures over the centuries have referred to me by many labels."

Yup, definitely older then he looked.

"Let me see if I can guess some of the others," I said, preparing to take a wild intuitive leap and use some of the information I'd picked up during my years of magickal research. "Iblis? Damballa? Samael? Belial? Serpent?" He smiled wider, making me realise I was on the right track. There were literally dozens, even hundreds, of other possibilities, but four sprang to mind as the most well-known and significant – at least to me.

"Mephistopheles, Beelzebub, Satan, Lucifer?" I said these last in quick succession and he nodded, devolving into full-on laughter as I finished.

Confirming exactly who I was facing definitely raised my pucker factor by – at a conservative estimate – about a billion, and I almost turned to sprint out. Only the knowledge that we needed powerful allies and *he* had contacted *us*, then inviting me here, kept my feet in place.

"Let me guess, not exactly how you envisioned me?" he said, once his laughter stopped. "Would you like a more...*traditional* image?" So saying, his outline began to flicker and I saw the ghost of a much bigger form with horns and goat feet begin to take shape – the ancient 'Devil' based on Pan, the form Satanists and the Roman Catholic Church had used for centuries.

"No, no!" I blurted out, throwing my hands forwards and sending Gauvain soaring off my shoulder. "Really, I'm good. The average Joe look actually suits you!" He laughed once more, ceasing his transition and appearing once again as the guy I'd first seen.

"Thank you," I said, genuinely grateful he hadn't continued shifting. I think coming face-to-face with the physical embodiment of the Devil would have been too much for me, and probably left me gibbering in a corner. "I guess none of those are who you really are. So if Isis is real, does that make you Anubis?" I asked.

"Surely you must realise that Isis is not her real name?" he said. "I seriously doubt that anyone in Aaru trusted you enough to give you their *true* name. Even if you proved yourself a decent man, you *are* still human at the end of the day. To them, giving you their true names would be like you handing a chimp a rocket launcher and then standing right in front of it."

I was a little taken aback by his abrupt insult, but I could see his point. Whatever they truly were, be it gods, angels, demons, even aliens, they had vastly longer lifespans than us along with powers most humans couldn't even imagine. I now had many of those abilities, although I was completely new to them and was still stumbling along compared to them, but that didn't mean they had to fully trust me.

I nodded to him, and he looked surprised that I hadn't immediately taken offence and started yelling at him. His gaze turned shrewd and calculating, assessing me more intently than he had initially.

"So what should I call you?" I ventured, immediately sure that I wasn't going to use 'my Lord' or 'Dark One'.

"Lucian will do for now," he replied with another smile, no doubt thinking of all the titles that had been lavished on him in the past. He waved a hand and another chair, comfortable but certainly less ornate than his own, appeared at the bottom of the dais steps.

"Let's talk."

Chapter 3

I walked forwards carefully, keeping my eyes on the being in front of me. He was clearly at least as old as Isis, since Judaism was around four thousand years old and they had stories of the Devil in the Torah.

I reached the chair he had manifested for me and looked at it. Then I looked at him, up on his dais. Then back at the chair. Then back at him, with an eyebrow cocked up and my head tilted. I didn't say anything, simply crossed my arms.

He laughed uproariously and slapped his knee, leaning forwards and bracing his elbows on his knees.

"I'm sorry," he gasped out finally. "It's been so long since I spoke to anyone who truly knew who and what I was. I got used to dealing from a position of power rather than talking to an equal. Not that I think of you as such, but you're certainly closer than anyone I've met in a long time."

"Does that include Elrulin?" I asked, still not sitting down. "He got kicked out of Aaru by Isis and the other council members for murdering children, then *somehow* he learned more advanced magick. I *wonder* how he managed to do that?" I continued sarcastically.

He actually looked sheepish at that. His smile slipped away and he closed his eyes, took a deep breath and shook his head slowly.

"I felt him arrive when he was expelled," he said sadly. "I had been here for millennia already, so I thought I could help him."

"But you must have realised that him being cast out meant he'd committed murder, or at least been abusing his magick enough to fall foul of the council's rules!" I yelled. I was astounded that he'd been so short-sighted as to offer assistance to what was, in effect, a newly convicted and punished criminal!

I stood there with my mouth open in disbelief at his sheer stupidity, eventually reaching over and sliding into the chair next to me. I completely ignored the height disparity in my concern over the more egregious error being discussed.

Gauvain landed on the back of the chair but didn't relax. I could feel his disquiet and tension mirroring my own, rebounding back and forth between us.

Lucian sighed and nodded, finally opening his eyes again and looking up towards me. He winced slightly at the indignant accusation in my eyes, which struck me as totally surreal: I was sitting here scolding *the fucking Devil himself* for his poor choices!

The freakish situation seemed utterly hilarious, and I struggled to keep a straight face. My lips quirked despite my best efforts, and the laughter bubbled up. He looked confused at my change in attitude, so I explained myself.

Lucian snorted into laughter as well, and our combined mirth fed off of each other until we were both gasping for breath.

"Jesus Christ!" I exclaimed, in disbelief at the absurdity of the situation.

"Nope, that was *definitely* not one of my names," he deadpanned, prompting another surge of mutual hilarity.

"'You're not the Messiah; you're a very naughty boy!'" I misquoted in a particular angry, high-pitched, raspy voice. He immediately caught the Monty Python reference and roared again, slapping the arm of his throne.

Soon enough we both calmed down, the gravity of the situation reasserting itself, and we each took a few deep, calming inhalations.

"I haven't laughed like that in centuries." He sighed, leaning back. His dais had lowered into the floor as we were laughing, and now we were level with each other.

"Well that was a great ice-breaker and tension release," I remarked, catching my breath and sitting back in my chair. "However, it doesn't change the fact that you took a proven murderer under your wing and taught him even *more* ways to use his power, giving him even *more* incentive to steal the energy from others. So let's take this from the beginning, shall we?" I crossed my ankles, interlaced my fingers and waited, ready to hear what I was sure was a tale no one else had ever heard.

"You already deduced, that I was cast out millennia ago. Over that time my stories have been corrupted, though I will freely acknowledge I was going down a dark path," Lucian began, sitting back in his chair and mirroring my posture. "I had learned the advanced magickal techniques and been told that further development would come through practice and experimentation.

"Back then, I wasn't the best at using elemental energy. As you've no doubt discovered yourself, vital or life energy is significantly more potent. It's also much easier to access."

I recalled my own early failures with elemental energy. I said nothing, however, fearing to interrupt his tale.

"I started drawing from others in my impatience to find new techniques and abilities. I eventually caused my closest friend significant harm, although fortunately he didn't die. I was brought before the council and warned to stop my experiments, but I was young and impetuous.

"I was caught drawing energy from others again not long after that and cast out. My crime wasn't as severe as Elrulin's, so I was allowed to take form. I was forbidden to return, though, and for centuries I wandered Earth pissed off at my situation.

"I knew many of my people came here periodically, often finding their way into local mythologies and legends as gods, heroes, even monsters. I decided to carve out a similar niche for myself, setting myself in opposition to them for obvious reasons.

"If there were humans struggling and my kind merely watched, I taught the primitive people what I felt they had been denied. Hence the legends of the Devil teaching beautifying of eyelids and making things, or of Prometheus bringing fire. Since I was opposing those viewed as gods, I came to be viewed as 'evil'.

"The facts were embellished and altered with each retelling, becoming the twisted legends you now know. Thus everything I had taught became evil. Pride in one's appearance and desire for material things became 'deadly sins'.

"I became 'The Prince of Darkness' from whom all evil arose, and somehow they got the idea that all wicked men were condemned to an afterlife of eternal torment at my hand. It was the most outrageous form of telephone (or in this case, celestial) whispers I'd ever experienced.

"After being here for a millennium or so, my anger cooled and I became more pragmatic about my situation. I started trying to simply make my own way, as it were, no longer trying to upset the apple-cart at every turn.

"Once I looked at humans as individuals, rather than merely a means to take out my frustrations against my own kind, I started to see the charm in your species. Eventually, inevitably, I fell in love. I spent over forty years with her, falling into a deep depression when she died." He fell silent for a while. His chin sunk onto his chest, clearly remembering the woman who had captured his heart.

"I've fallen in love several more times over the years, each time experiencing the pain of loss at the end, though learning more and more about the value of life. I understood how wrong I had been in my behaviour, finally coming to agree that the council had been right to exile me.

"When I sensed Elrulin being cast onto this plane, I realised he must have been on that same path. I had no idea just how far down it he'd gone, though. I wanted to save him my centuries of struggle, so I offered to teach him what I had learned.

"I recounted for him the nobility of spirit I had witnessed among humans in their darkest hours, and the purity I had felt in their souls. I never imagined he would view that as a new source of power. He seemed to listen to what I said, so I started helping him with his magick as well.

"One day, he entered the room I was in and I turned to greet him. Instead of the ball of energy he had been up to that point, he stood there encased in the flesh of a young man from the nearby village. I reached towards his mind and discovered the twistedness you experienced when he reached for you." Lucian's eyes grew dark, he furrowed his brow, and hints of the devilish visage he had earlier shown shimmered in sinister fashion momentarily, clearly forced up by his disappointment and anger at his erstwhile apprentice.

I shifted nervously in my seat, drawing his attention, at which he veiled his fury from me once again. He resumed the tale as if nothing had happened, though the image was burned into my memory.

"I think it had something to do with his taking possession of a human body; he had to find his way past the flesh, which required more effort than he was used to. He tasted his first soul and became addicted to the power it had provided.

"He decided to try and use that power in an attempt to break back into our home dimension – what you call Aaru. I sent him away, disgusted by the direction he was taking and refusing him any further teaching or help, then watched as he set up his 'Order of the Nine Seals'.

"He learned of the legend of the Veil of Isis, immediately deciding it was his ticket home. He searched in vain, none of his minions able to locate it. Eventually he started sending anyone he could, which is where you finally joined the narrative."

He finished his tale and waved his hand, manifesting a table between us complete with two crystal glasses and a bottle of Ardbeg 1965. He reached over and poured for both of us, then tapped my glass with his own and sipped. I tasted my dram, then looked in wonder at my drink.

He chuckled at my expression.

"When you're around as long as me, you can pick up some pretty nice vintages!"

"If this is anything to go by," I replied, "I'd love to take a tour of your wine cellar when all this is over. Maybe we can have a whiskey, wine and cheese evening." He smiled, and I continued. "For now, though, we need to focus on bringing your protégé down. How can you help us, and what do you want in return?"

"Well first off, let me make one thing absolutely clear: I won't fight. I have no intention of stepping in like some avenging angel – or demon, given my history – and simply wiping out your enemies. This is *your* fight, not mine.

"I can offer knowledge and advice; I can show you some more advanced techniques you didn't have time to learn from your teachers; I might even be able to track down a couple of other...let's call them 'entities' who have been hiding to avoid being bothered or snatched up by the Order. But that's it. Think of me more in a support role. No direct conflict.

"As for what I want, that's much easier. I want you to speak to Isis on my behalf, vouch for the fact that I've changed. All I want is a chance to show her what I have learned and how it has affected me."

Now his side of the bargain made sense. He had been exiled from his home for over four thousand years, alone. He wanted contact with his own kind, and to show that he had learned from his mistakes. Show that he was no longer the adolescent hot-head who had broken the rules all those millennia ago. It was a reasonable request, but at the same time quite a big thing to ask.

He wanted me to stand up and say, to a *god,* that he really had changed and deserved another chance. Yet all he was going to do was essentially a little light tutoring, *maybe* some matchmaking, and basically be a cheerleader? This was feeling kinda lopsided, and I definitely wasn't on the good side of the deal.

"Ahh," I exclaimed, thinking fast. "Now I understand. This has nothing to do with you *actually* wanting to help at all, does it? It's a means to an end for you. You're still only thinking about yourself after all, aren't you? After all your protestations of enlightenment, it's still all about what you can get from others. Maybe not their energy any more – you *have* learned that at least – but you're still the same selfish a-hole who got himself exiled!"

Chapter 4

I'd been trying to rile him to see if he would get angry, reacting like the Devil he'd been portrayed as, though I now worried I'd gone too far. His face darkened and his hands gripped the arm rests of his throne. I felt him gathering power, and he looked like he was about to attack me.

I braced myself and reached towards the power stored in Seren, but deliberately didn't move.

Just as I thought my little speech might have worked, he relaxed. He sat back in his chair with an assessing look on his face, then the corner of his mouth twitched up.

"Nice try," he said, regarding me with a new look of appraisal. "You're not getting me that easily. I have to say, it's been a number of centuries since anyone's tried to push my buttons quite that hard. Fortunately for you, I *have* actually learned a few things.

"Back then, I'd have simply incinerated you where you sat for that display of impertinence. Now, however, not only am I somewhat calmer and more reasonable, I am also willing to try to see things from your point of view.

"I will allow that from your side, I am taking little to no risk and have everything to gain from my proposed arrangement. Still, you must allow that this is, in fact, your war and not mine. Also, you are currently unaware of both what I can teach you, and exactly *who* and *what* I can bring to your aid."

Now it was my turn to nod in consideration. After millennia, I was quite sure he had knowledge, resources and contacts I couldn't even dream of. Even if they weren't the demons of religious legend.

"Fair enough," I allowed, "but I still think this deal is significantly weighted in your favour. If your contacts are hiding from the Order and we win, they'd be able to stop hiding and live their lives; and they'd have you to thank for that, at least in part, so you stand to gain even more favours in the future."

Lucian stared at me, clearly impressed.

"I think you need to sweeten my side, especially if I'm going to be taking all the risk. Not only in the fighting, but then in talking to Isis and the council on your behalf."

I crossed my arms and looked at him. Gauvain, who had been sitting quietly on the back of my chair while we had been talking, began preening my hair in silent approval.

Lucian, on the other hand, looked thoughtful, clearly considering what else he might offer to level out the two sides of the equation. Suddenly, he smiled and looked straight in my eyes.

"I have the perfect thing!" he said, actually snapping his fingers. I had to smother my eye roll and smirk at the clichéd movement. "While I currently have all external links blocked, I know you have at least one to an individual who established that link for their own ends, not yours."

I immediately thought of a certain creepy little skeletal fucker, remembering its eyes as it licked my essence off of its finger.

"I can educate you regarding the individual, possibly giving you certain advantages in your dealings."

Even though the link was apparently suppressed in his home, Lucian still spoke in nebulous possibilities. That alone gave me some idea of the potential power of the being in question, in which case I could use all the help and information I could get.

I sighed, trying to act as though I was reluctant to accept a deal that was only *barely* approaching a level playing field. I doubted he would be fooled, but I couldn't appear to be too eager. This was a chess game with a being who had been honing his skills for generations.

"Fine," I grumbled, "I guess that kinda brings things a little closer to even. So now what?" I continued, wanting to get things finalised so

I could get back to Serina's. I was acutely conscious that everyone would be waiting to hear what I had learned.

"Do we memorialise our deal in blood, written in ancient Aramaic on a lambskin?"

Lucian sighed and rolled his eyes, shaking his head at *my* cliché this time.

"Hysterical," he drawled. "Your wit is truly dazzling."

Gauvain sniggered in my head and I joined him, sounding like a couple of naughty schoolkids.

"We shake hands, swearing on our power to abide by the terms of the deal."

I sat forwards, feeling a tug as the strand of hair G was preening pulled due to my unexpected movement. I knew of this kind of magickal pact from my reading, but I'd never performed one myself before.

Lucian recited the particulars we had discussed, and I paid careful attention to ensure he didn't change the descriptions to give himself a loophole to wriggle out through.

He listed everything accurately, even making my side of the deal a promise to *attempt* to stand witness for him to Isis; and that only *after* he fulfilled all of his conditions.

Then he had me reach for my power, as I sensed him reaching for his. We grasped wrists and swore to abide by the terms of our deal, at which I felt something settle around my shoulders like a scarf.

The sensation lasted for a moment, then eased, leaving an awareness of yet another link. This one was more of a sense of familiarity, however, not anything approaching my link to Gauvain or Iyrin.

I looked deep into Lucian's eyes and saw true gratitude there, at least as far as I could tell. I was probably the first, in his entire lonely exile, who had been in a position to help him in this way. Even for an immortal, four thousand years was one hell (pun intended) of a long time to be without one's own kind.

"How can I contact you?" I asked, eager to get on now that our deal was made. "Also, when were you planning on teaching me these new techniques? And how much can I tell the others?"

"I'll text you in a couple of days so we can sort out a time. The text will include my number this time, so you'll have it. Now that you've been here, I grant you access for future visits, either via teleporting or by portal. Just think of the pyramid. I'll get hold of my 'acquaintances' in the meantime.

"As for the others, you can tell them what I'm going to be doing to help you, but I'd appreciate if you'd keep my origins to yourself. That means you'll also need to keep your side of the arrangement quiet. It's none of their business anyway, and I don't exactly want everyone knowing my past mistakes. I prefer to keep the mystery and the legend, so feel free to share some of my more...*notorious* names with them."

He laughed at his comment and I joined in, thinking of the expressions when I told the group that I had gone out on a limb to make a deal with the Devil himself on their behalf. Talk about putting yourself on the line! If that didn't prove how much I was prepared to risk for them, nothing would. It might even be enough to seal the alliance.

I thanked him again and called Gauvain, who flew over to my shoulder. I promised to keep my phone close, said goodbye, and teleported myself back to the car. I got in, G hopping over to his perch as I did, and then focused on the gate to Seirina's house.

I extended my awareness to include the car and transported us back. I lowered the window and pressed the intercom, imagining the uproar that was about to happen.

"Aye, wha' d'ye want?" came a familiar Scottish voice finally.

"I want to tell you what I found out," I said simply, laughing as I heard the surprised squawk through the speaker.

"Gavan?" The accent disappeared but the octaves definitely jumped up. "Is that you?"

"Yup," I replied. Thinking to prove it before she asked, I added, "The same guy who fell on his ass in shock when you offered to be mine forever." I heard her "Humph" at the memory, along with an outraged "WHAT?" from the background.

The gate clicked and swung open so I drove through, slightly slower than normal until I traversed the ward boundary. I negotiated the parked cars, showing that everyone was indeed waiting to hear my tale. As expected Mrs Wilson opened the door before I could knock.

"Oh, Mr Maddox," she exclaimed, "did you forget something?"

I furrowed my brow at her question.

"Erm, no…" I replied, "I've been away, had my meeting, and come back." I had a sneaking suspicion of what had happened.

These Aaruans were always futzing with time, and I had no doubt that Lucian was quite capable of creating a time distortion within his home. That was definitely going to be one of the techniques on my list to learn from him. Her next words confirmed my supposition.

"But you've only been out of the house for ten minutes!" she objected. I sighed, slowly shaking my head a couple of times.

"They do say time is subjective," I quipped, at which she gave me a very old-fashioned look. Something about the whole ten minutes thing tickled my memory, then I realised: That was how long my sojourn in Aaru had lasted in Earth time. Was that significant somehow?

"Fine, keep your secrets." She smiled. "They're obviously all still in the study. I guess I should be used to odd occurrences and comments after all these years…" I heard her mumble as she walked down the hall ahead of me, and I smiled fondly. I could understand why Seirina kept her around. I would have to be careful not to get too comfortable here.

I reached the study door, took a deep breath, squared my shoulders and walked in.

Chapter 5

Everyone was facing the door as I stepped into the room, clearly alerted to my return by Seirina's answering of the gate intercom. The level of disappointment was almost comical, as clearly they all thought that my trip had gone precisely nowhere.

"Wow," I said, "the level of confidence in here is simply staggering. Glad to see you all have such faith in me, and in our potential ally." The amount of shifting in chairs spoke volumes.

"You know, if you're not going to trust each other, this whole undertaking is doomed to failure before we even start," I continued, deciding to find out here and now if there was any point in continuing. Better not to lose lives in an ill-fated enterprise.

"I think we're all just a little...*surprised*...to see you back so soon," Serina said.

I knew I had to give them an explanation, but I was well aware of 'Lucian's' request to obscure his *true* origins. I decided to use his mythical Earth legend, since it would probably be quite intimidating and would therefore reduce the likelihood of too many probing questions.

"Well, your 'Mr. B' turned out to be a little more than you were aware of," I told Serina. "I know you call him that, but you were right that he had other names. Would you like to hear some of them?" Everyone leant forward in their chairs.

I looked over at Sovereign. "You might know him as 'Mighty Damballa'," I told her. Up to that point, I had no idea a skin as dark as hers had the ability to pale so dramatically. I moved on to Kazemde. "As an Egyptian, Set would probably be most appropriate." To Cheveyo, "I'm afraid I haven't studied much Native American lore, but maybe Coyote would suffice?"

As I spoke, those who understood the significance of each name looked shocked in their turn. I knew my next words would seal everyone's suspicions. "To those who haven't got it yet, how about Satan, Lucifer, or Beelzebub?"

When I used those ubiquitous names, everyone's thoughts were confirmed and the facial expressions were almost comical. I had to struggle not to laugh, being closer to the truth of who he really was and remembering the amusement we had shared.

Then for some reason, a tiny voice in the back of my head reminded me that most legends have their basis in fact. Maybe I shouldn't abandon my natural anxiety quite so eagerly. He had offered to help, but it *was* in return for something he wanted. Plus, he was a renowned master of the contractual loophole. I was going to have to keep my wits about me when I was dealing with him.

"So you're saying you went and spoke to…" Aurora looked like she was trying to back away *through* her chair, so I smiled reassuringly.

"Let's just say we were able to come to a…" I tried to come up with an appropriate term. "A mutually beneficial arrangement," I finished, attempting to appear more relaxed than I felt. Dominic leant even farther forward, putting his elbows on his knees and his fangs erupting in his excitement.

"Are you telling us you *literally* made a deal with the Devil?" he asked, sounding impressed for the first time since he had arrived. Then again, vampires thought of themselves as evil. I guess the purported father of evil, ol' Scratch himself, would be his ultimate boss.

"So exactly what kind of hole have you dug for us with him?" Seirina asked, practical as ever.

"Don't worry, I made sure I was the only one responsible for our side of the bargain," I reassured her, "and even that's only *after* he helps us out."

Angelica looked at me squarely for the first time since I'd returned.

"I still don't get how you were able to get to him, talk, hammer out an agreement, and then get back, all in ten minutes," she said.

"I guess when you've been around for more than four thousand years, you pick up a trick or two," I remarked calmly, refusing to rise to her baiting. "He admitted he taught Elrulin when he first got cast out." *That* got their attention. "That's probably where the scummy little shitbag learnt some of his more advanced abilities."

Everyone went quiet, and I could almost hear the gears turning. Help from the individual who taught Elrulin could reveal weaknesses, give pointers on how he thought, maybe uncover a way to take him down.

Dangerous or not, we looked to benefit significantly if he came through. Plus, since the deal I had made rested squarely on *my* shoulders, they had nothing to lose and everything to gain.

I could see variations of the same thought process running behind almost every set of eyes in the room. The only exception was Angie, who had simply looked away and refused to turn back.

My heart shrivelled a little more, but I reminded myself of my resolution from when I had left. No personal entanglements until this shit was done. I screwed the lid back down on my emotions and looked around at the others, ignoring Seirina's look of sympathy.

As the web-head was fond of remembering, 'With great power comes great responsibility,' and I seriously doubted Isis had given me mine as a dating tool. There was always Tinder; maybe Craigslist if I got *really* desperate.

Nah, even self-winding was better than that. You never knew *what* you could pick up on the internet.

Gradually they all seemed to come to the conclusion I had already reached – namely, that they would be foolish to refuse the opportunity. They all apparently had reasons to hate the Order, which was why they had agreed to this little summit meeting in the first place. Between my new abilities, help from the Devil himself, and inside knowledge from the members I had already liberated, they would never be in a better position to strike at the heart of the organisation they so despised.

As they made their decisions, they began to look at each other and I saw heads bobbing. They sat straighter and prouder, hope shining through their eyes. Cheveyo spoke up for the first time since he had arrived.

"Obviously, we are only here to represent our various peoples," he began, surprising me with the depth of his tone. His voice had an almost resonant quality that clearly surprised many of the others, if the expressions were anything to go by. "We'll have to go back and talk to our respective groups, but I think I can safely say we'll be with you in this."

The other delegates nodded, and I felt such consolation at the knowledge that I wasn't alone in this, my throat tightened. I swallowed convulsively to ease it, then met everyone's eyes in turn.

"I know you all have your reasons for being here, and I have no intention of prying into your personal pain, but I want to express my thanks," I said to them all. "I want to promise you all that I'll be in this to the end, either the Order's or mine, and I will do my utmost to justify your faith in me." Kazemde looked approvingly at me, and many of the others smiled as well.

"I think we should agree to meet again in a week," I went on, "to give you all a chance to liaise with your people, then we can work out precisely how many are willing to fight and how best to split them up. We can then start to actually plan our assaults on the various sites around the UK.

"America will be last, I think, given it is apparently being set up as the new site for their headquarters. From what Angelica and the twins have said, it's an isolated location that's easily defended and popular with some of the more monstrous Order members. I think we'll need everyone together for what will hopefully be the Order's last stand."

As I started laying out my strategy, expressions around the circle became more intense. There was a palpable resolve in the room, and I even saw Iyrin incline its skull out of the corner of my eye.

Gauvain's approval washed across our bond, and his meant more to me than anyone else's.

"While you're all having your individual powwows..." I realised what I'd said and faced Cheveyo to try to extract my size twelves out of my mouth. "Sorry, Cheveyo, no offence meant, it's just a common expression..."

He smiled at my discomfort and stumbling apology. "Don't worry," he reassured me, "I quite like the fact that such terms are in common use. It means my culture hasn't been quite as obliterated as the invaders attempted. It's not a derogatory term, so there's no offense or need to apologise."

I bowed my head in gratitude and continued.

"Yes, so, while you're all talking to your people, I'll contact Lucian again to see what he can teach me. With his time distortion abilities, I'll probably be able to learn what I need by then anyway. Then we can have our war council. It's summer now," I concluded, "let's hope that we can have a truly happy new year without the Order in our lives!"

Chapter 6

Everyone stood up, saying their goodbyes and shaking hands. I had a thought about the next meeting and spoke up before everyone left.

"If everyone's willing, I'll set up portals next time to bring you here. It'll save time and travel, plus there's less chance of you being followed. I'll need a photo of where you are, so I can teleport to you and then open a doorway back here." The five newcomers stared at me, making me realise I hadn't told them I was capable of such an advanced ability. They soon recovered, seeing the benefits of what I suggested, and agreed.

"Since you came here by conventional means this time, it's best to go back the same way. That way, if anyone *has* tracked you, you can always say you came here but weren't interested in what we discussed. The subterfuge will only have to stand scrutiny for a week or so, after which the fighting might kinda give the game away."

My touch of humour lightened the mood and got a couple of chuckles, then the five liaisons headed for the front door. I could hear Mrs Wilson showing them out, so I slumped back into my chair in relief again. I have allies, thank God!

My unconscious use of the term made me think. If 'Satan' was an exaggerated legend, *were* there actually 'gods'; or even more, capital G 'God'? My head hurt even considering the possibilities.

I decided it was something I could look into if I came through the upcoming conflict intact. I apparently had a significantly extended lifespan ahead of me, so such metaphysical and philosophical investigations would be an interesting way to fill a few centuries.

But that was for later. For right now, what I really needed was a good night's sleep. From my perspective, it was about three in the morning. Maybe once I learned how to create temporal distortions myself, I'd be less susceptible to the lag effect. Until then, it was kicking my ass.

I said my goodnights and headed upstairs. Until our next meeting, we were in something of a holding pattern. I brushed my teeth and got ready for bed.

Gauvain decided to sleep snuggled up like we had in Aaru, wanting to be close after the events of tonight. I lay down and he crowded up against my chin, then he was soon asleep.

My head was still spinning with all the revelations from the meetings; both with the delegates, and then with the Devil himself. Nothing like an interview with a legendary figure to mess with your head, right?

My whirling brain eventually turned my thoughts into dreams and I fell into a somewhat troubled sleep, imagining potential futures and battles.

★

I woke up to find that my disturbed sleep had caused G to fly back to his perch. I was laying across the bed, my head hanging over the edge and a crick in my neck as a result. Nothing like a good night's sleep to refresh you!

I yawned and stretched, then went to get a shower. The hot water at least unwound my neck muscles, and my toothbrush finished making me feel at least somewhat human again. I got dressed and headed downstairs for the ultimate morning power potion: coffee.

I stopped in surprise in the doorway to the kitchen, seeing that the table was already occupied. Apparently the twins and Angie had stayed last night, rather than heading back to their temporary lodgings, and they were currently having breakfast with Seirina.

After my epic failure with Angie last night, and my resultant resolution to ignore my feelings, I decided instead to head outside for some fresh air. I'd get coffee later, when the coast was clear. Yes, OK, call me a coward if you like. I prefer to say that discretion is the better part of valour.

I turned away, only Mrs Wilson having seen me, and headed down the hall to the front door. I couldn't go out the back, since I'd have to go through the kitchen to get to it. I stepped out, Gauvain soaring down the stairs and over my shoulder as I did. His wing ruffled my hair as he went past, and he wheeled up to the limits of the wards to spiral back down.

I closed the door quietly, then simply breathed in the morning air. Watching G's aerobatics calmed me and restored my good humour. I hoped that Lucian wouldn't take too long to get back to me, since I wanted to learn as much as possible from him before the next war council.

Now that I'd made the decision to fight, I wanted to get on with it and have it over and done with as soon as possible, so I could go back to living my life. After all, no matter how dramatic all this was becoming, I still had a business to run and bills to pay.

That reminded me, it had been a couple of days since I'd checked in with Summer. I pulled my mobile out of my back pocket and rang the shop.

"Dinas Affaraon, how can I help you today?" Summer's relaxed tone immediately confirmed that everything was safe and normal, at least in some part of my life. A reflexive smile lit up my face.

"You just did," I replied, chuckling. "I wanted to say hi and check you were alright. No more unwanted lurkers outside."

"Gav!" she shrieked right in my ear, making me jerk the phone away before I was deafened. "What's going on? Have you had your meeting? What happened? Who was there? What's next? How long d'you think it'll all take? When will you be back? Have you worked things out with Angelica? Have you slept together yet?"

Her typical machine-gun delivery had me laughing at first, although I winced at her last couple of questions. I already knew that she'd say it was all my fault, so wasn't particularly relishing my up-coming ass-chewing.

"The meeting was last night," I started, trying to take her list in order, "and it actually went OK. There were five delegates, each of a different magickal faction, and they agreed to join together to fight the Order. We're meeting again in a week, once they've spoken to their people, to plan things in detail.

"I want to get it done as soon as we can, precisely so I can come back to the shop. If you can believe it, I'm actually missing the simple act of paying bills. I'd like my life to return to something approaching normality as soon as possible."

I stopped there, hoping she might focus on what I *had* said, rather than what I hadn't. That hope lasted about two seconds. I should have known better, having been around her for all these years.

"Great," she said, sounding pleased that things were looking positive so far. "And the Angelica side of things?"

Bollocks, the woman was like a missile; once she was locked on to something, there was no shaking her.

"Um, she's still getting over what happened..." Once again, partial truth was easier than full disclosure. "I'm giving her some time and space, although I *have* told her I'm here for her. Better not to rush her." I crossed my fingers and held my breath, hoping she'd accept my answer and let it go.

"Hmm, that's probably a good idea. Especially given what you said she went through," she replied thoughtfully. "You went in and rescued her, so she'll know how you feel; I'm sure she'll come 'round soon enough."

I released my breath, and hoped she was right.

"Everything else OK?" I changed the subject, and fortunately she went with it. "Any problems?"

"Well, there were a couple of people who looked like your protection spells were keeping them out the day after you escaped, but that's it." A chill ran up my spine at her innocent comment. Thankfully, my precautions seemed to have worked. Those wards were definitely going to be a permanent fixture now.

"Glad that's been it. I'll keep in touch. Hug Emily for me, and make sure to get yourselves a nice bottle of fizz with the weekend groceries from me." I said goodbye and hung up, feeling better after having checked on my friend.

Gauvain swooped down and landed on my shoulder. Via our link he was aware of my conversation. We stood for a moment, simply enjoying the sunshine, then I turned to go back inside. Occupied or not, I was heading into the kitchen. I needed my caffeine!

Chapter 7

Thankfully for the sake of my sanity and my addiction, the ladies had left the kitchen. Mrs Wilson held out a mug with a smile.

"I saw you earlier," she remarked. "I knew you'd be back when the coast was clear. I've not known you to miss out on your coffee yet."

I chuckled softly, inhaling the aroma of Cafegeddon thankfully and sighing in relief.

"You're truly a treasure, Mrs Wilson," I said. "Has anyone ever tried to steal you away from Seirina?" Inexplicably, she suddenly looked absolutely terrified.

"Oh, I could never leave!" she said in alarm. Something was very off here, in a way I never expected. I had made a throw-away joke and she was petrified. What exactly was I missing?

"I was only joking, Mrs Wilson," I reassured her. "No one's going to make you leave." Again, the relief on her face was way out of proportion to the situation. Since I was stuck waiting for Lucian to call me, this little mystery was exactly what I needed to keep my mind off more sensitive topics.

"If I could ask," I queried gently, "what made you so upset? I hope you know by now that I would never do anything to hurt you."

"Of course," she said, looking relieved but still somewhat secretive. "It's just, I've been with Ms Crow for so long. We've bonded in unusual ways," she explained, although her story was so superficial as to reveal almost nothing. I nodded, though I decided to speak to Seirina to try to get a fuller picture.

I finished my coffee and handed the mug back to Mrs Wilson, smiling in reassurance. She weakly returned the expression, then I left to see if I could catch up with Seirina. Hopefully, the twins and Angie had headed out while I was in the kitchen, as I didn't fancy another to-do this morning.

Even my limited male brain realised no woman wanted to be told she was less important than something else, especially by the guy who had expressed feelings for her in the past.

Gauvain chuckled in my head.

Indeed, if you plan to have a conversation of that nature, please forewarn me, so that I might make myself scarce.

I snorted in agreement.

"Turncoat, coward, bloody chicken!" I groused, much to his ongoing amusement.

I believe your eyesight may need assessing, he joked, *and you may need some corrective lenses if you consider me to be similar in appearance to barnyard poultry.* He posed with his beak raised and his eyes closed in self-appreciation, and I had to laugh.

Which was when the study door opened and I came face to face with Angelica. The laughter died in my throat, and I stepped aside so she could get through the door first. I tipped my head but said nothing, as I had no idea what the right words would be.

I heard Gabby and Izzy asking what was wrong from behind her, so she walked out of the room and turned away from me to head towards the front door. The twins stepped out and caught sight of me.

"Oh," said Gabby.

"Indeed," said Izzy.

"That seemed a little uncomfortable."

"It certainly did."

"We thought he had feelings for her."

"That's certainly the way it appeared previously."

"Though she's been quite distressed since we got away."

"She's definitely been suffering some reaction to her experiences."

"She certainly seems to have been through some trauma at Atma's... I mean *Elrulin's* hands."

"But Gavan put himself at significant risk to get us all out."

"He definitely showed how much he felt for her."

"Even Seirina picked up on his feelings for her."

"She didn't seem in any doubt, you're right."

"We were expecting a different kind of reunion yesterday."

"Absolutely."

"But it didn't happen."

"No, they seem to be very strained."

"He doesn't seem particularly happy with the situation."

"She doesn't seem to be wanting to give him a chance anymore."

"Mind you, she's still grieving over what happened to her mother."

"That must have been hard, especially after losing her father to cancer."

I froze, hearing what the twins must have learnt when they scanned Angelica before we escaped the holding cells. The twins realised they were speaking out loud and clapped a hand over each of their mouths.

Angelica had stiffened but not turned around as she headed away, and the twins looked guiltily at her back. Then they glanced almost apologetically at me before hurrying after Angie, placing an arm around her shoulders when they reached her and leaning in to murmur something.

She nodded and they all headed out the front door, closing it behind them. Mrs Wilson came out of the kitchen, drying her hands having apparently been washing up from breakfast, and checked that the door was closed before going back in and bustling around again.

I let out a breath I hadn't been aware of holding, and my shoulders drooped. Gauvain nibbled a strand of my hair in sympathy, then headed back upstairs to our room. Probably going to preen and nap, I thought. Must be nice not to have these emotional minefields to navigate.

I stepped into Seirina's study and closed the door, turning around to see her looking at me pityingly.

"I know I told you not to pressure her," she remarked ruefully, "but I didn't think it would go like this."

Oh good, if an enchantress could get it wrong, at least I didn't feel quite so inept myself.

"Yeah, I was hoping she might want to talk at some point too," I replied. "I've decided I'm going to focus on the fight, and if she feels differently afterwards that's up to her. I'm done apologising for something that wasn't my fault, and the next move is hers to make."

"I see," said Seirina, but I could almost hear her mind churning. I had a feeling there might be a phone call in her not too distant future. Still, I had another woman to find out about just now.

"Talking of complicated relationships," I remarked, making her look at me curiously when she heard the change in my tone, "what's the story with Mrs Wilson? I made a remark about her being a treasure and asked if anyone had ever tried to steal her away from you.

"Anyone would think I'd asked her about a murder. I know she's not entirely 'normal', based on when I sensed her coming to the door that first day, but what gives?" Seirina smiled as I mentioned her housekeeper's expression and nodded understandingly.

"She was with my family from the time I was a child," she began, appearing to reminisce as she spoke. "She must have been in her early twenties when she came to work for us, and I grew up with her. When I left my parents' home to strike out on my own, she came with me to help run my house. I think she wanted to keep an eye on me, too," she whispered.

"As she wasn't magickal, she soon aged and became ill. She knew what I was, so came to me one day to ask me a favour. She wanted to die while she was still relatively healthy, then have me bring her back. That way, her illness wouldn't take hold and she could stay with me. I agreed, and she used an overdose of a sedative to end her own life.

"When I brought her back, I made sure she was independent and as close to alive as I could make her. Despite that, she always believed that if she left me her life would end and I'd take back the life I had given her. I never would, of course, but I'd definitely miss her. We've been together so long, I don't think either of us would feel right without the other."

Suddenly their relationship made so much more sense. Why Mrs Wilson was so attuned to Seirina's wishes, why she always seemed to know exactly what was needed, when and where. And, of course, why the poor woman had seemed so terrified at my innocent remark.

I smiled at this new evidence of this softer, more human side to Seirina. It was endearing that she was so attached to her childhood nanny. I was also glad to finally have a reason for that odd feeling I'd had when I sensed Mrs Wilson that first day.

I hoped all of my undertakings could be so successfully resolved. I had a feeling I wouldn't be quite so lucky in my next endeavours, however. Still, hope springs eternal.

Chapter 8

I decided to spend the rest of the day trying to store energy in Seren. I'd realised over the last week or so that unlike non-magickal folk, and even most magickal individuals, I had the advantage of being able to 'recover in advance'.

I could pour my strength into my heart-stone, then have a nap to recover. That way, when I went into a situation such as, oh I don't know, a war for example, I'd already have extra stores on hand.

Despite napping about half a dozen times per day recently, I was still nowhere near making a dent in Seren's capacity. I was beginning to think I could drain the entire planet of energy and still not have filled my ring. I snorted in juvenile amusement, then went back to my cycle of draining and replenishing (as opposed to the more recognised binging and purging).

After nap number seven, I didn't have the mental strength for yet another round, so I got up from the bed and went to stretch my legs outside. Gauvain roused himself from his perch as I went past, jumping across to my shoulder to hitch a ride along with me.

I went out through the kitchen this time, smiling at Mrs Wilson on my way. I remembered Seirina's tale of her origins and swallowed away a little tightness at how sweet it was that they had stayed together so long. After all of Seirina's loss and misfortune in relationships, I was glad she had at least one person left who meant so much to her.

Gauvain flew off my shoulder as soon as I was out the door. He rapidly climbed up to the peak of the area enclosed by the wards, then simply rode the air currents. I could feel his joy at being out and flying tinged with frustration that he was restricted by the wards.

It was like an itch across my shoulders, making me unsettled as well. I was actually quite glad to have the sensation, as it made me less likely to become overly comfortable here. I may have enjoyed being where Seirina could protect me and Mrs Wilson could look after me, but I couldn't ignore what the Order had been doing within the magickal community for so long.

Like every war in history, I had to balance the risk of people getting hurt against the likelihood of the Order continuing to go on harming, killing and coercing for centuries more if I did nothing. It was the lesser of two evils in the long run, though it might not feel like it to those of us fighting right now.

The breeze was picking up a little this evening, so I stilled the air within the wards and poured the energy into Seren. Every little helps, and I'd probably need every drop during my lessons with Lucian and the following fights.

I wondered idly if Lucian would allow me to use the heat and light of his home to increase my stores. With how uncomfortable I'd been before getting inside, I'd probably get quite a bit by comparison with what I could gather here.

I was so sunk in introspection, I wasn't paying attention to where I was walking. I strayed from the path onto the grass and the toe of my shoe snagged the turf. I stumbled forwards and fell to my hands and knees, grazing the palm of my right hand on a stray pebble.

I brushed it off, both figuratively and literally, and stood back up. Gauvain flew down in alarm, but as soon as he saw I was OK his concern changed to amusement.

From your perusal of Facebook, as your closest friend and partner, I believe my comment here should be 'Walk much, dumbass?'

The incongruity with his normal speech, combined with his perfect timing and assessment of the situation, made me burst out laughing.

"Thanks for the sympathy, butthead," I replied, making him bob up and down on my shoulder as he chuckled. It was nice to enjoy a moment of relative normality amongst the weirdness that my life had become recently.

As I'd said to Summer, I was truly missing some of the simple, day-to-day tasks and activities like my morning run and the routine of managing Dinas Affaraon. I'd even enjoy doing the inventory right now, not that I'd ever tell Summer. I knew that would be a one-way ticket to doing it alone again!

I headed back inside, going to the sink and washing my hands to clean off the grit. I saw that my right hand was oozing a drop of blood, so made sure to wash well and get rid of any residual dirt. I squeezed out a couple of drops of blood to ensure nothing was trapped inside, then dried my hands on a paper towel. (I didn't fancy pissing off Mrs Wilson by getting blood on one of her clean towels.)

She walked in as I was finishing and she must have seen me wince as I dried my palm, since she came over and took my hand.

"How did you manage that?" she asked, sounding like every long-suffering parent when they see their child do something daft. I chuckled at her tone, as did Gauvain.

"I wasn't watching where I was walking," I replied honestly.

She tutted and shook her head.

"*Boys*," she said, exasperated, "you may get older, but you never truly grow up do you?"

"My mother used to say, 'Little girls grow up, little boys just get bigger,'" I said.

"Sounds like a very wise woman," Mrs Wilson replied, and I grinned in response, feeling five again for a few moments.

My eyes watered slightly, as they always did when I remembered my mother.

She had been killed by a drunk driver running a red light when I was twelve, after which my father had raised me and my sister alone. He had employed a series of live-in housekeepers and nannies to help until we were old enough to be alone after school, and my mother's sister would have us to stay when he had to go away on business trips.

I had been more sensitive, like my mother had been, which I think always reminded my dad of his lost soulmate. Now that I was older, I realised that was another possible reason we had a rocky relationship. He wanted me to do well in honour of her memory, but it was also more painful for him to be around me.

My sister, being more pragmatic, had been more like him. Also, her dyslexia had been a challenge for her, so he was more encouraging with her, rather than driving her the way he did with me.

That difference had ended up pushing my sister and me apart, as he tended to hold each of us up as an example to the other. He had extolled my academic achievements to my sister, while praising her solid work ethic to me. My intellect had meant that school came much easier to me so I didn't appear to be trying as hard as her.

I had contacted my father a few years ago and we now had conversations several times a year over the phone, much more cordial than in the past, and we were both glad to have our new more equal relationship.

My sister and I, however, hadn't spoken for years. She had asked me to help her out with some money right when I was setting up my shop, and I had refused since my funds were tied up in my new inventory.

She had gotten angry and we hadn't spoken since. I actually viewed it as a lucky escape, since if I *had* helped her once she probably would have been back again and again until my shop started suffering. Never mix money and family!

While my mind had gone wandering down memory lane, Mrs Wilson had been getting on with putting dinner together. Looked like it was lasagne tonight, and I could smell the garlic bread warming in the oven.

I got some unused raw beef mince that she'd put aside for Gauvain and took him upstairs, putting the meat in a dish that I'd attached to his makeshift perch. Then I headed back downstairs for dinner.

Back in the kitchen Seirina was already sitting at the table. I pulled out my usual chair and sat down, giving a deep sniff of the enticing aroma coming from the oven. Seirina rolled her eyes at my dramatic sigh while Mrs Wilson smiled affectionately, getting out the dish and cutting a large slice to put on my plate.

We enjoyed a peaceful, cheerful meal and I headed up to my room to get an early night. I got my phone going on my YouTube playlist, setting it to stop playing after an hour. I lay back in bed with my hands behind my head.

I closed my eyes and thought back over the memories that had flooded through my mind earlier that evening. I realised that even though I might not get along with them all the time, my father and my sister were still my family and bringing down the Order as fast as possible would be the best way for me to protect them along with the rest of the world.

With yet another reason to fight set in my mind, I turned over and drifted off to sleep to the dulcet strains of Meatloaf's *Bat Out of Hell*.

Chapter 9

I was woken by the intrusive beep of my text message alert at the ungodly (how eerily appropriate) hour of twenty past four in the morning. I checked my phone and yes, it was Lucian. He told me he was waiting for me, so I texted back with what time it was and that I'd be there as soon as both my eyes were open and I'd had a shower.

He promptly replied that he was quite prepared to wait, since he'd prefer to teach me without having to put a clothes peg on his nose. Devil or not, he had a sense of humour. I texted back with a few choice emojis, then went to get my shower.

I managed to stub my toe on the leg of the bed as I passed, making me swear under my breath so as not to wake Seirina and Mrs Wilson. I hopped a couple of times, rubbing my foot, then finally made it into the bathroom without further incident or injury.

I performed my ablutions then headed back into the bedroom feeling slightly more human, although still wishing for a few more hours of sleep. I got dressed, then braced myself for my next scary chore: waking Gauvain.

For goodness sake, he groused, nipping my finger firmly in protest as I stroked his head, *can a body not get an uninterrupted night's sleep? What on Earth is so important to deny me my beauty rest? I realise it's a bit late for you, but I at least have an image to maintain.* He was always grumpy when I woke him early.

Gee, thanks for the compliment, ya fluffy grump! I replied – mentally so as not to wake the rest of the house. *Are you coming, or do you want to stay here and go back to sleep? Lucian texted me.* He shook himself, yawned and stretched his wings straight up.

I'd best accompany you, or who knows what trouble you'd get yourself into, he said superciliously. Sometimes I really wished I'd been partnered with the wolf that I'd seen when I first arrived in Aaru. At least *dogs* formed a bond where they were loyal and happy to see you!

My snide thoughts made it across our link to G, and he eyed me beadily. I knew I'd pay for that little comment at some point, but for right now I had places to go, a devil to see and things to learn.

Gauvain jumped across onto my shoulder, then I set off downstairs. I was yawning as I went, so pulled a little energy from Seren to make up for my lost sleep. I looked longingly at the kitchen, knowing I couldn't have my Cafegeddon this morning, but then I had a thought and went in.

I went over to Mrs Wilson's shopping list board and wrote a quick note, so she and Seirina would know where I'd gone when they found me absent. I grabbed a bottle of cold water from the fridge and headed to the front door.

Of course, the door was locked and the key had been taken out. To find it, I'd probably have to turn the lights on instead of using my phone's flashlight function as I had been to get down the hall.

I decided to get magickal with it, so I unlocked it telekinetically like I had with the cell door when I had escaped from the Order headquarters. You know, I was really starting to love these abilities.

I went out, relocking the door in the same way behind me. Now I had another problem: the gate was closed, the wards were up, and Seirina was still in bed. I suspected Lucian had done this deliberately, simply to see how I'd get around it. Either that, or he had simply forgotten the time difference from where he was.

Then again he *was* the Devil, so maybe he just wanted to be an asshole and force me to get everyone up. I knew Seirina had set up the wards to prevent teleportation, but had she known enough to block portals?

Crossing my fingers, I opened myself to my magick and focused it on a point about six feet ahead of me while thinking very clearly of Lucian's pyramid. I pictured the curtain Danu had described, using the power to cut through the fabric of the world and link me to where I wanted to go.

Thanks be to Isis, Ra, Odin, Jesus, Allah, Yahweh, and every other deity and pantheon I could think of, the wards didn't fry me and the portal actually opened.

I breathed a huge sigh of relief and Gauvain released some of the grip he'd had on my shoulder – a grip that had been firm even through my magickal reinforcement.

I stepped through into the grounds of the pyramid, and my shirt was stuck to my back with sweat inside of twenty seconds. I remembered the image Gauvain had supplied me last time, plus my own recollection of the top of the pyramid, then transported myself up.

I really needed to find a decent magickal term for that. Teleportation sounded too 'sci-fi' for my taste. Shifting was possible, although that sounded more like what weres did. Maybe I should ask Lucian what he called it.

I walked into the stone tunnel again, relieved to be out of the direct sun. I hadn't wanted to absorb the heat and light without asking permission first, so I simply endured for now. I looked at the different panels of writings again, wishing I could understand what they said.

"Hail, Satan," I exclaimed as I walked into the throne room, seeing Lucian on his golden chair. I noticed this time, he'd forgone the raised dais and had his chair on the same level as the rest of the floor.

"You're hysterical," he intoned, before breaking into a huge grin. "You have no idea how nice it is to talk to someone who knows who and what I really am. OK, I haven't told you my real name, but at least you know I'm not actually the biblical father of all evil that everyone else I've ever dealt with considers me to be."

I suddenly understood why he had helped Elrulin when he had first been cast out of Aaru. How lonely must he have been for the last several thousand years? When Elrulin had landed, it must have been a chance to have at least some kind of contact with home again. Now I understood my side of our bargain even better than I had before.

As I got closer, a strange look came over his face and he reached out to shake my hand. I was surprised, as he hadn't done that last time, but I thought nothing of it and gripped his hand firmly. I winced slightly as the pressure reminded me of my fall the day before, but it was a fleeting thing as he shook and let go with no further ado.

He waved his hand and created a more comfortable seat for me this time, so I went over and sat down. As I turned back to him, I saw him putting a handkerchief into his pocket and sitting back himself.

I didn't think Aaruans had a problem with hay fever or other allergies, but what did I know? I forgot about it and relaxed in the chair, Gauvain hopping off of my shoulder onto the back of it as I did so.

"Before we get started, there's a couple of things I wanted to ask if you don't mind," I said. Lucian nodded his permission, so I forged ahead. "Would you mind if I drew from the heat and light here to store some energy?" He raised his eyebrows and his eyes widened, so I explained. "The more energy I can store in my heart-stone..."

I jumped slightly as he sat forwards so quickly, I thought he was going to come completely out of his chair.

"You have a heart-stone?" he asked, to which I held out my hand with Seren glittering on it. I told him the broad strokes regarding the story of the stone's creation, followed by Master Harfi's help in forming the ring itself.

He reached for it magickally, then admitted he couldn't even feel it which explained why he hadn't been aware of it the last time I was with him. He waved his hand in unspoken permission when I reiterated my energy gathering request, then waited for my other question.

"The other thing I wanted to know was, what do you call moving from place to place without a portal?" I asked.

"Walking," he replied, so I rolled my eyes.

"Funny," I said, "you know what I mean. Teleportation sounds kind of 'Star Trek' rather than magick, and I wondered if you knew of another term for it?"

He shrugged and shook his head.

"You can call it what you like," he said, "but teleportation is the best name for it I've ever heard. Why worry about a name? Be more concerned with what it is, than what it's called." His comment reminded me of Isis' remark about humans needing a name and a box for everything when I asked what I had become.

That gave me another thought, and I tucked it away to consider later. For now, it was time to find out what exactly Lucian had to teach me.

We spent the next couple of hours reviewing what I had learnt in Aaru, with Lucian testing me each step of the way.

"How long did you say you were there?" he asked when we were done, and I decided to use his own sarcastic answering style on him.

"About ten minutes," I replied with a straight face. He looked startled, then realised what I'd done. Now it was his turn to roll his eyes.

"Very clever," he remarked, "you know what I meant."

I chuckled and shrugged.

"Their time, about ten months or so," I admitted. His look of shock was worth it, and I had to struggle to keep my laughter under control.

"Are you really telling me that you learnt everything you know in under a year?" he asked, ominously quiet and calm.

His tone sent chills up and down my spine, making me sit up straighter and think carefully. I needed his help, so I didn't want to piss him off by sounding cocky about my own abilities, but I couldn't lie to him now.

"Well, I was only taught the absolute minimum of the advanced abilities," I temporised. "My instructor told me that since I was worried about what was happening back on Earth, I'd set my own deadline so I'd have to practice by myself."

Despite my explanation, his brow remained creased and his shoulders appeared tense as he considered the implications.

"So how long did that 'minimal teaching' take you?" he asked. I could actually *hear* the air quotes he used, and knew I was on very thin ice.

"Umm, I'm not *exactly* sure..." I started, but one look at his face with the tightening around his eyes told me not to bullshit him. I felt him reach towards my mind and stabbed back hard, making him jump slightly and look even more askance at me.

"OK," I admitted, "I learnt the basics of the advanced techniques in under a week." I spoke quietly and openly, to be rewarded by seeing his eyes widen to a degree I was worried might cause physical pain. He gripped the arms of his throne so hard his knuckles went completely white.

"That's...not possible!" he whispered in shock. "Even Isis herself took longer than that!"

"Yeah, but she *was* only twelve at the time," I said self-deprecatingly. He shook his head in amazement, and I saw his lips twitch in amusement.

"Under a week…" he muttered, just loud enough for me to hear. "Well, now I understand a little more. If you're that talented, what I have to teach you shouldn't take very long. To be honest, having heard what you already know, there isn't actually that much. I'll probably do the same as your other teacher and show you the basics of the techniques, then leave you to practice by yourself."

He clapped his hands, startling Gauvain who had dropped to sleep after his early morning wake up. Lucian pushed himself up out of his chair.

"Let's get started!" he said.

My pulse pick up in anticipation. Here we go!

Chapter 10

"I have to be honest with you," Lucian said as he stood up, "I made this deal thinking I'd have a lot more to teach you." He looked somewhat sheepish, perhaps realising the deal wasn't quite as equitable as he thought it might have been.

"I thought you understood, from what I'd said in the meeting, that I'd had teaching in the advanced techniques," I remarked. "I definitely remember telling everyone I'd gone on to the higher level education." I looked at him questioningly. Then I remembered how I'd phrased it. "I never actually said what techniques I'd learned though, did I?"

He smiled and shook his head.

"Nope," he confirmed, "you were quite discrete about your abilities. You merely said that you'd impressed your teachers and had a solid grounding..." He trailed off, and I latched on to where he was going.

"A solid grounding in the advanced abilities, which you're quite aware of," I finished. "I *knew* I'd said enough to be clear to someone in your position! So don't try squirming out of this. If you don't have as much to teach me, you need to square this deal up some other way.

"I know you're going to put us in contact with a couple of 'entities' to help us in our fight, but that's not even close to equating with what you want to get out of this arrangement." I crossed my arms and cocked my head to the side, looking at him with the question clear on my face. "What else can you do for us?"

He looked back at me, assessing what would be acceptable to add to his side of the deal.

"I said I could give you information about Iyrin as well, don't forget," he stated, which I had certainly *not* forgotten, "but I'll go one better: I'll teach you how to defend your mind against him, and as a result how to sever your link with him."

A chill ran over me and the hair on my arms stood straight up. That was it, the one thing I really needed from him. Given how long Iyrin had been around, plus how long I could potentially live now, he could be attached to me for centuries against my will unless I found out how to break free.

Queen's *I Want to Break Free* started running through my head, making me laugh. Lucian raised his left eyebrow as my laughter bubbled up, clearly thinking I'd have jumped at his offer rather than dissolving into hilarity.

I hastily explained what had flitted through my mind and I saw his lips quirk up in amusement.

He shook his head slightly and sighed.

"You humans," he said, "your brains really are odd. We're talking about serious, life-altering things and you start coming up with a soundtrack! No wonder most of you have trouble following a single train of thought from beginning to end.

"If your kind had a little more mental discipline," he finished superciliously, "you might be able to solve some of the problems that are so rife in this world."

I raised my eyebrows and sat back in my chair at his disparagement of my species.

"Do you really think you're so superior to us?" I asked. Hey, I may not have the greatest opinion of the majority of humanity. Especially when you consider the wars, racism, exploitation, persecution of all kinds, and generally poor behaviour which humans exhibited on a daily basis. Still, I wasn't going to let someone who was thrown out of his entire native plane of existence run us down!

"Let's be honest here," I continued, "you behaved so badly, your own kind disowned you and threw you out of your entire dimension. Then, when you came here, you continued to act so poorly, you ended up getting a reputation for yourself that caused you to be painted as the Prince of Darkness, father of evil, ultimate corruptor...pick your moniker, none of them are especially flattering.

"Now, simply because I thought of a song that fit particularly well with what we were talking about, you feel the need to insult my entire *species*?" I got quite heated as I was talking, working myself up in my irritation. I abruptly realised I was telling the Devil off again and snapped my mouth closed – especially since I did want his help – but I didn't get the giggles this time.

Lucian sat down with a thump, his shock at my tirade easily discernible on his face. Without any warning, he flicked his wrist and I flew across the room to slam into the wall.

Gauvain shrieked in outrage and launched himself off of the chair. I called to him to stop his potential retaliation. I didn't want him getting hurt, plus I knew I had probably pushed Lucian's buttons quite hard with my comments.

I picked myself up with a groan, sore all down my left side and across my back. I glared at Lucian, then quite pointedly held up my right hand to show Seren. I reached into the store of energy and repaired the bruising I could feel.

I then created a shield around myself, along with a matching one around Gauvain, that deliberately had a slight rippling effect to it so that Lucian could see it.

I walked slowly and deliberately back to my chair, then sat down while staring straight into Lucian's eyes.

"That was your one and only warning," he said coldly. "You may have knowledge, ability, and even a reasonable amount of power, but you *will* show me the respect I deserve. I've been around for thousands of years, and you actually *need* my help. I would *like* your help with my situation, but I can survive quite easily without it. Remember your place, human!"

I narrowed my eyes, a whole host of arguments and counterpoints running through my mind, but for a change I decided to hold my tongue. He was right to a degree, I did need his help.

I knew he was downplaying quite how badly he wanted mine, but there was no point in playing every card in my hand in one go. I was better off keeping my powder dry until the most advantageous time. Make no mistake though, I would remember this moment.

We looked at each other for a few minutes, Gauvain still flying around the room and shrieking occasionally, then I raised an eyebrow.

"So then," I asked calmly, despite what I really wanted to say, "where does that leave us?"

He sighed and nodded slowly a couple of times, so I continued.

"I know you're older, more knowledgeable and more experienced than me. You know I'm prepared to actually step up and act to take Elrulin and his cronies down, but I need help to do it.

"I have access to Aaru and Isis, you want a chance to have your case reviewed – a parole hearing, if you will. You need me to get that for you and to be a witness on your behalf; I need you to teach me whatever I don't know and get extra allies to help in the fight."

I laid out our situation as pragmatically and fairly as I could, highlighting the vulnerabilities on both sides, and Lucian gradually relaxed as it became clear how dependant on each other we really were.

"You make valid points," he allowed. "You know, you *do* seem to be more logical than most of the humans I've come into contact with up to now. We got on so well last time you were here; perhaps we should start today over again?"

Gauvain finally calmed down as he felt me relax, so he flew back to my chair. He flapped his wings a couple of times and shrieked once more at Lucian, then settled back to a watchful alertness.

If he tries that again, I'll claw his eyes out! G raged in my mind, so I sent calming thoughts across to him. As sweet as his outrage was, I didn't want him getting hurt by punching above his weight class.

I refashioned his shield to be undetectable, then made it permanent. We were about to head into a war and I wanted him safe. This way he could still fight, as I knew for certain he would want to, but he'd be safe from enemy magick or weaponry.

Lucian smiled as he noted my alteration, then again as I dropped my own shield. I was going to have to trust that he wasn't really the evil demon he'd been painted. To be honest, I'd always thought the idea of a permanently evil devil, as the Bible described, was faintly ludicrous.

I much preferred the school of thought that said the Devil was a *punisher* of evil, rather than a perpetuator of it. I couldn't see an immortal being failing to learn over millennia; it had simply never made sense.

The story he'd told me last time fit far more with a reasonable, intelligent being who'd screwed up when he was young. It also correlated with what I knew of the rules of Aaru as Alex and Liam had laid them out for me.

That didn't mean I wanted to hold hands and sing *Kumbaya* with Lucian; I *would* give him the benefit of the doubt for now, though. I'd also, however, keep both eyes wide open for even the slightest sign of treachery or underhandedness. I was trusting, not a moron; and while people may learn from their experiences, rarely did they ever change their entire personality.

"So, what *do* you have to teach me?" I asked, trying to get back to the reason I'd returned to him.

"Good idea, let's get on with this," he said. "The easiest thing first, how to use a portal to bring someone to you rather than going to them."

I sat up straighter and leant forwards. I'd thought this would be a useful trick when he'd used it to bring me here last time.

"So what's the difference from opening the portal the normal way?" I asked. "I mean, normally I think about where I want to go and use magick to open the doorway."

"Exactly," he said, "and the same principle holds for opening a passage in the opposite direction. You need to picture where you want to bring someone *from*, hold in your head that you want them to come to you, then open the portal as before."

"Sounds simple enough," I said, "are there any risks to be aware of?" When Lucian looked at me oddly, I went on to explain. "The first time I opened a portal, I accidentally time viewed an event in my store. My teacher forgot to explain that the fourth dimension was breachable, and my first attempt went through more than just space."

To my surprise, Lucian looked quite impressed. I hadn't seen that look on his face before, and it was actually fairly empowering.

"Well, if you can achieve time viewing, a reverse portal should be easy for you," he remarked. "Do you think–"

"Nope!" I interrupted immediately, already knowing what he was about to ask. "I already know that time travel is a no-no, and time viewing is almost as bad."

He huffed in disappointment and I almost laughed.

He looked like a frustrated five-year-old, and it was kind of surprising in its apparent naivety. Over four thousand years old and he still looked like a child when things didn't go his way.

"Then no, if you're already aware of that, there's nothing else you need to worry about," he grumped.

"Anyway," I said, fighting back my laugh, "what's the other one?"

"Oh, this one is *far* more difficult," he stated, sounding excited again, "but infinitely more satisfying and useful: how to manipulate time."

If he meant what I thought he did, this one I *definitely* wanted to learn!

Chapter 11

"Obviously," Lucian took on a classic lecturing tone as he sat back in his chair, although his eyes still sparkled with his enthusiasm for the topic, "when I say time manipulation, I'm talking about creating a time distortion like I have around this pyramid or like there is between Earth and Aaru.

"I am most definitely *not* talking about trying to alter events in time (since you've already said no, you spoilsport)." He said that last under his breath, although loud enough for me to hear and I fought back another chuckle.

"Oh good, since I left my sonic screwdriver in my other jeans," I quipped, "and my other car is definitely not a blue police telephone box!"

"Well an Eye of Harmony wouldn't help you here anyway," he riposted, at which I raised an eyebrow.

"OK you lost me," I admitted with a grin. "I don't know as much *Doctor Who* as that, I was always more of a Trekkie."

"When you have unlimited time, you can catch up on your watching," he joked, and I laughed on cue.

"Well that's a reason for a distortion I hadn't considered." He joined me in my laughter.

"To be honest," he continued, calming and getting back on topic, "creating a distortion field like this takes a great deal of preparation and focus, so it's not something to try on a whim. For your current purposes, you might consider creating a distortion around an Order building before assaulting it. That way you could have your fight without drawing the attention of the civilian authorities. You certainly don't want to sit down to attempt it in the middle of battle."

I sobered, keen not to miss anything in his explanation if it was that complex.

"Fair enough," I said, sitting forward myself now. "So how does one go about it?"

"Well the first thing you need to do is make sure you have enough energy to complete the field," he told me, which made perfect sense.

I realised that having Seren would actually put me a step ahead of most magick users in this, since I would (hopefully) always have a store of energy on hand. I glanced at my hand, causing Lucian to follow my gaze.

"Indeed," he acknowledged, sounding almost jealous, "having a heart-stone will certainly make that first step easier for you. Just be aware that even with that, there are risks. You should know that if you try something too extreme, you can still drain your store and then yourself."

I nodded, sobering as I understood the potential risk.

"So I shouldn't try to bubble the whole of Europe away from the rest of the world," I snarked, "or make it so that one night outside my bedroom is five thousand years inside?"

He rolled his eyes at my absurdity.

"Indeed," he remarked again. "Covering the whole of Europe on your own would definitely be lethal," he agreed. "On the other hand, if you only want to include your bedroom, a significant distortion is very possible. Bear in mind, you experienced a difference of a month in Aaru equating to a minute on Earth, and that's an entire dimension."

"Hang on," I said cautiously, still thinking through the brainwave that struck me, "since it's the entire dimension, they're not actually altering time *there*. All they have to do is alter the equivalency with Earth, sort of like changing the settings on a pressure lock or one of those chambers they use for divers who get the bends, right?"

Lucian regarded me with shock, something I certainly hadn't expected to see.

"That's an impressive deduction," he breathed. "Even with all my years to think about it, I'd never even considered it like that!" He looked introspective for a moment, then looked back up at me. "You have a very unusual mind for a magick user," he commented, and I smirked as I remembered Danu saying much the same thing. I somehow doubted she'd be overly impressed with me comparing her to Lucian, though, so I'd make sure *not* to mention it the next time I saw her!

"You have to remember," I explained, "I lived over thirty years without magick. I had to go through regular school, learning to understand the world through science, mathematics, and logic.

"That's why I apply those ways of thinking to my magick, which was what made me able to learn the advanced techniques so quickly. My teacher was so impressed, she even said that your kind could stand to learn a thing or two from my human way of thinking."

I could have bit my tongue as I realised I'd said 'she'. Then I realised that Danu wasn't even 'her' real name, and after seeing 'her' shape- and gender-switching there was no telling what 'she' really identified as – not that it made the blindest bit of difference.

In fact, knowledge of that ability would probably make humans look at gender and sexuality very differently. It could probably cure a great deal of bigotry and prejudice, getting rid of a significant amount of unnecessary persecution and suffering.

For all I knew, Aaruans might not even *have* assigned genders. Being formless, they might merely be discrete entities who eventually find their partners and procreate. It was the *mind* and *personality* that mattered, after all, not the damned plumbing! I remembered considering something similar about Iyrin, too.

Wow, talk about a tangent! Still, I *am* a guy. Aren't I *supposed* to think about sex every six seconds or something? *Pay attention*, I thought.

Fortunately for me, Lucian had completely ignored my pronoun usage and seemed to have sunk back into thought himself. As I looked back at him, he appeared to come to some conclusion from his considerations and looked back over to me.

"Sorry," he apologised, apparently not having realised I had also spaced out for a moment. "Your interpretation has raised some previously unconsidered possibilities. Anyway, back to it…"

★

By the time Lucian had finished explaining everything, and I had managed to create even a small time distortion field, I was exhausted. No wonder he'd said not to try this lightly!

"I think that's quite enough," Lucian said, already impressed that I'd achieved my first success. "As with the rest of your abilities, you can continue to practice and refine your skills in your own time.

"You now know every ability I know, though you're not *quite* as proficient yet. Four thousand years of use does make one *slightly* smoother in the execution." He winked with his outrageously understated proclamation.

"Oh really, ya think?" I put my hand on the centre of my chest dramatically. We both laughed, and Gauvain *skree'd* as he stretched. He had been observing carefully, linking with me to see exactly what I was doing since a second observer was always a good idea in this situation.

I stood up and arched my back, stretching after my exertions, and Lucian rose from his throne to walk me out. G flew around the room a couple of times then landed on my shoulder again. As we walked out, Lucian looked sideways at me.

"I must say, I can understand now why Isis chose you across the centuries," he remarked. "Even with your late awakening to magick, I have never, outside of some of the most powerful and proficient of my kind, met anyone with a greater affinity for magickal ability and learning.

"I'll look forward to seeing what you'll become in few centuries; provided, of course, you make it through your upcoming battles." I stammered my thanks and he waved them off.

As we reached the opening to the outside, the heat and sunlight hit like standing in front of a furnace door. Since he had given his consent, I gathered the majority of both into Seren, leaving it more comparable to a dull English day and just warm enough to be comfortable without a jacket.

"If you don't mind," I said, sitting down on the top step of the stone staircase, "I'm going to recover here for a while, plus restock my ring with some of what I've used today."

"Good idea," he agreed. "You'll need all you can get for what's to come. You might even want to reach out to some of the bigger trees.

They'll give you significantly more power and they're old enough not to suffer, as long as you pay attention to how much you draw from them."

I lifted my head, not having considered that as an option. That would definitely be more potent. I thanked Lucian again for the tip.

"Meanwhile," he told me, "I have some friends and potential allies to track down, as promised." I remembered he'd said he knew a couple of entities who could help us in our fight. I nodded, and he waved as he disappeared off to wherever he was going.

I reached out and was almost overwhelmed by the intensity and richness of life around me. Even taking a few hours-worth of whatever energy the surrounding vegetation could obtain from the sun would be thousands of times what I could get from the sun myself.

I released my hold on the light and heat, then went in a circle around the pyramid. I only took from the largest, strongest plants so as not to cause any lasting damage. By the time I'd finished, I had stored many times everything I had gathered up to that point, including all my stores from Aaru and what I'd obtained since getting back.

I might have filled almost one percent of one percent of Seren with this session. If I could come back here once a day between now and the start of the fighting, I'd be in a much better position to take the Order down.

It was time to start accumulating my nuclear arsenal. Still, for now I should be heading back. Hopefully I'd be in time for breakfast and, more importantly, coffee!

Chapter 12

I managed to get back to Seirina's safely via portal again and decided, while it was still on my mind, to talk to her about the wards. If I could use portals so could anyone else, which left us vulnerable. The Order apparently didn't have anyone we *knew* who could use them; still, they could have picked up someone with the ability.

Judging by how dark it still was, I hadn't been away for very long relatively speaking. I opened the front door with my mind again, went in and locked it behind me. Since it looked like I had time, I decided to go back to bed to get a few more hours' shut-eye.

I poured some of my energy into Seren as I had been doing yesterday. Once the fatigue set in, I cut off the stream and closed my eyes, drifting off to sleep with Gauvain watching over me.

I woke up to see the sun streaming in through the window. I checked my phone – since I had given up on my watch due to the recurrent time distortions I had been going through – to see that it was just after half past eight.

I sat up, yawning and stretching, then got out of bed. I followed my nose down to the kitchen, smiling as I walked in. Mrs Wilson started, causing Seirina to turn and then also show her surprise.

"Oh, Gavan, we saw your message so we didn't think you were here," Seirina remarked, reaching for the coffee and drawing it closer to her. She obviously hadn't forgotten my hostage taking and caffeine leveraging.

I laughed at her attempt at reciprocity, accepting my mug from a smiling Mrs Wilson and sitting down at the table. I looked at Seirina who didn't move, then I raised an eyebrow. I looked pointedly from my mug to the cafetière and back again, saying nothing.

Seirina took a page out of my playbook, refilling her own mug and putting the coffee back out of my reach. I shook my head and sighed; a pox on all women who learn too fast and use your own tricks against you!

"Fine, fine," I surrendered, holding out my hand for the coffee pot. "Lucian still has the time bubble, so I returned while it was still dark and went back to bed. I completely forgot about the note I'd left, sorry."

Seirina shook her head, drawing the pot back towards her right as she'd been about to hand it over.

"Nope, try again Maddox," she remarked dryly. "'A' for attempt, 'E' for execution."

"'B' for bugger it," I snarked. "See, I can spell too." She laughed, so I motioned to the pot and continued talking. "That reminds me, we need to review your wards." Seirina's eyes widened and she sat back, so I rushed to explain.

"When I left this morning, I remembered you saying that you'd blocked teleportation so I was worried I'd have to wake you up to get out. Fortunately I tried a portal and it worked, so I was able to let you sleep–"

"Always a good idea," she interrupted. Mrs Wilson nodded vigorously behind her.

I smothered my grin and grabbed the coffee pot as Seirina finally relinquished it.

"Anyway, I realised if *I* could get in and out with a portal, the Order might have picked up someone in their American recruiting drive who can too. We need to upgrade things to block that, though I'd appreciate if you'd leave me the access. It'll be helpful since I'll be going to Lucian's every day from now on, and I certainly don't want to disturb you every morning when I go."

I didn't tell them it was simply for energy harvesting. Instead, I made it sound like a regular lesson plan. To my surprise, Seirina's eyes widened and her pupils dilated when I mentioned the loophole in her security.

"I didn't even know it was necessary to specify both methods!" she observed. Well that explained *that,* then. I hurried to reassure her.

"The twins said that the Order didn't have anyone they knew of who could even teleport, never mind use portals, so there was no reason for me to think any more about it. It wasn't until this morning I even considered the possibility that it might work. I'm happy to do the update and check the rest of the wards for you, if you'd like."

Seirina looked sideways at me. I wasn't completely sure why, though I had an idea, and she confirmed it with her next comment.

"This isn't some devious excuse to examine my wards so you can get through them is it?" She eyed me beadily and I smiled.

"Hey, I could have just left myself the portal ability and said nothing," I stated, making her sit back and humph. "If I tweak the wards so *I* can get through with either method, but everyone else is blocked, surely that's better?"

"Oh, fine," she grumped eventually. "I suppose it'll make my life easier as well, with you being able to let people in if I'm busy."

I extended my awareness to assess her security spells. It didn't take me long to see how she had them set up and make the necessary adjustments, linking with her after getting her consent so she could see what she'd missed. That way she'd know in future.

I then stood up, glad I could finally do something I'd been wanting to do for days now. I teleported home, directly into the kitchen, and grabbed the container of Cafegeddon. We had been running low, and I knew the order Mrs Wilson had placed hadn't arrived yet. I popped back to see Seirina's eyes blazing.

"So," she stormed at me, "the second you adjust the wards, you start running off without so much as a by your lea..." She trailed off midword as I held out the opened container and she smelt exactly what I'd gone to get.

"I thought we might need a restock until your supply gets delivered." I shrugged, and Mrs Wilson snorted at Seirina's dilemma: be grateful for the coffee or be pissed about the wards. With typical female sneakiness, she did both.

"I'm grateful for your willingness to share," she said, crossing her arms and tapping her foot, "but the ends don't always justify the means.

You could have told me." Mrs Wilson shook her head resignedly out of Seirina's eye line, clearly familiar with this particular mood.

I knew I was going to lose whichever way I tried to argue, so I did the only safe thing: I apologised.

"Sorry Seirina," I said, "I'll make sure to let you know in future. I will say that the rest of your wards are very well put together. I have boosted the power a little more, but other than the portal thing, there were no other holes I could find," I finished.

She eyed me shrewdly. "I know what you're doing, so you can stop laying it on quite so thick."

I saw her smile despite herself as she turned away, so I breathed a little easier again. Mrs Wilson got on with clearing the table, so I snagged my coffee mug and the pot to get whatever dregs were left.

"Meet me in the study," Seirina called, sticking her head back into the kitchen. "We need to start some planning ahead of the next meeting."

I drank the remains of my coffee and went to the fridge to get Gauvain some breakfast. I took it up to him and made sure he was settled with his meal, then headed to Seirina's office.

Having learnt my lesson already that morning, I knocked on the door and waited to hear her call out before I opened it. As I entered she was smothering the smile I had already heard in her voice, so I walked up to the chairs by her desk.

Once again I stood and waited until I got permission, raising an eyebrow and nodding at the chair in front of me when she said nothing.

"Oh sit down, you drama queen!" She finally gave up and laughed, and I joined in. My link to Iyrin tingled as I heard a rustle from behind her, and it climbed up the branch into view. It was no less creepy than the previous times I'd seen it and I shuddered.

There's no need to be distressed, it said in my mind, at which I saw Seirina. *I told you I'm willing to help you.*

"Sorry," I replied, "your appearance does take a little getting used to. Plus I still remember the way you 'tasted' me and then grew veins and stuff." Even Seirina grimaced at that, no doubt remembering her own experience of linking with the watcher.

I didn't actually grow them, it replied. *You were simply more attuned to me once I established our link, so you saw more of me.*

OK, that actually made sense.

"Fair enough," I allowed, "but do you always trick people into your links? Wouldn't it be better if it was a more willing partnership? This way feels almost like you're a parasite, what with you not giving me the choice."

I am NOT a parasite! Iyrin stood straight up against the glass. *Apologise!*

I had to stop breaking out into laughter in the face of his anger, remembering a particular film clip.

"OK Venom," I said, "I'm sorry. Just don't touch my pancreas; or anything else for that matter."

Seirina slapped her hands over her mouth at my snide remark and I smothered my grin.

I could feel Iyrin searching through my memories this time, so I deliberately brought up the relevant recollection, pairing it with my image of its tongue when it licked its finger.

Oh, I see, it said eventually, and to my relief its amusement seeped across the link. *I suppose I can see the similarities. Regardless don't ever call me a parasite again. Or Venom, either. Now, if you're quite finished with your juvenile humour, shall we get on with our discussion?*

"Surely we need to see how many troops we end up with," I reasoned. "It'll depend how big a force we can muster as to how many sites we can attack at once. Ideally I'd like to go after all four in the UK and Ireland at once, to prevent them regrouping each time, but we need to see the breakdown of our collective abilities to assess the viability of that."

Seirina was nodding but Iyrin shook its head, allowing its disdain to colour our connection.

You're showing your mundane roots, it said, making me sit up in irritation. *You already have a much better option. Why not keep your entire force together for maximum effect, then simply portal them from one site to the next?*

With overwhelming numbers, each fight would be faster and easier. Then by using your portals, you can attack all four sites in quick succession so they don't get the chance to regroup.

I stared at Iyrin with my mouth open. Seirina's expression was much the same as mine. I hadn't even considered that option but Iyrin was right. We gave ourselves the best chance of success if we could have our entire force for each fight, and I could simply open a portal for everyone to file through after each one.

"Brilliant," I breathed, my face lighting up. We had our plan, now we just had to wait a few more days to see how many answered our call to war.

Chapter 13

Over the next few days, I developed a routine for myself. I would get up, put on my running gear and transport myself and Gauvain to Lucian's pyramid. I would go around the entire periphery, absorbing energy from all of the large plants to store in Seren.

The image of wings gradually began flaring in the stone for longer as I finally started making a dent in the seemingly limitless capacity of my heart-stone. Even so, I could tell it would take years if not decades of gathering like this – with no demands on the store due to fights – to come close to filling it.

Once I had completed the circuit, I would draw the worst of the heat out of the area so that I could finally get back to having a daily run. I would then run the outer limits of the cleared area around the pyramid twice which, given its size, came to around six miles by my reckoning.

Gauvain would hunt while I was gathering and running, usually catching a small monkey or good sized lizard. He was overjoyed to be flying more freely and hunting for himself again, and his joy washed across our bond to put me in a good mood as well.

Once I had finished my run and Gauvain had eaten, I would take us back to Seirina's and have my shower. Then it would be time for breakfast, after which I would spend some time studying a few of Seirina's less gruesome magickal texts to see if there was anything useful for the upcoming battles.

The afternoons were spent trying to destress and occasionally meditate. Sometimes I'd practice katas in the garden, a couple of days I went into the kitchen and did some baking with Mrs Wilson.

The day I made salted-caramel-topped salted-caramel-centred chocolate chip chocolate brownies, Seirina refused to let me out of the kitchen until I'd written down the recipe for Mrs Wilson. We'd had them as dessert with some vanilla ice cream, and Seirina had pronounced them officially better than sex (at least without a soulmate).

It had taken me a full ten minutes to be able to breathe and see well enough to write it, I was laughing so hard. Mrs Wilson had had to walk out of the kitchen to compose herself.

I was also still keeping up with putting some of my own energy into Seren, napping at various points throughout the day. Between that and my sessions at the pyramid, I was hoping to have enough energy for all four fights plus the portals between sites with enough left over to shield and heal as many of our allies as possible.

I was determined to bring down the Order, but I was worried about the potential casualties involved. I was even keen to try to make our assaults as bloodless as possible, capturing rather than killing. Gauvain, however, had a different view.

Exactly how many repetitions will be required for this idea to penetrate your seemingly impervious cranium? he demanded when we were discussing things one afternoon. *Every time you leave an enemy alive, you run the risk of them coming after you in the future. Even the mundane thug who had his eyebrows burned off by your shop wards could be a problem later, though I appreciate your desire to send a message back to the Order.*

You have planned to attack each site in quick succession to prevent the survivors from regrouping and making things progressively worse each time. Yet now you wish to spare as many lives as possible? For the love of Isis, why?

"The two...three...two...oh, whatever!" I snapped, frustrated by the ongoing difficulty of counting heads vs. bodies. "The *people* we've rescued from the Order so far were coerced into working for them. How can we just head in and kill everyone when many of them could be in the same situation? Don't they deserve a chance as well?"

Gauvain sighed and cocked his head, looking at me pityingly. I could feel his mixed emotions across our bond, but my own were so conflicted I couldn't even begin to interpret his.

Your compassion does you credit, Gavan, he began, at which point I could hear the 'but' coming from a mile away so I braced myself. *Still, we are severely limited in our opportunities to conduct research and interviews to differentiate between the willing members and those who are involved due to pressure exerted by the Order.*

'Still' was only 'but' in a fancy suit, if you ask me. However (yeah, yeah, shut up) the little feathered philosopher wasn't wrong. We may have no option other than to, as so many have said, 'kill them all and let God sort them out'.

The only thing I could think of was to speak to the twins and get as many names as possible. There was always the hope that when the fighting started, those who weren't fully committed to the Order would surrender.

Gauvain was right about everyone else. If they fought, I had to be prepared to finish the fight. Even those that did surrender would have to be scanned. There were plenty of instances where bad people acted to save their own skins when things went sideways, so the simple act of surrendering couldn't be taken at face value.

"I have a funny feeling that some of it will be taken out of my hands," I mused to G. "I doubt that any vampires fighting on our side will have my qualms, nor the weres. I'll have to set some ground rules for the more aggressive fighters before we begin our assaults.

"That reminds me, I'll also have to look into finding a way for the vampires to be protected against the sun, or they'll be virtually useless."

It may be advantageous to create a portal inside in order to prevent them being exposed, Gauvain proposed thoughtfully. It was a valid option but unless we could get an image of every interior before we attacked, the vampires would only be able to help once we were already inside each location.

If I started scanning minds at random to get a clear enough picture, every magick user or magickal being would know we were there before we made a move.

My phone rang and I saw it was the shop number, so I hit the answer button.

"Hey, Summer, what's up?" I asked, hoping it wasn't another pointless assault by some gormless thugs.

"Well, I'm not a hundred percent sure," she replied hesitantly, sounding very unlike her usual self. "I *think* there's someone outside assessing the shop. I've seen the same woman go past the door three times in the last twenty minutes, actually looking at the windows and the door each time rather than the things in the display." I had a sneaking suspicion that her description meant the Order had sent a magick user this time. Well, at least they were learning.

"On my way," I told her. G landed on my shoulder and I teleported to my office again. I walked out into the shop, noting that Summer didn't so much as twitch this time. It seemed as though she was getting used to my abilities too.

"So, when did you see her last?" I enquired.

Summer glanced at the clock above one of the bookcases.

"About five minutes ago. She's wearing a purple t-shirt and jeans. Blonde hair, quite pretty if you like that California girl kind of look."

I looked sideways at her and smiled.

"Careful, or I'll rat you out to Emily." I teased her, but she was too canny to fall for that.

"Pft, she'd probably agree with me," she observed, making me shake my head. Those two really were perfect for each other. One of these days I really was going to have to get one or the other of them to propose. Just then I saw a girl fitting Summer's description meander into view.

"That her?" I asked, glancing at my friend, and she nodded. Right, time to put an end to this shit once and for all! I strode angrily to the door, yanking it open and stepping out onto the pavement.

The bell above the door chimed, and the young woman turned around. Her eyes widened, apparently not having expected to see me there. If that was the case, though, why *was* she here?

"I thought I made my position clear last time some of you turned up," I stated, at which she visibly paled. Clearly she had heard exactly what had happened to the petrol-flinging pricks. "What the hell do you want? Let me guess, your boss wants you to try to break my wards?" Her guilty, shifty face confirmed exactly what I thought.

"Well good luck with that," I told her. "Have you had a good enough look? Go on then, make your attempt. I'll just stand here and watch." I saw her shakily raise her hands towards the shop window, then she closed her eyes and took a deep breath. She started muttering some kind of incantation, advancing towards the glass.

As she turned away and I saw her profile, a vague sense of recognition washed over me. Then, once she closed her eyes, I realised where I knew her from. She was the girl I'd knocked unconscious outside the prison vault under Bolton Castle!

And this is exactly *why everyone keeps telling you to finish your battles properly!* I heard Gauvain say through our link, from his perch inside. He must have felt my rush of recognition. I acknowledged his statement in grim silence, keeping my eyes on the blonde.

The resistance was building up in the wards, and the longer she kept going the more it grew. It felt like pressure building up in a wound rubber band, so I took a cautious step back to avoid the backlash I knew would be coming.

A soft lilac glow, similar to her shirt colour, appeared between her hands. I wondered idly if the colour of her magick was due to it being hers, or because she specialised in breaking wards, or was merely a random reflection of her top.

She took a final step and I winced in anticipation, already expecting the reaction as she placed her hands on the window. With a huge flash, she was flung backwards across the street to slam into the wall under the sandwich shop's window. Fortunately the guy who worked in there seemed to have gone into the back.

I jogged across the road, dropping into a crouch as I got to the girl. Her nose was bleeding, reminding me of my early efforts in Aaru, and her eyes were unfocused. I helped her up, using the contact to sense her consciousness and strengthen the connection.

"Well that went well for you," I observed, making her pull away from me at my sarcasm. "I tried to make you people understand, I won't tolerate any attacks against my business or those I care about. Now I'm going to show you what happens to those who ignore my warning."

I reached into her mind, searching for the spark that Gonpo, the guardian monk I had met in Tibet, had told me about – that seed where her magick had taken hold. I had an idea that required close access. It was the only thing I could think to try that would let me send her away having been definitively punished by me, though I wasn't sure it would work. Still, it was better than simply killing her outright.

I located it easily, just as the monk had said, then reached in and closed my mental fist around it. I pulled at it, feeling a tearing sensation as I managed to start removing the ability from her mind.

I flayed her magick away, slowly so she would be aware of it, and I felt her anguish at the loss. Then I withdrew from her head and stared into her eyes.

"Please, NO!" she begged, and I glanced into the window next to us in case the sandwich guy was back. Fortunately not, I didn't need him thinking I was trying to do something inappropriate here. I stored the magick I had taken in Seren, then stepped away from her. She dropped to her knees and sobbed.

"Please," she begged again, "I'm already in trouble for not stopping you when you broke in. If I go back having failed again, I'm likely to be executed!"

"With no magick," I replied coldly, "they might consider what I've done to you as a fate *worse* than death for a magick user. Maybe now you can get away from them, since you're of no further use, and you'll be able to get your life turned around.

"If you do, come and find me again. Remember, what is lost can sometimes be found again." I saw her eyes widen as she understood precisely what I was saying: if she pulled herself together and got on the right path, maybe she could earn her magick back.

"Let this be the final warning," I finished angrily. "Go back and tell your *master* that next time, I'll take more than just magick from whoever he sends. I'm done being merciful, now I play for keeps." Then I turned on my heel and walked back to Dinas Affaraon, hearing her still sobbing.

No more mister nice guy!

Chapter 14

I went back into the shop and told Summer the bare bones of what had happened, reassuring her that hopefully this would scare the Order enough to make them leave her alone now.

"Still, keep your eyes open, just in case," I told her with a hug. "I've already told her to tell them the next person *won't* be making it back, so hopefully they'll finally get the message." Her wide eyes made me realise this situation was definitely changing me, maybe more than I would like. Then she shocked me with her comment.

"I was wondering how long it would take," she said. "You've always been such a softie, I was worried you wouldn't be able to do what was needed in this thing you've started. Now I can stop worrying about you quite so much."

Gauvain's approval and agreement filtered through as he flew back to my shoulder from the perch where he'd been observing the proceedings.

I must say, I was impressed with your solution of removing her ability, he remarked. *Though her return to report failure may yet lead to her death, even with the fate you have already settled upon her.*

"At least then it's not me killing a young girl," I replied, recognising my own soft-heartedness. I was getting there, but baby steps made it easier. Gauvain tutted softly in my mind, Summer shaking her head slightly as she apparently heard him too.

"Maybe you're not quite as hardened as all that just yet," she said, "but at least I know you're still you. I'd hate to think your magick had turned you into someone I didn't recognise at all. Now get out of here, I've got work to do." Summer shooed me away, though she gave me a tight hug before walking back to the counter. I smiled at the subtle admission that she had been worried about my mental fortitude, shaking my head.

"You *do* remember who the boss is, right?" I joked, holding my hands up as she spun to narrow her eyes at me, as she did every time I commented about it. "Oops, look at the time, must dash!" My last sight was of her laughing face as I shifted back to my room at Seirina's.

"I hope that puts your mind to rest about my willingness to do what I have to," I said to G as we arrived, and he nipped my ear softly in agreement.

After I'd spent the rest of the afternoon in my usual manner, another thought came to mind with regard to our upcoming assault: What about weapons? I hadn't used any up to now, but a big fight was different from a brief one on one. Even a four on one was easy enough if they didn't have magick. Going up against the Order was a whole different ballgame.

The weres and vampires pretty much *were* weapons, and most of the rest were magick users, but I needed to talk to Seirina about other weaponry.

I don't care how good you *think* you are, a shotgun to the face will still screw up your entire day. Weapons would also mean we wouldn't have to exhaust our own energy stores in every situation. Any few advantage points were worth chasing.

I made a mental note of my idea, then got ready for bed. Gauvain finished his evening preen and settled down on his perch for the night, meanwhile I closed my eyes and drifted off to sleep.

My night was disturbed by dreams coloured by the discussions of that evening. I watched battles but was unable to help, I lost my magick and tried to run from monsters but couldn't move my legs; you know, restful and peaceful stuff.

I was glad when my alarm finally went off and I could head off to Lucian's pyramid. I felt much better after my energy collection, and my run left my head clearer and more grounded. I headed back to Seirina's house where I finished the cure with my shower, then went down for breakfast.

Despite my energy collection and exercise remedy, my lack of sleep must have shown in the dark circles under my eyes.

"Good grief," Seirina exclaimed, "you look like crap. Did you get *any* sleep last night?"

I grimaced, reaching for the coffee pot.

"Meh, not much," I replied, yawning. "My brain decided to treat me to a full-on worst case scenario montage. Not exactly the sweet dreams I was hoping for." I yawned again then sipped at my coffee, sighing in satisfaction as the first hint of caffeine reached my bloodstream.

"I'd be surprised if you *weren't* feeling some anxiety about the fighting to come," Seirina stated sympathetically. "Only an idiot isn't worried by the prospect of war. You may be powerful and talented now but all it takes is one lucky shot."

"Talking of shots, I've been meaning to ask," I said. "What kinds of weapons do you have around here? I was thinking last night, we'd be best off not relying purely on magick and brute force if we don't want to exhaust our forces in the first battle."

Seirina agreed, tilting her head as she wondered where I was going with this.

"So, what have you got around here? You wouldn't happen to be a secret doomsday prepper with a huge underground bunker filled with guns and explosives would you?" I finished jokingly hopeful, not really expecting anything of the sort.

"This isn't Hollywood, I'm afraid." She smiled, shaking her head. "No hidden stash of grenades and Gatling guns. My name's Crow, not Schwarzenegger!"

"Damn, we could have used a terminator or commando on this." I laughed as I continued the film reference. "Even a xenomorph or a predator would have been useful!"

She rolled her eyes.

"Why do men always think that *guns* are the way forward?" she asked rhetorically.

I shrugged.

"They may not be the be all and end all, but they certainly help in a fight. Hell, I'd even settle for a decent sword or a crossbow. Anything so I'm not going in there with nothing to wave at them other than my brain."

"You're probably right," she said with a wicked look in her eye. "After all, we wouldn't want them to humiliate themselves by laughing so hard they just fall over!"

"Oh, that's really nice," I grumped. "Just for that, I'm not going to save Elrulin for you." I stuck my tongue out, the true epitome of maturity. "First come, first served, and I'll be keeping score like Gimli and Legolas!"

Seirina smiled as evil a smile as I had yet seen from her.

"Oh, a contest is it?" she taunted. "They *do* say that competition brings out the best in a man. I'll look forward to seeing if it's true!"

She scanned me up and down, almost as if I were a horse that she'd previously thought was a riding school hack but suddenly won the Grand National first time out of the gate with the Derby coming up.

"I think a few weapons might actually make this more interesting," she considered aloud. "Firearms are a bad idea. You see, magick tends to make them jam and malfunction far too easily.

"Your throwaway comment was quite right: A sword would be your best option. I'm sure we can locate a suitable blade for you. I already have my own." She looked at me in a way that made me realise that whatever her chosen weapon was, I probably didn't want to know it's origin story.

"So where do I find an appropriate blade?" I asked, kind of getting into the whole bloodthirsty spirit of the competition.

"In mind, magick and metal," she replied.

Oh, this could be interesting…

Chapter 15

"So are you saying," I clarified, "that the only way for me to get a suitable weapon is to make it myself?" I had never been great at metalwork when I was at school, so the idea of making a sword for myself may be fascinating as an abstract concept but was somewhat concerning in actuality.

"What, you thought magickally attuned weaponry was available on Amazon?" Seirina asked incredulously. "We're not talking about a knife for skinning a rabbit or gathering firewood when you're camping.

"This needs to be something you can use to channel your power through. A weapon that will resist enemy magick and enable you to cut through unfriendly shields. To do that, the sword – or dagger or knife or whatever – has to be in synch with you and your abilities."

It made sense but wasn't something I had considered before. Then again, I hadn't exactly been planning things out since I got my magick. This had more of a 'flying by the seat of my pants' type of operation, as exemplified by my fantastically detailed planning before heading to the Order's headquarters.

Maybe one day I'd actually get the chance to plan more than a week ahead. For now, I needed to figure out how to craft a sword in the next forty-eight hours. Unless, of course, I wanted to stroll into the upcoming war with nothing more than a stick for a weapon.

I suddenly understood why Seirina had given me such a wicked grin when talking about her own weapon. She had probably made it centuries ago, back when she could still go to a friendly blacksmith. Since the industrial revolution, blacksmithing as a trade had declined significantly.

Nowadays, most knives were made by large companies in robotic foundries. There were still working blacksmiths but I doubted that many of them were armourers. Those that *did* have that level of knowledge and skill probably worked for museums or maybe Renaissance fairs.

I was quite certain that if I walked up one of those artisans, they would have been far too curious for comfort. It would also take too long to make and I doubted they would allow me to be actively involved in the process. I voiced my concerns to Seirina.

"Not a bad assessment of your situation," she concurred. "You're right in that I had my sword created a long time ago. Given my magickal affinity, I had blood and death involved in the forging. You won't need that, fortunately."

A chill ran down my back as she spoke so casually of killing for the sake of creating a weapon that would be used for yet more death.

"Who..." I moistened my suddenly dry mouth and tried again. "Who did you kill in the forging?" I whispered. To my relief she rolled her eyes and sighed.

"How did I know you'd immediately go there?" she asked. "This is why necromancers don't advertise. All anyone thinks is that we're out killing anyone we want and making hordes of undead slaves! Not all of us want to end the world, you know!

"Why do you think I refused the Order's advances?" she continued heatedly. "I've always tried to use my abilities for *good*. For your information, Mr High-and-Mighty Maddox, it was a *sheep* that was sacrificed for the creation of my blade.

"I used it's blood to quench the steel, instead of wasting it as often happened during butchering. Then the meat went to feed the hungry of my village as mutton stew, so it was a *positive* death that served life!"

I felt like a truly humungous judgemental asshole right then. I was just as guilty of judging her because of her abilities – something she had no choice over, having been born that way – as everyone else who had ever persecuted her.

"Please accept my sincerest apologies, Seirina," I said. "I should have known better. Everything I've seen since I met you has proven you're a good person."

She nodded gratefully, although still looked grumpy.

Since I needed her help to make my sword, I stepped forward and put my arm around her shoulders. She patted my hand and then stepped away.

"OK, no need to get mushy," she said, though I had a suspicion she was genuinely moved by my apology. I certainly *hoped* she was, as I didn't want to be on the wrong side of someone with her combined skill sets.

"So how can I create a weapon in such a short time?" I asked. "I've never made more than a wonky candlestick, back when I was about fourteen. I've watched a few YouTube videos of people making knives, but I have nothing like their level of skill."

"The first thing to remember is, you'll be using magick to make the blade," Serina told me, taking on a more instructional tone. "Remember what I said: mind, magick and metal.

"You have a huge advantage over me in your level of power and ability, so you should have no problem making your sword in only a few hours. The thing that will probably take you the longest is *designing* your blade in the first place. Do you have any idea what you want it to look like?"

Every sword I had seen or read about in fiction or history started running through my head. Did I want a katana? A broadsword? A claymore? Would something like Sting or Anduril, Orcrist or Glamdring be best?

What about Blade's blade (badum bum, tsh)? The Highlander's sword? Something from *The Inheritance Cycle*? The swords from *Forty Seven Ronin*? Stormbringer? Excalibur? Inigo Montoya's sword?

Having only ever used a bokken during my martial arts training, never a live blade, I had no idea what kind of sword would feel right for me. My wooden practice swords were obviously most similar to a katana, but I didn't want to be limited in my design.

"I think I have some research to do. I'll go and have a think, then meet you for lunch to go over my ideas." I headed upstairs to contemplate my options.

After some consideration I decided on a double edged blade rather than single, simply for the greater adaptability in combat. That already eliminated several famous blades from the creative process, so the next step was to go online and see if I couldn't narrow the design specs further.

I decided I didn't want to copy *any* blade exactly. If this was going to be a weapon for me to focus magick through, it had to be *mine*. Imitation might be the sincerest form of flattery, but it wasn't necessarily conducive to the most natural feel when it counted.

I looked at several different hilt designs. I wanted to be able to use my sword either single or double handed, so a hand-and-a-half (also known as a bastard) sword hilt would be best. I wanted the pommel to be a solid cone of metal so I could use it for a reverse strike if needed.

Next was the crossguard. I wanted something more useful than a simple crosspiece and the functionality of a sai appealed to me. The three prongs allowed the wielder to lock an opponent's blade and potentially wrench it out of their hand. That was a useful little trick, so I sketched a compact crescent-shaped crossguard on the hilt I'd already drawn.

Last but certainly not least, the blade itself. I decided on a triangular blade, something like Anduril from Lord of the Rings but not as long. I thought around forty inches would be about right, since most katanas were that sort of length so it would feel similar to the bokkens I had practiced with in the past.

Since it would be reinforced by magick, I thought about two and a half to three inches wide at the crossguard would be sufficient. Any wider and the blade would become too heavy to use one-handed, any narrower and it would start looking like a rapier. Plus if it was too narrow, it wouldn't have the weight for powerful strikes.

I originally wanted a Damascus steel blade, multiple layers like the very highest quality katanas from the Middle Ages. After some research on sword-making sites, however, I discovered that modern ten-ninety-five carbon steel was vastly superior and didn't actually benefit from the folding process. Now I had to hope Seirina had access to the materials I needed.

After all my research and planning, I was definitely ready for lunch so I headed down to the kitchen. Mrs Wilson had put together some mushroom and Swiss cheese omelettes, the smell of which had me salivating from halfway down the stairs.

Seirina was already sitting down, so I slid into my seat eagerly as my plate was set down in front of me. I recounted the results of my research and design thoughts, to which Seirina responded with a thoughtful "hmmm".

"You've obviously considered this quite carefully," she said eventually, her speech pattern slowing as she apparently considered the options. "I have one question for you in order to know if this is possible in the limited time we have. You learned transmogrification, correct?"

I nodded, already thinking I knew where this was headed. Her next comment confirmed exactly what I thought, with one additional twist.

"If you examined a knife made of the right carbon steel," she continued, "could you replicate it out of a lesser steel and charcoal?"

I had never considered fusing the two materials together. That would be less like transmogrification and more like magickal baking, taking the ingredients and fusing them in the right proportions to get the desired result. It should certainly take less energy than turning some of the lower quality metal within the substance of it *into* carbon.

I explained my interpretation to Seirina at which she pursed her lips and looked down at her plate thoughtfully.

"Transmogrification would be more like turning some of the steel into carbon, which takes much more energy," I told her. "If you've got some reasonable steel and some good charcoal, blending the two takes only a fraction of the effort. If you've got a way to heat it up, it might be even easier." I was a little disappointed, but not surprised, when she shook her head.

"Sorry, but blacksmithing was never a passion of mine," she laughed. One look at her delicate features would tell anybody that, so I joined her amusement. "Unless the oven is enough, you're going to have to come up with another way."

Now it was my turn to roll my eyes.

"You made a crack about guys always wanting guns," I said. "In the same vein, why do women think that you can simply stick something in the oven?" I snickered, my amusement dying away as she narrowed her eyes to glare at me.

When she broke into an evil chuckle and pointed at my nervous face, I tutted and flapped a hand in her direction.

"Stop trying to scare me," I said. "I'm nervous enough about all this already. If you can get me the steel and carbon, plus some wood for the hilt and leather strapping to wrap it in, I *think* I could use magick to accomplish the rest."

I already knew the best place to do this, now it was time to get to work.

Chapter 16

Seirina got up and handed me a kitchen knife from the block on the counter. Meanwhile Mrs Wilson left the room and gathered up a few steel rods and a bag of charcoal from somewhere, returning to put them on the floor next to me in the kitchen. I tilted my head and raised an eyebrow.

"Umm, not to seem ungrateful or anything," I remarked, "but is there a reason you have stuff like this lying around?" She didn't exactly seem like the DIY sort, so why the metal?

"The charcoal is for the barbecue," she explained, which made sense and was the bit I *had* figured out. "As for the steel, it was left over after I had some workmen in to repair Ms Crow's greenhouse."

At least it hadn't been part of Seirina's supplies for her necromancy. I didn't want anything distorting or corrupting my magick when I made this sword. Well intentioned or not, necromancy was not something I wanted to have to contend with when I was doing something complex for the first time.

I thanked both of them and gathered up my supplies. Mrs Wilson handed me two old leather belts, telling me that Seirina never wore them any longer. I knew I could find wood where I was heading, so I now had everything I needed for my project.

I said my farewells, called to Gauvain, and we returned to Lucian's pyramid for the second time that day. It was the logical place for me to work, since there were plenty of sources to bolster my energy.

Before I tried doing anything with the steel, I practiced collecting and focusing the heat in the area into a discrete location. If I could use it almost like a blowtorch, I could heat the metal to enable me to work it effectively. Gauvain went off to fly and hunt while I set to work.

It took a little practice but I soon managed it by thinking of a focusing lens, much as I had when I was first starting to learn to move a rock in Aaru. Given the intensity of the sun, I figured I should be able to direct quite a bit of heat into the steel. Then I could use telekinesis to manipulate the metal into the shape I wanted.

Thankfully, since I was using magick, if the sword wasn't quite right I'd be able to reshape it. It wouldn't even weaken the steel, as I shouldn't need to heat it as much as a regular blacksmith. Once I was happy with the shape, I could use the heat to temper it.

I was sure Lucian would have a source of water somewhere nearby that I could use to quench my sword, then I could sharpen it with magick. I reached out with my power to check for water in the area, remembering its feel from my transmogrification lessons.

I located a stream running through the forest not far from the western perimeter of the pyramid's grounds. I found a block of stone and used magick to mould it into a trough, then telekinetically brought some water from the river to fill it.

Once I had made my preparations, I took the knife Seirina had lent me and sat down on the steps of the pyramid. I extended my senses towards the blade, trying to identify the particular feel of the high carbon-content steel.

I compared it to that of the steel in the rods Mrs Wilson had given me, along with the carbon in the barbecue charcoal. After a while I figured out the particular characteristics and magickal signature of the good steel and the required balance of the basic steel with the carbon.

It was almost like trying to work out the spices in a cookie recipe, only easier because I could examine it on a molecular level with my magickal sense. I placed the steel rods on the ground near the water bath and began to heat them.

I reached out and collected some of the charcoal, fusing it with the metal as it became hot. Once it matched the feel of the knife blade, I melded the rods together into a single bar of high quality steel.

While it was still warm and reasonably pliable, I drew the steel out into the shape I had envisioned for my sword. I swung it experimentally but unexpectedly found it was a little too light for my taste.

Instead of tapering all the way to the tip like an extended triangle, I made it more like a narrow broad sword until about four fifths of the way up. From there it tapered to a point as before, like a slightly narrower and longer Roman gladius. As I worked, I embedded some of the runes I had learned from Master Harfi – the jeweller in Aaru who had made Seren for me – into the steel to help strengthen and protect it.

Once I was happy with the look and feel of the edges and the central fuller of the blade, I created the curved crossguard. I made it into a single piece of steel with the body of the sword, then found some dry hardwood and fashioned it into a hilt.

Before I attached the wooden hilt, I heated the steel as my research had indicated to temper it, then quenched it to strengthen it properly. I had learnt this allowed the sword to flex when needed, but still be hard enough to hold a sharp edge.

I made sure the wood felt right, if a bit narrow, in my hands then created the conical pommel of my sketch. The lump of steel helped counter the weight of the blade, balancing the sword almost perfectly.

The final touch was to bind the handle in leather. The belts weren't exactly suitable for wrapping a sword handle but, as with the steel, they provided me with the raw materials I needed.

I was able to compare them to my own leather belt, then adjust the structure and finish of the leather to a more appropriate condition. I wound the resultant material around the hilt of my new sword, bound it to the wood firmly, and it was done.

I found some more wood and created a scabbard for my sword, compressing and polishing the wood to a high sheen both outside for the look and inside so that my sword would glide in and out (ooh-err, missus).

I could tell I was tired after my efforts by the fact that I was making juvenile off-colour jokes. Gauvain snorted in my mind as he flew towards me, knowing through our bond that I was done.

You know full well that fatigue is not a prerequisite for your typically puerile humour to make an appearance, he remarked, and I had no option but to agree. I refreshed myself with a little more energy from the sunlight, then headed back to my temporary home base.

As usual when I went to the pyramid, even though I had been there for several hours only a few minutes had passed here. That was another reason I had decided to work there: I hadn't been sure how easy I was going to find it to make my sword, so extra time might have been needed.

Seirina was glad to see me return with news of success. Mrs Wilson, on the other hand, was more pleased to see the return of her favourite knife. It was nice to know where I ranked in the grand scheme of things!

Both of them expressed their admiration for the appearance of my sword and its scabbard. Seirina assessed it magickally, telling me that she couldn't even touch it which I found reassuring. Thankfully, it seemed that I had absorbed the metalworking techniques in Aaru well enough to replicate them as needed, even if I had first seen them in jewellery rather than weaponry.

I took my new weapon out into the garden and went through some of the sword forms I had practised with my wooden replicas in the past. The balance was exquisite, making the weapon feel like an extension of my arm exactly as it should.

Gauvain watched from a nearby tree, occasionally making a few suggestions on my form based on what we had seen during our online research.

Sometimes one's body didn't quite follow one's mental image, so an objective external view prevented me from fooling myself and developing bad habits. The other thing that he suggested, which I had already considered, was that I needed a name for my sword.

All of the great weapons in fiction and legend had names; now I had to come up with something appropriate. I didn't want to use a name from a legendary weapon, since it would create unrealistic expectations and I hadn't recreated any of them anyway.

I wasn't sure whether I wanted a Gaelic name, a Welsh name from my own heritage, an Arabic name in honour of Isis... Did I want an aggressive name, a hopeful name, a symbolic name? Finding the right name for something could try the patience of a thousand saints and the wisdom of five hundred wise men.

After I finished my sword practice, Gauvain and I went up to my room to try to come up with a name. I got out my phone and went to Google to look up some boys' names. I found a few that sounded alright, but none seemed to be quite what I wanted.

There was one that made me smile since it was far too literal. I made a note of it to mention later at the right time, since a little humour could be a good stress release.

Next I went to Google Translate to see if any sword names I could think of sounded good in other languages. Names like Battle Dragon or Soul Fire came to mind, but none seemed to fit. Finally Gauvain decided to chip in.

Perhaps you should consider precisely what you wish your blade to symbolise, he suggested. *After all, are you truly doing this to be a conqueror or to embody the fury of the gods? Or do you have loftier aspirations for the outcome of this conflict?*

His different perspective struck a chord in my mind. I *wasn't* doing this out of a desire for conflict or glory. I was doing this to attempt to free the magickal community from the threat the Order represented, to free my friends from the fear of reprisal.

That thought led me to translate the word 'liberator' into Welsh, Scots Gaelic, Irish, and finally Arabic. Scots Gaelic was saoradh. Irish was similar, translating to saoirseoir. They weren't bad but I was tripping over my own tongue saying them, so I didn't fancy trying to pronounce them to other people.

Welsh was even worse, without a single vowel in the entire word: Rhyddfrydwr. I took one look at the screen and burst out laughing, startling G. He joined in once I explained the joke, and we both struggled to say it, failing dismally.

After all that I didn't hold out much hope for Arabic but I checked the translation, nevertheless. When the word appeared on the screen, it resonated in my mind with the image of my sword.

I looked from the screen to my sword and sensed the rightness of the name. I held it in my mind as I touched the sword, my magick burning the name into the wood of the scabbard as I said it out loud.

"*Muharar.*"

Chapter 17

I told Seirina the sword's name at dinner that evening, explaining the translation when she asked. She firmly approved of my reasoning behind the choice, agreeing that this should be a fight for freedom not power.

As she said it, my mind flashed back to the image of the first time we met when she was using her Scottish accent. I swallowed the laugh that threatened to erupt at the memory.

I was glad I'd managed to get my sword completed before the war council, as I wasn't sure how much lag time we'd have between the meeting and the start of our assaults. I mentioned my query to Seirina but she only shrugged.

"It'll depend on how long it takes to get all the fighters gathered together," she replied.

I realised that I hadn't told her what Lucian had taught me.

"Umm, I know how to bring them all together through portals," I explained. "If someone can show me a picture of where they are, I can open a magickal doorway right to us. It's like I said I could do for the delegates for the next meeting."

"You know, just when I think I have you figured out, you surprise me again," she remarked. "Sometimes you're shocked by even the smallest magickal occurrence, then at other times you're completely unfazed by the most dramatic abilities. Wouldn't opening a portal for an army be a bit more difficult than for one person? You're a walking contradiction, a true oxymoron."

"Hey, I'm neither an ox nor a moron." I laughed, and she shook her head in despair. "But no, the most energy is actually used to *open* the portal. Holding it open only takes a minimal amount of effort." Her eyes widened but she leant forward in interest at my explanation after my comic riff.

"Why are you always such a goofball?" she asked in exasperation, and I shrugged.

"I find it easier to laugh at myself before anyone else does," I explained, thinking back to my time at school. "That way I can control the jokes and they hurt less." Humour had always been a defence mechanism for me, my anxiety often turning it quite acerbic.

"You need to learn there're more kinds of people in this world," she said, slightly more sympathetically than before. "Not everyone is an asshole who wants to hurt you in some way. I know kids are deeply unpleasant, especially up to a certain age, but *most* people lose that attitude as they grow up a little more."

I shrugged slightly, aware that she was right for the most part. Summer and Emily were prime examples of people being decent human beings. On the other hand, Ciarán Heffernan – the man who had pursued me to Tibet in search of the Veil of Isis – was the epitome of a schoolyard bully who stayed exactly the same as he got older.

"I prefer to play it safe and get the jokes in first," I reasoned. "I can always back down on the humour later if I need to. I prefer to disarm people with a non-threatening first impression and try to make a new friend, rather than wait for them to judge me and maybe end up at odds."

Seirina shook her head. "You really had a lousy time as a kid, didn't you?" she observed sympathetically but shrewdly. My spine stiffened a little at the pity in her voice.

I had been to another plane of existence, met goddesses, and returned with powers I had only dreamt of. I didn't need *anyone's* pity any more. I made the decision, in that moment of crystal clarity, that I would start trying to develop more self-confidence. I seriously doubted Isis wanted her chosen champion to be some timid little mousy guy, afraid of what everyone thought of him.

Seirina must have seen something change in my expression and she tilted her head, raising one eyebrow as she did so. I simply smiled slightly and raised my own eyebrow in reply, saying nothing.

"Oh, so you're going to try to be mysterious now?" she asked. "Really? After everything you've already shared, *now* you're going to play the strong silent card?"

I laughed, realising it was definitely too late to act mysterious and aloof around her (acting a doof, however, was still my go-to move).

Between everything she knew about my feelings for Angelica, my tales about what I'd learnt in Aaru, and all our discussions since I'd been here, she knew more about me than anyone else except probably Summer. Then again Summer had known me for years not days, so she did have kind of a head start.

"Fine," I allowed, "yes I had a rough time as a kid. With everything that's happened to me recently, though, I think I've finally found some self-confidence. Still, thirty plus years of personality doesn't just go away. I'll probably always be a bit of a goofball, but I can stop using it as quite so much of a defence now." I thought through it as I was explaining myself and felt more comfortable with my approach as I was saying it.

"You're probably right," she agreed, "your humour will always be a part of you now. It's like someone who was a late bloomer as a child – they always develop a more complex personality than the pretty or athletic kids who end up effortlessly popular, since they have to work harder to make friends."

Summer had often told me of her struggles as a child. I knew who she was *now*, and she was one of the most genuine people I knew. I sometimes envied Emily in her luck at finding someone like Summer, but they were so perfectly matched and happy together you could never resent their relationship.

My disastrous blind date with Summer's friend flitted through my mind again and I smiled at the total incompatibility we had discovered. I recounted it to Seirina when she asked what I was smiling at, which made her laugh.

"You should be grateful you found out early," she observed. "At least you didn't invest lots of time before you discovered you weren't right for each other. Plus now you have another interest, right?"

I winced, thinking of my last less than successful talk with Angelica, and Seirina put a hand on my arm.

"I know things are rough at the moment," she said. "Still, I know she really does care about you. She's still feeling very vulnerable after what happened before you got her out of there, so she's pushing away everyone with the power to hurt her right now.

"You just need to show her you're there for her when she needs you, while still giving her some space to work through her issues. The twins are helping, talking things through when she wants to. They also keep pointing out everything you went through for her and that anyone in your position would have done what you did, including her."

I felt a surge of gratitude towards Gabby and Izzy on hearing that, making a mental note to thank them the next time I had a chance to talk to them alone. I had a thought of something I could research as a way to pay them back, though it would take time and a serious amount of study and energy, if it was even possible. They might refuse the offer, but at least I could try to give them the option.

For now, it was time to get some sleep. Tomorrow was going to be a big day, what with the next meeting in the evening. I wanted to be as fresh as possible. I hoped we would have enough bodies to make this thing a viable plan. I didn't want to have gone through all this ultimately to find out we had no chance of success.

Hopefully, even if we didn't have an army of thousands, the combination of supernatural creatures with magick users and whatever Lucian came up with would be enough. We would have the element of surprise on our side as well, and that might be sufficient to give us the final edge we needed.

My sleep was about as restful as sunbathing naked in a patch of poison ivy infested with fire ants and with my genitals smeared in honey. More 'need to run but can't move' dreams, a few 'naked at the front of class', one or two of my favourite 'unprepared public speaking' montages, and a special guest appearance by 'falling without a parachute'.

Overall, I was pretty glad to get up and go to the pyramid for my daily collection and run. Gauvain flew up to start his morning hunt, then returned to me as he became alerted to Lucian's presence. At the top of the structure Lucian waved at me, so I teleported myself up to talk to him.

"Hello there, Gavan," he greeted me jovially, our last disagreement apparently forgotten or at least well hidden. I kept my alertness level high, however, as I didn't fancy another violent introduction to a wall. Although out here, he would probably just fling me off the top of the pyramid. That made me think…

"Morning Lucian," I replied distractedly, probably sounding as tired as I felt after my disturbed night.

He cocked his head to the side.

"You don't exactly sound enthusiastic for this evening's upcoming events," he observed, so I recounted a few highlights from my mental self-torture last night.

"Ahh, battle jitters," he remarked sympathetically, "everyone gets them. Well, everyone who cares about their troops and the outcome of the battle. It's merely your adrenaline kicking in, making your mind work overtime."

"Yeah, I kinda figured. Another reason to gather some last top-up to my reserves and then unwind with a run; try and burn off some of my nervous energy," I mused.

"I'll let you crack on then," he stated, surprising me with his use of one of my habitual colloquialisms. "I did manage to track down the two individuals I mentioned to you. They'll be ready to attend your little soiree, then be available when you need them.

"I had thought about a brother and sister that I know in Cornwall, then reconsidered. I don't think you're established and comfortable enough in your abilities yet to deal with them, especially in the midst of a war, plus they're kind of insular and don't really like to get involved with much outside their local area."

I thanked him and headed back down to ground level, momentarily intrigued by his mention of the siblings then discounting them as something to address after this was all over.

My first energy collection went directly to waking me up and replacing the sleep I hadn't had, so I soon felt better. I went on to complete my usual circuit, drawing slightly more than I usually did in the knowledge that I might not get another chance for a while.

Gauvain observed from the skies above, choosing not to hunt but rather lend me his silent support. When I started my run he stayed directly above me, banking and wheeling as we went, revelling in his mastery of the air.

I waved up at the top of the pyramid, unsure if Lucian were still watching, then headed back for my shower. I felt better after my morning wash, G also choosing to take a quick dip today. He then went onto his perch to preen (huge surprise) while I went down for breakfast.

I breathed in the divine scent of fresh-brewed Cafegeddon, stepping through the kitchen door with my eyes closed in anticipation of that first sip.

"Good morning, fellow caffeine addict…" My voice died in my throat as I opened my eyes to see we had visitors. The twins smiled and waved from their seats at the kitchen table. I raised a hand in their direction distractedly. My attention was firmly centred on the other intruder to my anticipated morning ritual.

"Hello Gavan," Angelica said softly. Well, shit.

Chapter 18

My shoulders tightened at those two simple words. If I'd known they were here, I would have gone into the study like I had on previous occasions. When had they arrived? My sojourns to Lucian's pyramid didn't allow much time to pass here, so they must have arrived while I was in the shower.

As I stood frozen in the doorway, Seirina came up behind me and shoved me gently.

"Shift, ye great lummox," she said, putting on her accent for fun. "Ah need mah coffee afore I kill ye!" I stepped aside, my face remaining blank.

Every time I thought I'd reached an equilibrium, come to a decision not to be affected, there she was. Today she seemed almost back to herself, which really didn't help as it brought back all the thoughts and feelings she'd aroused (in more ways than one). Angie.

I had known she and the twins would be here today, what with the meeting happening later this evening, but I'd expected them after lunch. Their early arrival, combined with Angelica's apparent recovery, had thrown me not just for a loop but a complete rollercoaster.

No matter how many times I made the decision to focus on what mattered, my damned emotions kept creeping up and giving me a sucker punch to the 'nads. There were *so* many other ways I wished my groin could experience Angelica, yet solid emotional kicking seemed to be all I got.

I took a deep breath, swallowed my testicles out of my throat and back down to where they belonged, and went and sat down at the table. My cheeks were tense as I smiled at everyone, then reached for the coffee pot.

"Well, now that everyone's completely uncomfortable," Seirina said, scanning the room, "maybe we should move onto something a little more productive?"

I glanced at the assembled women, feeling outnumbered as ever, and heroically looked deep into my coffee mug as I drank.

"Clearly Gavan has nothing to contribute right now," Seirina continued, making the twins snigger. "However I think we should probably all adjourn to the study so we can discuss a few details prior to the meeting this evening."

So much for me being the supposed leader of this little enterprise. Every time I saw Angelica recently, I felt like some inexperienced fourteen-year-old who'd never kissed a girl before.

I had made the decision to ignore my feelings and concentrate on the fight, which was great when I was angry and could use that to bury everything else. As soon as that clarity faded, everything came rushing back and blindsided me.

I hated that my emotions simply refused to listen to my intellect. I *knew* how important this fight was, how many people could end up being hurt if Elrulin kept on going the way he had been, but my stupid heart kept overriding me.

I needed to sort this out before it decided to crop up mid-battle and get me killed. Once we'd had our little pre-meeting meeting, I was going to have to talk to Angelica and work this out one way or another.

I nodded to Seirina, refilled my coffee and stood up. As I turned away from the table, I could have sworn I heard someone mutter "*Men!*" under their breath. I kept walking, afraid of my own reaction, but promised myself I would respond at the appropriate time.

I was sick of being surrounded by a sea of oestrogen in this house, which was another good reason to get this underway. I missed my shop and my home – though come to think of it, I was outnumbered there as well. I really needed more guy friends.

I went into the study and chose the love seat in the bay window, making sure to sit squarely in the centre so no one else could join me. Seirina noticed immediately, rolling her eyes and shaking her head slightly as she went around to her chair.

The twins came in and went straight to one of the chairs in front of the desk, tilting their heads in sympathy to me as they went. Angie, on the other hand, looked as if she was about to walk over to me. I twisted towards the desk, rather than out into the middle of the room, and put my left knee up onto the seat. I looped my foot under my right thigh, thus claiming the entire area. Male inelegance at its finest saves the day again.

She'd pushed me away last time. Now she was going to have to make more of an effort if she planned on there being anything between us. She paused briefly, so I sipped my coffee to break any eye contact.

Finally she accepted the inevitable, walking over to the other chair next to the twins and sitting down. They reached over and squeezed her hand, then Gabby and Izzy suddenly glared at me. She'd yelled at me last time, how come *I* was suddenly the bad guy?

Seirina glanced over at me with one eyebrow raised and her hands clasped in front of her on the desk, probably waiting for me to ask my questions, but I kept drinking my coffee. OK so I was being childish, but why should I have to be the one to make the effort here?

I had already shown how I felt by putting my life on the line during my rescue effort. If women wanted equality, that should apply to all areas. I could never understand why there had to be equality in the workplace and home, but as soon as it came to dating it was always ladies first, the man should pay, hold the doors, make the running and the women can sit back and shoot down any corny pick-up lines.

I was a firm believer in chivalry but once a woman made the decision to walk away, shouldn't *she* have to make the next move? Otherwise the guy runs the risk of being seen as harassing or being called a stalker.

As far as I was concerned, the whole damned thing was more dangerous than a tightrope on fire over a minefield floating on a shark tank. Moreover, I considered myself to be about as clueless over how to negotiate it as someone in a blindfold and noise cancelling earphones with their hands tied behind their back.

Look, all I'm trying to say is I thought it was safer right now to not get involved in the whole deal. From the looks of things, however, that was clearly the wrong position to take if the twins' expressions were anything to judge by.

To quote my mother, 'I was never right but I was wrong again'!

Seirina, apparently realising I was going to be about as useful as a comb to a bald man, took charge of the meeting.

"So we'll be having the second meeting this evening as you know," she began. "However, there was something that Gavan mentioned a day or two ago." The twins and Angie looked at me but I stayed focused on Seirina's face. She narrowed her eyes at me then continued.

"All of you were coerced in one way or another into working for the Order, so how can we be sure there aren't more in your situation? Do you know of anyone else in the same position?"

They all turned back to her and the twins were quick to confirm exactly what I'd thought.

"There's almost certainly quite a few members who are there reluctantly," Gabby began.

"Though we have no idea who or how many," Izzy chimed in.

"We didn't even know about Angelica's situation."

"At least not until we scanned her."

"Not really something we could do in the middle of a fight."

"Certainly not with the speed and accuracy that would be required."

"Or in enough numbers to make any significant difference."

"We doubt even someone as powerful as Gavan could manage it."

"And he's the most accomplished telepath we know."

I finally unwound enough to nod to them in thanks for their compliment, though they had confirmed exactly what I had suspected.

"That's pretty much what we thought," Seirina remarked.

"Then we've only got two choices," I decided to finally chip in, ignoring the faces turned towards me and speaking straight to Seirina. "Either we kill everyone, or we allow for surrenders but scan everyone who does. I'd be more inclined to the second course of action, but I'm not about to try to force vampires and weres to do the same.

"We can talk about it tonight, maybe ask the representatives to talk to their troops," I continued. "At the end of the day, though, this is about long-term gains. Even if we end up having to kill everyone we find, it'll finally put an end to the threat the Order represents. I'm not about to risk that just because I want to give people a chance.

"I was told during my time in Isis' dimension that I had to learn to finish a fight properly," I said, remembering Danu's unwelcome comments after my spat with Oli. "It's necessary to prevent future problems that might be even worse. I've only recently started paying attention."

With that decision made, and my line in the sand drawn, I got up and left the study. I took my mug back into the kitchen, calling Gauvain as I went. I heard him soaring down the stairs as I handed the cup to Mrs Wilson.

I went out into the back garden to stretch and clear my head from the blind-side I had received – seeing the twins and Angelica before I'd had a chance to prepare. G stayed perched on my shoulder rather than flying off, preening my hair and lending me his silent support. I closed my eyes and lifted my face to the sun, breathing deeply in the fresh air.

I heard the door open and close and felt Gauvain turn to see who it was. He showed me an image of Angelica and my shoulders tightened involuntarily.

I understand you had previously decided to compartmentalise your emotions, G commented softly in my mind, *and to set aside your personal desires in favour of the larger scope of what we are attempting to accomplish. Still, it may be advantageous to clarify your situation prior to embarking on such a perilous endeavour. That way, you should be less likely to become distracted at an inopportune moment.*

He was right, but it didn't mean I had to like it. I had, after all, decided I needed to talk to Angie even before our little session. G was merely pushing me to take my own advice, as any good friend would.

I took one more deep breath and turned to face the scariest opponent any man could ever encounter: a beautiful woman for whom he had feelings, and who was aware of that fact. That was someone who could rip your heart out of your ass, stick it in a blender and hit frappé; then drink it in a vodka cocktail with a paper umbrella and a huge smile.

I shook my head at my super-encouraging imagery and braced myself.

"Hello Angie," I said. "I guess we should talk."

Chapter 19

"Just wha-"

"I need-"

We started talking at the same time and then stopped just as quickly. Since I prided myself on being a gentleman, I motioned for her to go first. After her first few words, I was glad I had.

"I need to apologise for the way I treated you last week," she said softly, and my eyebrows headed for my hairline. She smiled at my expression. "Yes, a woman *can* admit when she's wrong, you chauvinistic ass!" She laughed as she said it, her eyes sparkling like they had in my shop that first day.

"How did I go from being a gentleman to a chauvinist in three point four seconds?" I asked in mock indignance, hiding the sudden leaping of my heart. Maybe the caffeine hadn't been such a good idea this morning. She chuckled again, then continued.

"I was dealing with a lot, but that was no reason to take it out on you," she observed, much to my relief. "I've been talking things through with Gabby and Izzy and they've helped me to put things into perspective. In your position, I would have done exactly what you did and kept my own counsel.

"You had no idea what Atma...I mean Elrulin," she corrected herself, her face showing determination as she firmly named her enemy, "would do when he didn't get his way. You didn't even know who or what he really was. I mean, how could you if no-one in the Order even had a clue."

She was obviously going through a speech she had thought about and prepared in advance, so I kept still and quiet. I was barely breathing at the possibilities this was indicating, though my heart raced, and the hair on my arms and the back of my neck stood up.

"You came after me with no thought for your own safety, as soon as you couldn't contact me the same day as your meeting," she went on, her voice growing stronger and more positive as she did. "That proved you didn't want anything to happen to me. The only one to blame in all of this is *Elrulin* –" she stressed his correct name this time, the refusal to be cowed any longer evident in her demeanour – "not you.

"I am *so* sorry for what I said to you. I *should* have been thanking you for getting me out of there. If you hadn't arrived, I'd probably still have been in that damned room. So I know it's hugely overdue but thank you, Gavan. Thank you for rescuing me, thank you for freeing me from that son-of-a-bitch, and above all thank you for caring."

Once she finished, she stepped forwards and kissed my lips lightly. My brain promptly shut down as my hormones reacted like ten pounds of sherbet dumped into a lake of cola. Something in my chest cracked and crumbled away, releasing a tightness which I hadn't even been aware of.

Everything looked watery and out of focus as my eyes welled up (damn my hay fever; shut up Gauvain). I swallowed past the sudden lump in my throat and took a deep breath. To judge from the smile on her face and the sparkle in her eyes as she stepped back from the kiss, she knew exactly how she had affected me and she was incredibly happy about it.

I stepped towards her with my arms out, G giving up and flying off my shoulder *skree*'ing loudly. I ignored him and wrapped my arms around Angie, kissing her deeply then tucking her head into the angle of my neck. I held her tight, trying to communicate without words – I didn't fully trust my voice at the moment – that I would always be there for her.

She hung onto me like I was a life raft on the Titanic and I could feel her softly sobbing, her body relaxing as the stress finally bled away for both of us. Suddenly there was cheering from the back door and the open window of the study.

"It's about time!" came Seirina's voice.

"I'm so happy for you both," Mrs Wilson chipped in.

"You'd better look after her," Gabby or Izzy piped up.

"Or you'll have us to deal with!" Finished Izzy or Gabby.

We broke apart to face the house, though I kept my arm around her shoulders protectively, and we laughed together.

"Oh, I'll be keeping him firmly in line, don't you worry about that," Angie pronounced imperiously, making our little audience cheer and giggle.

"Oh great, gang up on the man," I groused happily. "I think I prefer the idea of the meeting this evening and the fighting afterwards. At least *that* I have a chance to come out on top with."

"We can discuss who's on top later," Angie whispered to me while pinching my ass, making the others whoop and holler again. I shook my head and lifted my chin in mock dignity, trying to draw attention away from the tightening in my underwear.

Even Gauvain was laughing in my head while warning me he was about to land on the shoulder that didn't have Angie tucked into it. I set off towards the house, bringing Angelica along with me, feeling as though I was ten feet tall and walking a foot above the ground.

We smiled at Mrs Wilson as we passed her, accepting her patting us both on the cheek like a kindly aunt. She bustled off to start preparing something for later while we continued on to the study.

When we entered, Angie stepped over to the twins and accepted their hug while I paid more attention to the rustling from Iyrin's terrarium. As it came into view, I could feel it reaching across our link. I bristled and made my position abundantly clear.

Remember, you so much as touch her or Gauvain and I'll not rest until I destroy you, I thought angrily. *In fact if you stick solely to your role as 'watcher' and nothing else, we should get along fine.*

Temper, temper, it whispered in my mind, transmitting its amusement at my aggression. It seemed Iyrin viewed my outburst in the same way as I'd view a little yapping Schnauzer jumping up and down at my feet. It was insulting but at least if I was that insignificant, hopefully it would have no reason to view anyone else I cared about as important either.

I was merely going to comment that your interaction was particularly fascinating, it continued. *Even Seirina's relationship with her husband didn't afford me such a feast of interesting emotions.*

A chill ran over my body at Iyrin's choice of words. Was it *feeding* off of my emotions? Was *that* why it wanted to be connected to people? It would explain why it had chosen an enchantress to link to, and why it wanted to be attached to me with the upcoming fighting and potential future conflicts.

Ah, I see you make connections and deductions faster than Seirina, it observed, coldly degrading her to me without a second thought. *Yes, your emotions are a source of energy for me and yes, that is why I chose both you and her.*

Having felt the recent surge from your interactions, I have absolutely no interest in harming those you care about. Your joy is far more potent than your misery, since you have had too much practice in burying and suppressing your negative emotions according to your memories. So please, feel joy and love as much as possible. I shall savour your experiences like a fine wine.

With that, it withdrew from our link again and climbed back down into the depths of the foliage, leaving me beyond creeped out but glad that my friends and loved ones were apparently safe. The girls had all been hugging and *kvetching* while Iyrin had spoken to me, although Seirina looked at me, having apparently felt something from her link with the skeletal little fucker.

I shook my head, indicating it was nothing for her to worry about, and her expression cleared, going back to the happiness she had been showing before. The twins released Angie and stepped over to me while Seirina took over the hugging.

"Just remember," said Gabby.

"We'll be watching," finished Izzy.

"We've become very close to Angelica over the last couple of weeks."

"She's become like a sister to us."

"We don't care *how* strong you are now..."

"You make her cry and we'll find a way to make you regret it."

Then they reached out and pulled me into a tight hug, each of them putting their head on one side of mine so that I was sandwiched between them. A totally unique experience I savoured for the affection it conveyed. I gave them one last squeeze and let go, stepping back and smiling at them.

"I have absolutely no intention of hurting her," I reassured them. "I'm happy to take things slowly and respectfully, plus I'm not sure getting distracted by a full-on relationship right now would be the best idea for either of us. Don't get it twisted, though. She's not getting away from me again."

"I'm sorry, what was that Gavan?" Angelica said from where she and Seirina had finished their hugging. They both looked at me, clearly having heard at least something.

"Who, me?" I fumbled. "I didn't say nuthin'!" Seirina sighed and shook her head in exasperation while the others all sniggered at my discomfort. I could already tell this was going to be like trying to date a sorority member: *Everything* would be discussed, analysed, reviewed and dissected, with me as the bad guy in any controversial event.

Oh well, she was worth it. Plus now I had even more to fight for, even stronger reasons to keep focused. I had always felt most powerful and determined when fighting for those I cared about rather than myself, and this would be the ultimate expression of that.

Gauvain gripped my shoulder a little tighter, allowing his happiness for me and approval of Angelica to wash across our bond. I was grateful for his approbation and support, as it would definitely make my life easier.

Now all I had to do was survive the next few weeks until the Order, and particularly Elrulin, were defeated. At which point I might be able to actually enjoy my new status. I knew Summer, for damned sure, would be ecstatic for me and want to hear *every* detail.

Come to think of it, she and Emily would probably team up with Angelica exactly like the twins had. Maybe I shouldn't be in such a rush to get them together. I could see this ending up with me in the dog house on regular occasions. God help me if their cycles ever synced up!

I snickered to myself at my juvenile thought and felt Gauvain's exasperated tolerance of my humour.

"Now that the mushy stuff is out of the way," I observed, trying (and failing dismally, if the expressions around me were anything to go by) to act as though I hadn't been through an emotional spin cycle, "I guess we should start getting ready for war."

After all, it *had* to be safer than the relationship minefield we'd just tap-danced our way through!

Chapter 20

We spent the rest of the morning reviewing all the information we had on the Order. Although the girls knew plenty about the Bolton Castle headquarters, the other three sites were pretty much just names at this point.

Given the danger of the other sites being notified once we started our attacks, I considered the best option would be to leave the main site until last. Elrulin was the most powerful of our enemies, so it would be best to see try to gain as much intelligence from the other sites as possible before facing him.

I decided the best way would be to start up north with Edinburgh Castle. Then we could swing out west, crossing the water to Ireland for Blarney Castle. Next would be back to the UK for Rochester Castle before finally heading north again for Bolton Castle.

"You did that on purpose," Seirina said, looking at the map.

"Did what?" I asked, confused. She held up the map with the sites marked on it, on which she'd connected the dots in the order I'd listed. I immediately saw what she meant and laughed, not having realised the sequence would make the rough shape of a G.

"Umm, totally accidental I swear," I protested, suppressing my laughter. "Still it *is* appropriate, don't you think?" I acted sanctimonious, immediately obtaining the expected quadruple eye roll from everyone. Gauvain chuckled in my head.

"I can see you're going to have your work cut out, making sure he knows his place," Seirina said to Angelica. I gasped indignantly and placed the fingertips of my right hand on my chest. I was determined to keep everyone's spirits up, since we all knew how serious this was about to get but it wouldn't help to dwell on it.

Mrs Wilson had put together a kind of buffet for lunch, with some antipasti, sliced meats and cheeses, crusty bread and salad. Even Gauvain joined us, nibbling on some beef as he hadn't hunted at the pyramid earlier.

Despite my efforts, the stress was starting to ramp up for everyone. As a result, we were all doing more picking than tucking in. At least everything could be saved for later, which was probably why Mrs Wilson had done it. She really was amazing; I had to remind myself of her unusual situation on a regular basis.

As we were eating, my phone beeped with an incoming message. When I checked, it was Lucian. He wanted me to come back to the pyramid right before the meeting so I could collect the two individuals he had rounded up to help us.

The news started a flurry of speculation as to who, or what, the Devil would have recruited to our cause. He hadn't exactly given me any hints before, so I was both excited and somewhat apprehensive to see our new allies.

After lunch, I popped home to grab something to occupy us all and raise some smiles: Cards Against Humanity. The sight of the box had everyone smiling and shaking their heads even before we started, no doubt thinking of some of the potential combinations. Gauvain decided to go up to our room and get some sleep.

I'm not even going to try to describe some of the hilarity that ensued but suffice it to say, we all ended up with sore ribs from laughing. I also gained an entirely new respect for the twisted workings of the minds of Gabriella and Isabella.

Some of their ideas could make a porn star blush, so I spent half my time unsure if I was even *allowed* to laugh, given I was the only guy in a room full of women. My discomfort definitely ended up increasing the hilarity level for the girls, but for once I actually enjoyed being the butt of the jokes since much of it was due to my budding relationship with Angie.

I was also able to get my own back on regular occasions, since this game made no bones about humiliating and poking fun at absolutely everyone. I even made a few mental notes of some distinctly interesting possibilities, using Angie's reactions and expressions as my gauge. I was now more eager than ever to get through the upcoming fight, so we could explore some of these ideas!

The afternoon passed quickly in all of the laughter and distraction, leaving everyone much more relaxed and prepared for the meeting. By the time Mrs Wilson said that dinner was ready, everyone was much hungrier than we had been at lunch.

I took some meat up to G and he nibbled my finger appreciatively. He decided to stay at Seirina's when I went to see Lucian, so his presence wouldn't colour any discussions.

After a nice vegetarian meal of mushroom stroganoff, I headed out with a kiss for luck from my new girlfriend. I got a warm, fuzzy feeling as I used the word, even within my own mind, so I still had the smile on my face when I entered the top of the pyramid. Lucian noticed the change immediately.

"Well, someone looks pleased with themselves," he remarked. Since I could hardly believe it myself, and the time distortion here would mean we had the time to chat, I was more than happy to discuss my good fortune.

As I recounted the day's earthshattering sea-change, I saw Lucian's eyes stare off into the distance with a soft smile that I never would have expected to see on the Devil. I remembered what it was that had made him more appreciative of the value of life: his first true love.

I apologised for flaunting my good fortune, reminding him of what he had lost, but he stopped me before I got more than a few stammering words out.

"*Never* apologise for finding happiness," he told me firmly, "as long as your joy doesn't depend on someone else's misery. The world needs as much happiness – even more so if it's from love – as it can get. I've discovered over the centuries that it's a magick all its own, and I only regret that it took me so long to understand it."

He almost sounded tearful for a moment, making *me* feel a lump in my throat, but both of us swallowed hard and pulled ourselves together. Lucian jerked his chin up once, cleared his throat and moved on to the business at hand.

"As promised," Lucian began, "I have two individuals to assist you. Neither of them are from Aaru, so don't expect them to react the same as you're used to. One of them has been around for a significantly long time and has made something of a name for himself.

"The second, by comparison, is a much *newer* being. It may sound like a strange description, but it's the best way I can put it. Let's deal with that one first since I don't think you want to force the other, older individual to wait around for you."

So saying, he reached behind his throne and pulled out...a brown paper bag, like you'd put your groceries in. I raised one eyebrow and furrowed my brow, no more shocked than if he'd turned into a frog and hopped around on the floor, at which he burst out laughing.

"I *knew* you'd have that expression," he said, putting the bag on the floor between us. As I reached for it with a doubtful expression on my face, he stopped me before I could pick it up. When I raised my hands in confusion, he explained.

"Think of this more like a wardrobe from Ikea or a kit car than a Victorian mahogany dresser or a Ferrari," he said cheerfully. "This is essentially an energy source to fuel your fight, so you can make it look however you want.

"It's the energy equivalent of a disposable razor, so I'm not expecting it back," he continued dismissively. "For all I care, you can make it look like a D cell battery and carry it in your pocket. Whatever works for you.

"You need to keep the bag closed until you're alone, as you don't want any outside influences when you're giving it its form. After that, it can obviously be around anyone else with no problem."

The dismissive way he spoke about what he'd previously referred to as another life form gave me slight chills, though I was careful not to let it show. That level of disregard showed me he hadn't evolved in his thought processes quite as much as he had tried to convince me.

He had been kicked out of Aaru for using other beings as energy sources. Then on my first visit here, he'd spent a lot of time explaining to me all the reasons he'd moved beyond that. Now here he was acting in the same way on Earth all these millennia later, despite all of his earlier protestations of reformation. Not only that, but he was also trying to get *me* to do the same thing.

Maybe he thought that me becoming accustomed to using another being like that would make me more sympathetic to his cause. Perhaps he felt I'd understand him better, so I'd find it easier to champion his case to Isis.

Unfortunately for him, I'd grown up with pets my whole life. They might not be as intelligent as some people (though others I'd met made the dumbest dogs look like geniuses), but I had no doubt so-called 'lower life forms' were as sentient and feeling as any human.

That didn't mean I was going to turn vegetarian, I just made sure not to get too friendly with any cows! On the other hand, I was in no way planning on being as dismissive about this 'energy source' as Lucian was being.

I'd deal with that later in my own time, once I was done with the meeting tonight. For now, it was time to meet this other individual and I was quite apprehensive.

"Fair enough, I'll sort something out once I get a moment to myself," I said, trying to appear as blasé about it as Lucian. "So who's this 'super-being who's made a name for himself' that you've tracked down? Have you got him stashed away in some infernal Tupperware back there?"

Lucian actually winced at my tone. Maybe I ought not be quite so flippant. He confirmed my suspicion in as many words.

"You might want to sound a little more respectful when you meet him," Lucian advised me. "You've probably read about him in *The Key of Solomon*, where he is referred to as Eligos, though he has also been called Eligor and the Demon Abigor.

"He usually gets called a Knight of Hell, though you now know those sorts of labels are inaccurate at best and insulting at worst. I have fought alongside him in the past, which is probably where those references originate, and he has some abilities that should serve you well in your upcoming battles.

"That being said, he is most definitely *not* a servant, nor is he someone to underestimate. He agreed to help you in return for a favour that I did for him centuries ago during the Crusades, but make no mistake: Once this is over, his obligation will be fulfilled and he'll go his own way.

"The books will tell you that he can 'see hidden things', 'knows what is to come' and 'knows all the secrets of war'. Some of that is true, and some is hyperbole. He can absolutely do what many have called 'remote viewing', which should be extremely helpful as far as teleporting or opening portals goes. He's also a masterful tactician, so I'd advise you to listen to him and involve him in your planning."

As he finished talking, hooves rang loudly on the stones of the corridor. They stopped and I heard a clanking, like armoured feet hitting the ground. Metallic footsteps came closer until a figure stepped out of the shadows and into the light of the room.

Chapter 21

Since *The Key of Solomon* and Lucian himself referred to Abigor as a demon, I wasn't quite sure what to expect from the new arrival. Would it be some giant, horned monstrosity? A suit of armour with only a cloud of darkness inside?

What I *actually* saw was the most pleasant interpretation of his appearance from the books; that of a handsome man. The one image I vaguely remembered from *The Key* was of a bald head, yet this guy had a head of thick black hair to make Tom Cruise jealous.

He was slightly shorter than me, maybe six foot, and wearing no armour. The metallic footsteps had been caused by his spurs and armoured footwear which shifted into simple modern hiking boots.

He smiled at my apparent surprise, walking in and sitting down in another chair Lucian had created for him. He looked like some GQ cover model chilling out before a photo shoot. The energy I sensed from him, and the magickal aura I could see around him however, warned me not to underestimate him.

"Greetings, Mr Maddox," he said. His voice was deep and mellifluous, like auditory caramel or silk. His skin was a shade I could only describe as ebony, making Sovereign's colouring look like a healthy summer tan.

"Hello," I replied, my mind racing to catch up with the reality of the situation. "Evidently Lucian has told you about me, so you have the advantage. What do you prefer: Eligos, Eligor or Abigor?" The last thing I wanted to do was piss him off by using a name he didn't like.

"Whichever is easiest for you is fine," he replied, "although I *would* prefer if you could choose one and stick to it. In battle, clarity is essential. The last thing anyone needs is to be yelling different names and confusing the issue."

"Fine, Eligos it is," I decided. "I'm grateful for your willingness to help us, even if it is only as a favour to Lucian. Despite what he may have told you, he does actually have an interest in this."

Eligos nodded.

I was unsure if it was because Lucian had told him, due to his legendary powers of battle knowledge and foresight, or simply a tactical awareness that most people had multiple reasons for their actions. Regardless, it was good to know he wasn't blind to all of the subtext.

"Indeed," he intoned, "as I am aware that you yourself have multiple reasons for what you are doing. Some altruistic and philanthropic, some more selfish. The end result is still the same, however. Elrulin and his forces must be destroyed." My eyes flew to Lucian at Eligos' use of Elrulin's true name and he shrugged.

"Eligos and I have known each other much longer than Elrulin has been around," he told me dismissively. "I told you we'd been involved in the Crusades together; Elrulin hadn't even been cast out then. Why *wouldn't* he know Elrulin's true nature? Only once he started working with – and more to the point using and preying upon – humans did Elrulin bother to hide his identity."

It made sense on one hand, but on the other I was confused. If we were so insignificant to him, why would he *need* to hide? Who the hell (pun intended, given present company) would be a threat to him?

Before I could say it aloud, I realised exactly who. Me.

Given that those I had met in Aaru had all known about Isis' 'chosen one', Elrulin himself would have heard about it before he was cast out. Could that have even influenced him, driving him to gather more power? Was all of this actually *my fault*?

I discounted the thought as soon as it occurred, since Isis was the one who had chosen to create a champion. If anything, it was *her* fault for making Elrulin feel as if he wasn't good enough.

Then again, assigning blame was about as effective as trying to baptise a cat. I once read a quote that basically said, 'When you're hip deep in shit, there's no point whining about it. The only thing to do is pick a direction and start walking.'

There was absolutely no point in trying to figure out whose *fault* it was that Elrulin went psycho; we just had to deal with him as he was now. Too many people spent far too much time weeping and wailing about who was to blame for their situations, especially considering in many cases it actually *was* their own faults.

Now the only way to dig ourselves out of the shitstorm that was the Order was to get the hell (look, I like the joke, deal with it) on with this.

"Fair enough," I allowed, "so let's get back to the important issue. How can you help us take down Elrulin and his flunkies?"

Eligos nodded, almost as if he knew every thought that had just flown through my head. Maybe he did, given the legends about him.

Maybe he could read my mind. It seemed like every other non-human entity I met lately could, so why not him? I really needed to find a better way to defend my own thoughts.

"There are many potential possibilities in a fight like this," he observed astutely. "We should go to this meeting you have planned and assess the size of your forces. We can't make any kind of sensible and worthwhile assessment until we have an accurate tally of our own assets."

"OK, that one even *I* knew," I riffed, making Eligos smile tightly but Lucian winced at my tone. I remembered him saying to be careful around Eligos as he was not from Aaru; still I wasn't going to pretend to be something I wasn't. I also didn't want Eligos to think I was completely inept at strategy.

"My apologies." Eligos nodded to me. "I sometimes forget not all humans are as incompetent as most I've met. Then again, it is said that war should always be a last resort. Yet so many of your kind appear to revel in it, making it their sole purpose in life rather than a means to an end.

"I am prepared to assist you, but my patience with your quest is limited. My main focus will be to bring this undertaking to a successful conclusion as swiftly as possible."

His mannerisms reminded me so much of Gauvain, I tried to double check that my link remained the same as it had before. Then I remembered all links outside the area were suppressed while I was here.

"I am grateful for your indulgence," I replied, my own speech becoming coloured by his archaic attitude. I shook off the feeling and continued. "I'm not interested in a long, drawn-out conflict. I want this over and done with, so I can go back to my shop and live my life."

Eligos looked at me, his eyes focused on some indeterminate point as if peering into my soul or my destiny.

"Any respite you obtain is likely to be fleeting," he informed me. "You are now a weapon in the eternal war, a soldier in the fight between light and dark. This is merely your first skirmish, practically a training exercise, virtually inconsequential in the larger tapestry."

A chill flew up my spine at his pronouncement. I knew I was supposed to be the so-called Chosen of Isis, but I had no idea she had doomed me to never be at peace again. I was going to kick her ass next time I saw her!

Still, if that *was* to be my destiny, I'd better learn as much as possible from any available source, and who better to start with than a legendary warrior? I might not have his gifts of foresight and remote viewing, but I could at least pick up some pointers on strategy.

No doubt a teacher like him could refine my tactical awareness to a degree that would make human war seem like a novice playing checkers instead of chess. He could teach me how to become the best warrior I could be, giving me the greatest chance to survive whatever it was Isis had planned for me.

"Good to know that my future is destined to be so cheerful," I remarked dryly. "Thanks for the pep talk. Maybe we should head to the meeting. Then at least we can get my first military action underway. The anticipation is becoming tiresome."

Eligos nodded, no doubt well accustomed to the joy (or lack thereof) of pre-battle anxiety. I had enough of the other kinds without adding that to the tally, thanks very much, so the sooner I got done with it the better.

I retrieved my paper bag, still a little weirded out that it contained a life form which Lucian had advised me to use as the equivalent of a Duracell and then discard just as easily. I promised myself if there was any legitimate way, I wouldn't be so callous.

I resolved to make it as fair and equitable a partnership as possible, though I had no intention of bonding to yet *another* life form. Gauvain was my willing bond-mate, Iyrin had forced a bond upon me. I would absolutely not act in the same way to the individual Lucian had given me as Iyrin had towards me.

Eligos and I said our goodbyes to Lucian and I took us back to Seirina's house, ready to assemble the delegates for our war council. It was time to get this mission underway.

Chapter 22

When we returned, the sky was beginning to darken. I had brought us into the back garden as a more discrete point of arrival, which was also where I was planning on opening the portals for the participants of this evening's little get-together. The last thing I needed was some random passer-by getting curious about the flashing lights of the gateways opening and closing.

Eligos looked around the garden when we landed, though I got the sense he wasn't admiring the flowers. His eyes narrowed as he examined sections of the fence, assessed the strength of plants, analysed areas of cover.

It was as if he was planning both an assault and defence in seconds which, given who and what he was, was probably *exactly* what he *was* doing. I stood quietly for a minute, then once he appeared satisfied I cleared my throat.

"So, do you do that every time you go anywhere new?" I asked. He looked at me, almost as assessing a look as he had just bestowed on the petunias. "You looked like you were planning the Normandy invasion just now, both attacking and defending, with the flower beds as the beach."

Eligos smiled, apparently impressed by my perception, and nodded in agreement with my interpretation of his activity.

"I find if one is aware of one's surroundings, one is far less likely to be taken by surprise," he explained. It made perfect sense, but did it mean he was unaware of Seirina's wards? Surely they made his tactical analysis of the compost heap somewhat redundant.

I posed the question to him and he sighed, shaking his head as he regarded me. It was as if I'd been doing well in class, then suddenly said something idiotic that made the teacher realise quite how stupid I really was.

"Do you truly believe I could be an effective strategist," he replied, sounding disappointed in my lack of faith in his abilities, "if I were unable to detect protective wards and enchantments? I can even discern they were originally cast by a necromancer, then altered and enhanced by you. I can tell exactly how to dismantle them, where any potential weaknesses might be…"

I pricked my ears up when he mentioned weaknesses and I narrowed my eyes at the perimeter. I thought I had closed off any holes, so I was quite disturbed by his disparagement of my efforts. He seemed to realise my distress and went to reassure me, exactly as any good general would.

"I said *potential* weaknesses, not *existing* ones," he remarked. "Your defences are actually quite comprehensive. However, for completeness, I should warn you that your access through the wards is a *potential* source of weakness for an enemy to exploit.

"The only way to have a truly impenetrable defensive system is to leave no points of ingress or egress. Just as a gate is the weak point in a wall, so your access is the potential hole in your wards. However the enemy would require your exact energy signature or DNA, which is why I said *potential* weakness."

I was more relieved than I had expected to hear that the wards were effective. As far as I knew, that meant no one else could get in without either my or Seirina's permission. I had never been a blood donor, so my DNA was safe. I didn't see how anyone could replicate my energy signature either, so hopefully that was all the bases covered.

We turned around and headed to the back door, Mrs Wilson opening it as we approached. Eligos stopped short of the door and turned to me.

"I'll stay outside until the meeting begins," he told me, looking around the garden again. "I prefer not to limit my awareness by enclosing myself unnecessarily. Although I can maintain an appreciation of external occurrences, it requires me to divert some of my attention away from those I am with. As you can no doubt understand, that reduces my situational awareness; not a good condition for a soldier to become accustomed to, whether with allies or not."

I wanted to be insulted by the intimation that he had to keep an eye on us, but unfortunately I was starting to learn that people usually had more agendas than they let on.

Ever since my abilities had been unlocked, I'd been thrust into a larger world. Things weren't simple anymore; there were always multiple layers to everyone's intentions. Even the simplest of messages could have a dozen different levels.

I was too used to the simplicity of my shop. People came in, they bought or they didn't, then they left. Now, even that was no longer straightforward. Were they there to assess my defensive wards? Were they trying to scan me or Summer?

I could get dizzy considering even the simplest of situations. No wonder I hadn't been able to figure out the dynamics of the relationship between Angelica and myself. Eligos regarded me again, raising his eyebrows and tilting his head.

"An awareness of the different implications of a situation is the first step to tactical awareness," he observed. "Even being aware that there *are* different nuances is a start. I'm impressed; maybe you *do* have more potential than I first considered."

I was too flattered by his comment at first to even be irritated that he was reading my mind again. Then I realised his comment might be designed for exactly that reason: to ingratiate him to me so I overlooked the fact that he was reading my mind. Then I realised I'd never actually asked him not to, though just thinking it meant he now knew how I felt.

He smiled, and I realised there was yet *another* layer to things: a test to see if I could analyse the nuances and be aware of them. He nodded as I realised that which made me feel good I'd passed the test, irritated there even *was* a test, and tired with a hint of headache at the constant multiple analyses.

I decided to head inside and leave Eligos to his watchdog position, so I thanked Mrs Wilson and went through the kitchen. As I reached the study door, it was flung open and I was greeted by a cloud of dark hair and a pair of arms wrapped around my neck. You know, this girlfriend stuff was alright!

"I didn't think I'd been gone that long, at least not here," I croaked out past the strangulation of a shoulder against my Adam's apple. Angie eased up on the death grip and leant back to look at me.

"You went to meet the Devil," she protested. "Of *course* I was worried about you! That's my job now, doofus," she finished cheekily and I laughed, my headache beginning to fade with the endorphins from being held by her. I heard Gauvain's chuckle in my head as he listened to her comment.

Oh, I shall definitely be using that appellation in the future! he crowed across our link. I rolled my eyes, both physically and mentally, getting much the same amused response from both of them.

Not unless you want to find out what it feels like to be plucked, I promised him. I detected his indignance but also reluctant amusement.

There is no need to resort to threats, he replied primly. I relayed the brief exchange to Angie and she laughed.

"You two really are like an old married couple sometimes," she joked, so I raised my eyebrow.

"Are you sure you want to get into a three-way relationship?" I asked, deliberately creating a phrasing violation to make her squirm. She slapped my arm and sighed, seeing straight through my ruse.

"*Men,*" she said, in that long-suffering tone all women instinctively use. "Why is everything about sex with you?"

"Not everything," I riffed back, "only the best stuff!" She heaved another long-suffering sigh and shook her head at my juvenile response, then I heard Seirina and the twins laughing behind her. "Umm, yeah, anyway, so, I need to go upstairs and sort out a couple of things."

I stammered out a few words and turned away, hurrying upstairs as my face blazed as hot and red as a road flare. I heard more giggles as I executed my strategic manly retreat (also known as running away), so I pressed my lips together and kept moving.

Once I reached my bedroom, Gauvain flew over to my shoulder and nibbled my ear in welcome. I sat on the bed, put the brown bag down in front of me, and stared at it thoughtfully. I had no idea what was actually inside, other than the fact it was the building blocks for a life form according to Lucian, but I had no idea how that actually worked.

I caught G up on what Lucian had told me regarding how to put the energy together, namely that I needed to be alone. Then I opened the window for Gauvain and he soared out into the evening.

I sat there and considered what I required from this life form. It needed to be able to stay near me and yet, ideally, be able to take care of itself if necessary. I remembered what I had thought when Lucian gave me this thing, and it suggested exactly what I needed to do.

I had never really been a cat person, plus they were a little too independent (read 'asshole') to be reliable. Why witches chose them as familiars was an eternal mystery to me, unless you considered their evil gaze and searing disdain as endearing.

Nope, canine and not feline was gonna be the way to go here. Also, I didn't need it chasing Gauvain; I didn't really think he'd appreciate it. I pictured something compact, kinda like a Jack Russell terrier since they were about ninety percent attitude, then opened the bag.

I tipped it up over the bed and scrambled backwards as nothing but a pair of eyeballs rolled out. They lay there, looking at me and blinking slowly, so I gingerly reached out and picked them up. I could sense the energy cloud surrounding them, eagerly waiting to be formed.

I sent it the image and emotional attachment I had brought to mind, feeling it accept my desired form. I placed the eyeballs back on the bed and saw a swirling vortex of power come into being around them, sweeping them up as it went.

It coalesced into the shape of a dog about an inch tall, then started to grow like a tree on a time lapse video. I expected it to stop once it reached terrier size but instead, it kept growing.

As it neared the size of an American Staffordshire terrier, I moved farther up the bed until my back was against the wall. It slowed down once it passed the size of a decent German Shepherd, finally stopping at about the dimensions of a large Irish wolfhound.

It still had the build and colouring of a Jack Russell, so I was really hoping it didn't have the attitude of one or we could all be in some seriously deep shit. I reached out to it mentally and felt it recognise me, welcoming my contact like a hug from an old friend.

I stretched out and laid my hand on his head (yup, those were some serious nuts at the back there). He pressed up to me, just like the puppy I'd had as a child, and I heard his voice in my head.

Hello Daddy, he said, wagging his tail. *What's my name?*

Chapter 23

As soon as I heard his voice in my head, so sweet and trusting, like I had always imagined from an animal (not Gauvain, of course), I was reminded of every one of my pets who had crossed the Rainbow Bridge. I swallowed past the sudden tightness in my throat and blinked to clear the tears I felt welling up.

I knew in that one moment I could never use and discard him, like Lucian had said. Anyone who *could* treat an animal with such disregard, whether mundane or magickal in origin, was the lowest of the low in my opinion. For Lucian to have suggested it merely confirmed what I had thought when he handed me the bag: he really hadn't evolved as much as he professed.

I stroked the new fuzzy head, murmuring some random comforting words, and felt Gauvain returning. He flew through the still open window to land on my shoulder, peering down at the 'dog'. He spoke directly to him, allowing me to consider a name for him while they conversed.

I could tell from his comments that the dog was nowhere near as sophisticated in his thoughts as Gauvain, yet still more intelligent than the typical family pooch. I put him at about the level of an average ten-year-old child.

I grabbed my phone and started searching for male dog's names. I considered Dynamo, but thought it was a little too on the nose, considering why Lucian had given him to me. I wanted him to know I thought of him as more than a mere battery.

Given his size, Hulk was a possibility too, but again kind of obvious. I liked Igor; most people thought of a lumbering servant with that name, though the list I was reading said it meant 'warrior of peace' in Russian.

Then I came across a name that resonated perfectly, as the name of my sword had. *Paladin*, a protector of a noble cause. I reached out and rubbed his ear, feeling him press his head into my hand exactly like every dog I had ever known.

"I name you Paladin," I told him, feeling Gauvain's approval of my choice. Paladin's tail was almost a blur, he was wagging it so hard and fast. He jumped up on the bed and clambered onto my shoulders, licking my face and ears. I laughed while trying to push him back, Gauvain joining in with the laughter even as he flew to his perch to avoid being squashed.

The three of us together made a powerful team, one which had a chance of doing some real good in this fight. As I pushed Paladin back, he sniffed at my right hand. He focused on Seren as if it was a strip of smoked bacon.

He *pushed* his energy through me into the stone, making me feel as though an icy river and a lightning storm were blending together to lend me their strength. I saw the wings of Isis shine like a sun from the depths of the stone, the metal warming to just short of uncomfortable.

He stopped after a couple of minutes and I felt his energy level dipping significantly as a result. He curled up on the bed and immediately dropped to sleep, snoring like a puppy after a big drink of milk.

I was staggered by the increase in the amount of energy stored in Seren once he had finished. It still only seemed like it was about four or five percent full, but that was several times my total energy gathering efforts since I first stored some in Aaru! No wonder Lucian used his kind as batteries if this was what they could provide.

Gauvain flew over and snuggled into the centre of the circle created by Paladin's body, soon joining him in slumber. I left them to their dreams, heading downstairs again to start gathering the delegates. I reached the ground floor at the same time as Seirina came out of her study.

"Oh, there you are Gavan," she said. "I was about to come and get you. I've started getting photos sent through from the delegates, for you to use for your portals." She handed me her phone with the first picture already cued up, so I took it and went outside.

Eligos turned as the door opened, nodding once to acknowledge me as I walked out. I told him I would be opening the gateways for the different representatives to come through, so he wouldn't be alarmed by my suddenly opening holes through the wards.

I cycled through the different pictures, opening a portal from each location in turn for the person who sent it to come through. Once they were through I closed their door, then proceeded to the next.

Each person gave me some kind of assessing look as they passed me, then went inside to be shown to the study by Mrs Wilson. Eligos had, quite sneakily I thought, moved to the far end of the garden to stand in the shadows out of the new arrivals' sight.

He looked to be remaining aloof until everyone was present. That way he didn't need to go inside until the meeting was due to start, which I understood given his previous comment. Once the last portal was closed and the final person was inside, he walked up the path to join me.

"I shall remain out here until you have completed your initial greetings," he informed me. "Once you have had your preliminary discussions, reach out to me with your mind and I shall join you at that time.

"I would advise you to inform them of who I am, in order to forestall some of the obvious questions. Then I can enter and we can strategize regarding the fight against Elrulin." I thanked him for his patience and walked inside.

As I went through the kitchen I had a thought and jogged up to my room rather than going directly to the study. I picked up Muharar and belted it on, smiling at the sight of my two friends snuggled up together. At least I didn't have to worry about any friction there, as they clearly got on well.

I left them dreaming together and went back down to the study. As I strode in, the low hum of chatter I had heard coming down the stairs faded away. A few eyes flicked to the sword on my hip briefly, though soon enough everyone was looking directly at me.

I welcomed everyone back, thanking them for their continued agreement to work with us to bring down the Order. Then Dominic, the vampire representative, spoke up.

"I see you've obtained a weapon for yourself," he noted, making everyone else take interest. "Would you care to share the details? I'm sure there's quite a few of us who would like the chance to get something. There're not many magickal armourers around."

"Unfortunately, I don't know of any either," I remarked regretfully, which caused a few eyes to narrow as they clearly thought I was being evasive. I hurried to explain. "I made this myself, using some of the techniques I learned while I was away."

There were several surprised expressions at my explanation, which made me smile.

"May we see it?" asked Kazemde politely.

I shrugged.

"If you wish," I replied. I was well aware that none of them would be able to use it due to the wards I had incorporated into its forging, but if they wanted to admire my weapon then why not?

I snickered in my own head at my deliberate phrasing violation, then drew Muharar with a flourish. I held it horizontally across both hands, displaying it around the room. There were some admiring mutters, then I re-sheathed it.

"And have you given it a name?" continued Kazemde.

"I have, actually," I replied. "I wanted to name it myself before someone else decided to, particularly since I didn't want something aggressive." I remembered my search and decided to have a little fun.

"I chose to look for a name in another language. I looked at Egyptian, in honour of Isis, and quite liked the boy's name 'Sefu'." Kazemde snorted in laughter, immediately getting the joke, which made everyone look at him curiously. "Once I checked its meaning, however, I realised it was a little too literal. Sefu means sword by the way, for those of you who don't speak Egyptian." At that point everyone got the pun, causing a few sniggers and a couple of groans at the corniness of the gag.

"I finally chose to search for the translation of a specific name into different languages," I continued. "I looked at Gaelic and Welsh, neither of which I could even pronounce, so they wouldn't work. Once I looked at Egyptian again, I found the right name.

"Since I'm doing this to help free everyone from the threat of Elrulin and the Order, I chose the name 'Liberator', which in Arabic is

Muharar." A couple of people raised eyebrows or widened their eyes, and there were a few nods of approval.

"I certainly approve of your sentiment and choice of name," Kazemde told me, "though you should know your pronunciation is incorrect. There are several forms of Muharar in Arabic, each with a slightly different intimation and pronunciation, each leading to a completely different meaning."

"Yeah, I found that out when I translated it the other way," I laughed. "I also wasn't sure exactly how to write the correct version in Arabic script, so I stuck with letters I recognised for the sheath." I turned so they could see the name. Kazemde smiled.

"No offence intended if I got it wrong," I told him, which made him laugh and he reassured me that it was fine. "So, now that's over with, let's get on with things."

I wanted to get the meeting back on track. The sooner we could work out a plan, the sooner we could take the Order down. Once that objective had been achieved, I could then get back to my shop and regular life, or at least as regular as it might be now I had unlocked my magick.

"Have you all managed to contact your respective people?" I asked, wanting to get a sense of what we had to work with. "What sort of numbers will you each be able to provide?" I realised we were about to start getting into the tactical discussion part of the meeting, so I should really bring Eligos in for this.

"Actually," I blurted out, cutting off Aurora as she started to talk. "My apologies Aurora, I just realised the ally we have been provided by Lucian should be here for this." There were some alarmed expressions at the thought of meeting an associate of the Devil, as I had expected.

"Some of you may have heard of him from various magickal texts," I continued, already getting an idea of what the reactions might be to the name. I even heard Iyrin rustling its way to the front of its leafy refuge, though sneakily staying low and out of sight of most of the room as it had before. I notified Eligos mentally that I was now introducing him, and I received his affirmative response.

"He has agreed to assist us as a favour to Lucian, not because of any obligation to us or desire to be involved," I elucidated for them, "and he has informed me that as soon as we're done, he'll leave. He has been known by a couple of different names but at his request, and for clarity during fighting, I have picked one for all of us to use.

"That being said," I prepared to sum up as I sensed Eligos approaching the door, "may I introduce you all to Eligos."

All eyes turned as the door swung open, varying degrees of apprehension and terror reflected on the assembled faces.

Chapter 24

As he stepped into the room, Eligos was already looking around the room at each person in turn. He narrowed his eyes at Iyrin's terrarium and I was startled to see the little skeletal shit scurrying back into the leafy depths.

As my gaze travelled over everyone else, there were significantly differing expressions on the various faces. Dominic, Kazemde, Seirina and Sovereign looked politely interested to see the new arrival. Cheveyo was supremely disinterested in everything, much as he had been last time except for the mention of the windigo.

Angelica and the twins seemed to be a little apprehensive, then pleasantly surprised when they saw him. Aurora, on the other hand, stared wide-eyed as the door opened, her feelings clearly magnifying when she saw him in person.

She scrambled backwards, knocking over her chair as she did so, and crab walked around Seirina's desk until she was in the corner of the office farthest away from the door.

"That's a fucking demon!" she cried out. I wasn't sure if it was because she knew of him from her reading, or if she was seeing him differently from the rest of us, but she was quite evidently not happy.

"Hold on, hold on," I said, holding my hands out placatingly. "Just because the books say he's a Knight of Hell, you need to understand something. First off, the Devil himself isn't what you've been told.

"Second, Hell is a human invention born out of a desire to believe nasty people get their come-uppance in the afterlife. Therefore, third, so-called 'demons' are merely individuals who have been known to associate with Lucian in the past.

"Since history is written by whoever comes out on top in any particular conflict, those on the losing side often get cast as demons, devils, and various flavours thereof. What Eligos *actually* is, according to Lucian, is a highly experienced warrior with unrivalled tactical awareness and a couple of abilities that could assist in our battle planning.

"As I said, he has agreed to help us only as a favour to Lucian, so please treat him with the respect he deserves. If you don't want to deal with him directly after today, that's fine. I'll happily act as liaison." At this point I glanced over at Angie and winked. She smiled and blushed at the memory of our first meeting.

I looked back at Aurora and she nodded carefully, although she kept a watchful eye on Eligos. When I turned around to look at our newest arrival he was regarding me with an eyebrow raised and a slight tilt to his head, along with a slight turn up at the corner of his mouth at my defence of him.

"So then, getting back to the *important* details at hand," I continued, stressing my words in such a way to communicate to everyone that the details of Eligos' background were inconsequential next to what we were doing. "What sort of forces have you each been able to muster up?"

Uncharacteristically, Cheveyo was the first to speak up. His answer, however, was less positive than I had wished and I was really hoping he didn't set the tone for everyone else.

"The shamans and medicine men support this effort," he stated, "but are unable to offer aid for the assaults in this country, so far from their home soil. If the efforts here are successful, I'll be able to gather the few who are still practicing to help with the fight in America."

While it was somewhat disappointing, I could appreciate his response. His culture and powers were closely tied to his home soil, so it made sense they would not be as comfortable or as powerful over here. Especially in view of the fact that so many Brits had been involved in settling America. We were descended from those who were responsible for such atrocities against the Native Americans, and the destruction and loss of so much of their heritage.

Thinking about it like that, I easily understood why he had been so stand-offish last time. I was actually surprised he was even willing to help that much, although clearing the Order out of America would no doubt be in his people's best interests. Maybe this could go in some small way towards repaying some of the karmic debt owed to his ancestors.

I nodded to him in understanding, and he looked at me with his head drawn back slightly, his brow gently furrowed and his mouth pursed, like a scientist examining the results of an experiment. It was as if he had been ready for me to call him out on his lack of help, then been surprised by the absence of my expected hostility.

Dominic was the next to speak, and we finally started to get some positive feedback.

"I have managed to recruit eight vampires to our cause," he told us. "Although I realise this sounds like a small number, all eight are old and powerful. Which is why they were able to deny the Order's recruiting efforts in the first place. With me, this gives us nine significantly strong vampires."

I looked over at Eligos and he already had his chin sunk towards his chest, as if he was planning exactly how best to deploy the vampires – which was probably exactly what he was doing. Kazemde spoke next, and I began to realise my idea of an overwhelming force was naïve in the extreme.

"I have spoken to the seventeen families I know of who have either resisted or fled outright from the Order. Fortunately, there are generally several members of each family who are blessed with our powers. I have therefore gathered forty-two weres of various kinds." Kazemde told us, quietly proud of the number he had recruited.

"The wolves make up the majority of the count, with a few felines and one clan of bears. They're already preparing themselves for our call." Relief surged through me: We finally had a promise of a reasonable number. Cheveyo and Dominic had made me worry I was going to be doing all of the fighting myself, and I was quite sure a plan along those line was pretty much doomed to failure.

"De obeahs of N'awlins offer six in addition to me," Sovereign said, her accent more pronounced than last time, no doubt due to her close contact with her fellow practitioners over the last few days. "De seven of us can raise a force to terrify dose *possede*'s in da Orda."

I had completely forgotten about that aspect: the voodoo practitioners could raise *zombies*. They would be the perfect cannon fodder, totally expendable and able to overwhelm defences without cost to us.

I smiled for the first time since Eligos had entered, finally seeing a glimmer of light and possibility in all this. That led me inevitably to Seirina, since her powers were so similar. She was already nodding, clearly anticipating my thought process.

"Absolutely," she affirmed. "I can certainly work with Sovereign's team to build an assault force. I doubt the other side of my abilities will be as much help, unless you think I can seduce an entire castle?" she joked.

I had to laugh.

"I guess that depends on how skimpily you're planning to dress," I riffed back. Dominic immediately looked significantly more interested in the conversation, while Angie simply slapped my arm.

"Typical man," she said, "always has to drag the conversation down to the gutter."

I winked at her and shrugged, smiling in acknowledgement of the truth of her remark. The way her eyes smouldered at me in response to my smile made me *really* hope this damned fight didn't take too long.

"I have recruited three full covens, each of a full sacred thirteen members," Aurora spoke up, breaking my train of thought before it ended up with naked tangled limbs and sweaty bedsheets (damn her). "We may not be the best fighters but most of us are accomplished healers, along with being remarkably experienced at protective charms. We do have other abilities, of course, but none that would be of much use indoors with minimal access to the resources of the natural world. One coven is my own, which gives us thirty-nine Wiccans."

"That's actually extremely helpful," I said to her, "thank you. Protective wards are always useful, plus they should hopefully reduce the need to call on your curative capabilities." She beamed at me as I praised the abilities of her associates and I saw Eligos winked at me and nodded his approval.

"OK, so that gives us...fifty-one powerful fighters, between the vampires and the weres..." A thought suddenly occurred to me and I glanced over at the two representatives. "Those two factions historically harbour significant animosity towards each other. Are you guys sure you can get your troops to work together against the Order, rather than fighting each other?"

Dominic looked insulted whilst Kazemde seemed vaguely amused.

"We are more than capable of maintaining focus," the bloodsucker stated indignantly, "as long as your animals don't attack first." He aimed his last pointed insult in Kazemde's direction, but the Egyptian refused to rise to the bait. Clearly his feline side helped him maintain a healthy detached disdain when required.

"The weres have no interest in the leeches," he intoned calmly. "They used to try to subjugate my kind to be their daytime guardians. As long as they don't try it again, we can live and let live."

I nodded gratefully at both of them.

"Fine, so fifty-one fighters, seven voodoo priests and priestesses, one necromancer and one independent magick user; plus, of course, Eligos and the abilities he brings to the mix." I summed up our numbers, then hurried on before I got hit again.

"I haven't forgotten you ladies," I said to Angie and the twins. "I need you three to help us analyse any information we recover from the sites, anything that can point us to the new headquarters they're establishing. Plus, of course, the thirty-nine Wiccans who can provide defence, healing, and other forms of support.

"Given the numbers we have, we'll only be able to take one site at a time," I said, moving on to the planning part of our little get together. "I can use portals to move us between the sites instantaneously, so we can hit each of them in quick succession. Eligos has the ability to see things remotely, so he can guide my gateways.

"Once we've taken down the three subsidiary sites, we can move on Bolton Castle. I don't have to tell you, each site is under a valued national monument. This means we can't simply march in and level the place. We're going to have to fight hand to hand, and we need to do as little damage to the sites as possible."

As I discussed how we would conduct our assaults, I glanced over at Eligos and was surprised to see him looking...bored. I had thought the tactical discussion would be his bread and butter, yet it seemed to be about as appealing to him as rancid sewage. Then again, maybe it was just my tactics that stank.

"Of course," – I swallowed my pride and deferred to Eligos for his input – "Eligos has far more experience in these areas than me. How do *you* think we should approach this?" I asked him. I couldn't think of any way a force as small as ours could take on four sites at once, nor even three and then one.

Our newest associate, however, came up with an approach I had never even considered, since I had discounted many of the legends surrounding him after Lucian's comments.

"Why don't you take Edinburgh and I'll take the other two, then we'll meet at Bolton," he said offhandedly.

All of us stared at him dumbly at this nonchalant intimation of his power. I couldn't *wait* to hear his explanation of this one!

Chapter 25

"Umm, not that we're ungrateful for the offer," I said, somewhat irritated by him waiting until we showed how small a force we had been able to muster before offering to help, "but I have a couple of questions. Firstly, how could you hope to assault and defeat two Order strongholds in the time it takes us to take on one? And secondly, is there some reason you waited until now to tell us about your capabilities?"

There were subtle noises of agreement from the rest of the room, which caused Eligos to glance around at everyone before looking back at me. He seemed to be supremely unconcerned at my accusatory tone and words, instead appearing to be almost disappointed that I hadn't anticipated his comment.

"After your remarks to Lucian when we met, along with Miss Aurora's reaction to me," he observed, "I thought you were more aware of my resources." My mind flashed back to what I'd read about him in *The Key of Solomon*, at which point I realised what he was referring to.

"But Lucian said that the whole 'Knight of Hell' thing was essentially adverse propaganda," I protested. "Are you saying that you really *do* have control of sixty legions of demons?"

I couldn't reconcile the disparity between Lucian's denial of *The Key*'s description of Eligos, then Eligos himself referring to the information in there as something to be relied on. That was just maddeningly unhelpful;

why were these things never clear? Next someone was going to tell me that up was down!

"Well I wouldn't necessarily call them demons," Eligos explained, "and it's not quite sixty legions, but I certainly have access to a significant number of soldiers that I can summon under my direction.

"As to why I said nothing until now," he continued calmly, "this *is*, after all, *your* fight and not mine. I therefore waited to see what resources the alliance as a whole was able to access. However, since I wish to be done with this as soon as possible, it behoves me to offer any necessary assistance to facilitate a rapid resolution."

I stared at him with my mouth hanging open, stunned by the revelation of what was, in effect, his own private army. I wasn't quite sure how to feel at that point. Glad, of course, that he was willing to support us and help achieve our goals by ending the fight.

Then again, pissed off that he'd waited until it sounded like we were going to struggle before offering in the first place. On the third side, I hadn't actually included him in the round robin of everyone saying what forces they had to bring to the effort, so was it really his fault?

In the end, we needed his help and he *had* offered as soon as I had included him in the conversation, so I was just going to be grateful and tell the rest of my brain to shut the hell up. Since he had already proven he was aware of my thoughts, I wasn't surprised to see him tilt his head and lift on corner of his mouth as I came to that conclusion.

Everyone else was looking between us in confusion at what must have seemed like a silent conversation, which I guess in a way it was. OK, it was me having the conversation with myself and him simply agreeing, but the principle was the same.

"I think we are all extremely grateful to you for that offer, Eligos," I said, deciding to get the meeting back on track. "I, for one, am definitely glad we won't have to draw things out like I thought at first. It will also be far easier to take Bolton Castle with the addition of your forces.

"I would, however, like to clarify a point of conduct for what we're about to do." Everyone looked at me curiously at that statement, including Eligos, and even Iyrin poked its bony face out between the leaves in interest.

"Since we've already established there are a number of Order members who are there under duress and coercion, we should at least give an *opportunity* for people to surrender. All those who do should be scanned by someone with reliable telepathic abilities, to prove they're not simply trying to save their own guilty asses.

"Those that genuinely *were* forced in some way, such as Angie and the twins here, should be assisted however possible. The liars and turncoats, feel free to eat," I stated, directing the last comment to Dominic, much to his amusement.

"Any that refuse to surrender," I continued, noting what seemed to be general agreement to my attitude, "we need to 'kill 'em all and let God sort 'em out', as a wise man once said." I saw Eligos nodding again, apparently fully on board with my tactical assessment of how to deal with the situation.

"Very wise," he said, at which everyone else was quick to murmur their agreement. "We should not give Elrulin's acolytes the opportunity to rebuild the Order at a later date. Your attempts at mercy are to be commended, since they show you have a generous heart.

"However, we should not lose sight of the danger posed by an enemy left alive to return at a later date, especially once they are in possession of the knowledge of who is now arrayed against them. That gives *them* the opportunity to attack, with surprise and numbers on *their* side.

"In the spirit of your merciful attitude," he continued, "I will require Iyrin to assist me." I was shocked that he was including the watcher. I couldn't think what it might bring to the party, other than the obvious creep factor. "Since I can only be in one place at a time," Eligos went on, at which I understood where he was going, "Iyrin can go with the other half of my forces to perform the scanning."

Seirina looked startled at the idea of Iyrin being involved, while the delegates mostly appeared confused since they hadn't heard Iyrin's name before. I was more surprised Eligos was comfortable enough to demand the little bastard's service, so it was just one more example of Eligos' power.

"Iyrin, maybe you should introduce yourself to the group," I said cheerfully, facing the terrarium. I could feel its irritation across our link, even as the rustling indicated it was making its way up to the glass.

I could also feel, even though it was trying to conceal it from me, that it was genuinely afraid of Eligos, which confirmed for me beyond a shadow of a doubt that Eligos was far more dangerous than Lucian had let on.

When it finally appeared up on the raised branch in full view of the room, there were quite a few gasps of surprise at its appearance. I could definitely relate, since I still vividly recalled my first experience with it.

At least they were all safe from its unwelcome advances, unlike me. Still, at least I had my deal with Lucian now. As I thought that I detected a thread of enquiry from Iyrin, so I sswiftly brought the assault plans to mind to cloud our link with noise and prevent it searching through my memory.

Our eyes met and even though it had no eyelids, I could swear it was scowling. I simply smiled at it, pleased that my strategy seemed to work. I might not be able to completely block it out, but it seemed like I could throw enough static its way to prevent it from freely perusing my mind.

"Iyrin, would you please not distract Gavan," Eligos called out and I heard a subtle warning in his tone that, while unspoken, nonetheless came across loud and clear. I saw Iyrin flinch and felt it immediately withdraw from my mind.

Everyone else looked at me with varying levels of enquiry, so I shrugged my right shoulder and waved it off as inconsequential. We had bigger fish to fry right now, in any case.

"So this is Iyrin," I told everyone, when it became clear it wasn't going to speak up for itself. "According to Seirina, it is something called a watcher. All I know is it has significant mental abilities and if you value your privacy, you'll stay away from it."

Seirina and Eligos echoed my sentiment, while Iyrin itself gave one of its bird-like head tilts. Kazemde, who was sitting nearest to the tank in our circle, leant away slightly, even though Seirina's desk was between him and Iyrin.

I had to smile at the evidence of Kazemde's feline attitude, that unmistakable standoffishness even housecats displayed. Unless you had a can of food in your hand, of course, or were trying to do anything even remotely important, in which case they found it necessary to present their asshole directly to your face for inspection and approval.

When he saw my expression, Kazemde sat back up straight and averted his eyes, as if he'd never been concerned in the first place. It was remarkable how you could see so many cat behaviours, if you knew to look for them.

It made me wonder if werewolves showed similar canine behaviours. I'd have to watch them when I met them. For now, of course, the main focus had to be planning the assault on Edinburgh Castle.

"So if you're not going to be with us in Scotland," I said to Eligos, once again trying to get back on track. – It was remarkable just how easy it was to get side-tracked right now – "can you at least help us to locate the entrance to the Order's tunnels underneath the castle?"

"It's possible," he replied thoughtfully, "although since I have never been there, I would require some accurate information on the site."

I opened the browser on my phone, looking up Edinburgh Castle to see what I could find.

I selected the official website and found, to my delight, there was a fully manoeuvrable three dimensional model with all of the buildings labelled available. I loaded it up and walked over to Eligos, showing him what I had found.

"You know, if this level of intelligence had been available at Troy, things might have gone very differently," he observed absently. "They might not even have needed to build the horse. The body count would certainly have been less, and it would have been more of a skirmish than a long drawn-out war."

"Umm, not to get off topic again, but you were at *Troy*?" I asked, amazed. "Did you meet Achilles? What was he like? Was Helen really that beautiful?" At that point I stopped talking as I heard Angelica clear her throat pointedly. Eligos locked gazes with me, and I saw the amusement in his eyes.

"To be honest, no," he said dryly. "I have merely studied the engagement in as much detail as I was able to find. It's a fascinating topic, one I highly recommend for anyone who wishes to study battle strategy.

"Now, back to the current question. I have examined this model and used it for the basis of my remote assessment, and now believe I may have located the entrance to the Order's underground locale. However, it will not be as easy to access as the tunnels under Bolton."

A chill ran down my spine as he said that, since I didn't think the tunnels under the chapel were exactly 'easy access'. What could make the Scottish tunnels harder to get into than a three ton block of granite?

"The Edinburgh tunnels have their entrance directly under what the model has labelled as the New Barracks. This indicates the probability that there will be a significant military presence around. I therefore recommend you teleport yourself in and then open a portal for the rest. I can give you a picture of the place to send yourself to."

Oh wonderful, nothing like making things easy!

Chapter 26

"So let me get this straight," I said to Eligos, still trying to wrap my head around what he'd told me. "You want me to take an image from you, that you're going to get by some method or other without even going there yourself, then teleport in simply *hoping* your picture's accurate and no one's in the vicinity?"

I was staggered by the level of blind faith he was expecting from me. I knew Lucian had vouched for him but I'd only just met the guy (demon, entity, whatever), so the degree of trust he was asking for was kind of a big deal.

"With every due respect," I continued, not wanting to piss him off but keen to make sure I wasn't planning to head directly into a shitstorm, "how can I know that your 'surveillance' abilities are reliable? You're asking me to bet my life on the veracity and accuracy of your powers, after having met you only a couple of hours ago."

I took a deep breath once I'd finished, then held it quietly as I waited for his response. If he was as tactically astute as I'd been told and the books reported, he should hopefully understand and appreciate my caution.

On the other hand if he was closer to the demon of lore, I could end up a smear on the carpet for my impertinent doubting of his abilities. To my relief, after a brief pause, he nodded.

"However insulting your doubts may be," he stated, "I would have less respect for you if you blindly trusted in someone else's assurances regarding something so important." I breathed again, glad he was reacting as I'd hoped he would.

"I can only offer you an example to try to reassure you. Your office at your shop has three bookcases, one on each side of the desk and one behind your desk." I saw his eyes become unfocused somewhat as he looked at some nebulous distant point for the image he was seeing.

"As you sit at the desk, the shelves on the right are your research volumes and magickal texts. To your left are fictional volumes, and behind you are items such as amulets, statues and such that you have collected over the years.

"Your desk has a green leather top and in a prominent position is the box you recovered from Tibet, in which you found the Veil that you had been sent to locate." I held up my hands in surrender, acknowledging the accuracy of his description. His gaze returned to the room and fixed on me.

"I like your decoration choices," he told me with a slight smile. "Your office has a very restful feel."

"Thank you; and thank you also for not being offended by my doubts." He waved away my apology as unnecessary. No doubt he would have had the same suspicions if he were expected to trust *his* life to someone else's abilities, particularly if he'd only just met them. It simply made good tactical sense to have a healthy degree of doubt in the unknown and unproven.

Everyone else in the room seemed relieved that we'd had a demonstration of the accuracy of Eligos' remote viewing. That meant we had our assault plan for Edinburg, while he could sort out his own plans for Blarney and Rochester.

"Excellent," I said, addressing the room as a whole. "So we have a plan. I'm presuming your team, Sovereign, will need a few days to create enough '*soldiers*' to be of help?" She smiled at my delicate term for zombies, and there were a few chuckles around the room as people realised what I meant.

"It definitely gonna take more dan a snap o' da fingers," she agreed. "If Seirina give us her help, ah t'ink we be ready in tree or four days."

Seirina nodded in agreement, whether to the request for help, the timescale, or both.

"Fine, so in four days I'll text everyone to send me a new picture and then open portals to bring your forces through," I stated, making plans so we could draw the meeting to a close. "I'll find a location somewhere out of the way that's big enough for everyone, a field or something like that." Everyone agreed and then started getting up and milling around, saying their goodbyes.

I walked out to the back garden with the departing delegates, opening portals for them to go home after checking the photos they'd sent me again. Seirina was planning to head to New Orleans tomorrow after a good night's sleep, and I would open a portal for her when she was ready. Once the last of them had departed, I went back inside to find Eligos in the hall looking like he was doing his distance viewing thing again.

"You look like you're detecting a disturbance in the force," I joked, causing him to break off, look at me and sigh.

"Lucian was right," he said. "You do seem to enjoy finding irreverent ways to say things."

I shrugged in acceptance of the comment.

"Hey, life is depressing enough without being serious all the time," I replied, at which he raised his eyebrows and sank his chin onto his chest in introspection.

"An interesting viewpoint," he observed thoughtfully. "It's true that this existence often requires you to deal with unpleasant occurrences. However to dwell on things you cannot change is unnecessary, poisoning the good times by considering the worst possibilities that may not even occur. Your attitude actually does have merit."

I was surprised but gratified by his analysis, since I had never considered my tendencies in quite that way. Still, at least it meant he wouldn't get upset by me being my usual self now.

"Before you distracted me," he continued, reminding me that he had in fact been doing something before I walked in, "I was observing an individual I think you should be aware of."

I pricked up my ears at his comment. Was this a potential ally or an enemy?

He vanished, only to reappear a few seconds later with someone curled in a ball at his feet. I realised that he had just teleported through the wards and immediately panicked about the potential ramifications.

"How the hell did you do that?" I stormed, inwardly surprised no-one came out from the study to investigate the cause of my raised voice. "I made sure *I* was the only one who could get through the defences, as you well know, so how come you can suddenly come and go at will?" I needed to identify any potential weaknesses and shore them up as soon as possible.

"Be calm," he told me reassuringly. "I would think you might understand by now. I told you someone with your DNA or *energy signature* could get through. Do you really think I would spend this much time around you, allowing you to trap me inside your barriers, without me assessing and remembering your presence so I could use it to get out myself?

"That would be ridiculously naïve, expecting me to allow you to essentially make me your prisoner. Of *course* I identified your energy, especially once I knew it was the key to my ability to come and go at will."

I sighed in relief as I realised the wards were still secure, then registered exactly what he had said.

"Sorry," I said. "I was just startled so I didn't think it through fully." He shook his head at this further proof of how utterly new I really was to this magickal world.

"Regardless, my ability to penetrate your wards was not what I wanted to address right now," he continued, glossing over my little hissy fit. I looked down at the huddled figure at his feet, curious as to who it was and quite why Eligos had found it necessary to abduct him into our little protected refuge.

The new arrival groaned, unfolding from his foetal position at our feet and rising to his hands and knees. Our eyes met and he started slightly, then quickly recovered and glanced around the hall. He fell on his ass and scrabbled away when he saw Eligos, only stopping once he reached the limit of the corridor.

He pushed himself up to standing, using the wall for support, and looked around wildly. Given how swiftly Eligos had gone and returned, I could only assume he'd simply clobbered the poor guy and yanked him back here without so much as a 'by your leave'.

"Who the hell are you people and how did I get here?" he demanded angrily, pressing his back against the wall. He *looked* distressed, but there was something in the tone of his voice that made me pause.

He was a fairly unassuming, nondescript guy; slim but not skinny, middling height of about five eight, with short brown hair. He reminded me somewhat of a young Robert Carlyle as he appeared in Trainspotting, although without the stubble or heroin-chic scruffiness.

"Um, Eligos, you wanna take this one?" I said, looking at the guilty party. The abductee started as I mentioned his kidnapper's name, which only confirmed my suspicion that there was more to him than he was letting on. Eligos ignored the guy completely, instead choosing to address his response to me.

"This individual has been observing this location for several days," he told me calmly. A chill ran down my back at the implications, as I immediately understood where he was going with this.

"But...the wards," I stammered out, concerned over how much might have been learned and relayed about our activities.

"The wards may have denied him close access to the building," Eligos explained, "and prevented him from observing anything behind the house. However he was still able to witness the arrival of certain parties in the past. His mind is guarded magickally, which was what alerted me to his presence. I *was* able to determine how long he had been watching you, though I have not yet attempted to access his full recollections of what he has observed."

Deliberately unassuming appearance and a magickally guarded mind, watching the house where we had wards up and were preparing to start a war with the only significant magick group I was aware of. The only logical conclusion was that he was a spy for the Order.

I glanced over at him and saw the anxiety he had been exhibiting drain away. He clearly realised that we understood what he was, so his pretence was no longer effective nor required. What he *didn't* do, however, was say anything else.

"So now what?" I asked Eligos, curious as to how he planned to get any information from someone with a mind so well guarded. His eyes went unfocused again as he looked into whatever other dimension gave him his special information.

"He is an agent for a special department within the Order," he stated. "Though any more detail, I am unable to discern. From the information previously relayed by your other informants, I was unaware that the Order had individuals with this level of ability."

The hairs on the back of my neck stood up so hard, a porcupine would be jealous. If the Order actually had people like this, it definitely had implications on what we were about to attempt. In all honesty, I had been starting to wonder how they had spread their insidious tendrils so widely with the limited abilities of the members I had encountered so far (not that I had any plans to say that to Angie or the twins).

"There is only one way I can think of to get the information we want from him," Eligos continued, at which point I balked.

"I'm not sure I have either the ability or the desire to go diving into the mind of someone with his level of training," I admitted. Eligos rolled his eyes at me and shook his head.

"Meaning no disrespect to your prowess," he told me, "but I had no intention of asking *you*. Our most efficient option, with the greatest chance of success, is Iyrin."

OK, I'll confess, I momentarily felt a hint of pity for the poor bastard at that point. It didn't last long, however. The son of a bitch deserved everything he had coming to him.

In fact, I was about to relish every horrific expression across his underhanded face.

Chapter 27

That the new arrival hadn't reacted to Iyrin's name told me he certainly hadn't been able to eavesdrop on our conversations. If he *had*, he'd have already been screaming, sweating, trying to run and shitting himself with fear.

Instead, the arrogant sneer on his face quite clearly communicated he had significant faith in his own mental defences. Since the twins and Angie hadn't described anyone they knew of with advanced magickal training, this guy must have worked for a clandestine department within the Order, secret even from the majority of the rest of its members.

Eligos grabbed him by the arm and marched him towards the study, leaving me to trail along behind like an obedient puppy. I ignored the ignominy of the situation, since it was the least of my worries right now, hurrying along so I wouldn't miss anything.

When we entered Seirina's office, she was talking to the girls. All of them stopped and looked at me, then giggled like a bunch of prepubescents at recess. I sighed and rolled my eyes, realising this was likely to be my fate for the foreseeable future. To my surprise, Eligos actually turned to regard me with a pitying expression which quickly disappeared into a smirk. Great, even *he* knew I was screwed!

"OK, fine, can we move beyond the schoolyard for a moment?" I said, *trying* to divert the attention away from myself. "Eligos found this guy outside on the street. He was apparently watching the house for the past several days, saw several relevant attendances, and has some kind of magickal defences around his mind."

The smiles that had shown up at my reaction soon disappeared as I spoke. The shock was evident as I mentioned his mental fortifications.

"Were any of you aware of the Order having a separate division for spies and special ops?" I asked, talking mainly to Angie and the twins. The confusion was obvious in their expressions, and they were quick to deny any knowledge.

"Well I have to say," I continued, "from your description of the diverse areas the Order is involved in, Angie, I *was* surprised at the lack of advanced magickal training within the members you *were* aware of.

"I thought maybe it was because even the weakest of abilities, no offence intended, would be a massive advantage over anyone who was mundane. Now it seems as though anyone with more significant levels of power was sequestered and squirreled away into a secret department.

"Hey," I said as I saw the indignation and disappointment on the faces of our ex-Order members. "It's nothing to be ashamed of. All three of you have significant abilities and if I were you, I'd be *glad* you didn't reach their cut-off for secret service duty.

"If you *had*, I'd never have met Angie. Then I wouldn't have come on a rescue mission, you two wouldn't be free and we wouldn't have the opportunity we currently do. Still, we need to find out as much as we can about them – including what kind of abilities these specialists actually have."

I turned to Eligos, locking gazes with him and nodding. He inclined his head once in return then stepped around me, still gripping the spy tightly by the upper arm. He approached Seirina's desk and looked past her at Iyrin's leafy refuge.

"Iyrin," he intoned, "I want you out here. We require the knowledge this man has locked in his mind." The familiar rustling sound indicating movement started immediately, once again confirming that the creepy little git was subservient to Eligos for whatever reason.

Maybe I'd find out when Lucian taught me about it and how to block it but for now, I was simply glad *someone* could command its assistance. If we were facing more powerful enemies, we needed as many powerful *allies* as we could get.

I turned away from the tank to watch the spy's face, not wanting to miss his expression when he first caught sight of Iyrin. I wasn't disappointed, not even having to turn around to spot the moment its skull came into view.

The bastard's eyes widened and he tried to back away from the desk as hard as he could. Unfortunately for him, Eligos was significantly more solid than he appeared and had placed himself right behind him.

Iyrin clambered up the branch and placed its hands on the glass, just as it had when it had drawn me in, only this time it didn't stop there. It passed through the pane and Eligos reached out towards it.

Under Eligos' power, Iyrin floated across the gap and landed on the surface of Seirina's desk. The twins and Angie had shifted in their chairs when it came into view, then had positively panicked and shot out of their seats across the room as it had left the terrarium.

Eligos pushed the captured spy forwards until the fronts of his legs touched the desk, then held him in place. Iyrin jumped towards him, latching onto the front of his shirt and riding him down to the floor as he stiffened, falling backwards.

Thankfully, the carpet protected the back of his head, because he was already completely unable to save himself. Iyrin had immediately begun delving deep into his mind and I could *feel* its relishing of the free reign it had been given flowing across our link. It was like seeing a glutton given unfettered access to an all you can eat buffet.

It was at that point even I started feeling sorry for the interloper, so I crossed the room to join the girls and was immediately grabbed. Angie pulled me into a hug and the twins crowded close. All of them hid behind me but peered over my shoulders in morbid fascination, like children covering their eyes at a horror movie yet continuing to watch through a crack in their fingers.

Although my link with Iyrin was nowhere near as powerful and free-flowing as my bond with Gauvain, I could still get a sense of it rummaging through the guy's memories. His defences, while undoubtedly sophisticated and formidable if Eligos couldn't fully breach them, were utterly useless against the alien nature of Iyrin's mind.

I had experienced that weirdness myself when it linked to me. I previously thought my mind was well buttressed, which had been confirmed by both Lucian and Eligos recently, yet Iyrin had simply strolled past my walls as if they weren't even there.

Eligos was evidently aware of that difference, which must have been why he chose the little skeletal oddball instead of me to access the spy's memories. After that brief reflection, I no longer felt slighted by the choice of psychic interrogator.

After only a few minutes, Iyrin's sense of satisfaction washed through me. I guessed that meant it had found what it needed, so I indicated to Eligos with a tilt of my head things might be drawing to a close. He stepped over to the strange tableaux and crouched down.

"Have you ascertained all relevant information, watcher?" he queried, to which Iyrin lifted its head and nodded. It looked over at me, and I then realised I was going to have to be the go-between. Eligos apparently wasn't going to allow Iyrin into his mind, so I was required to be its human Bluetooth speaker.

I've got him held unconscious for now, it said through me, *and I've established a link. To make it stronger, and allow for control over any distance, I want a bone from him.* I was shocked that it was planning to take a bone while the spy was still alive, though I continued to relay the remarks to everyone else in the room.

If her face was any indication, Seirina echoed my alarm, though she held her tongue and didn't get involved. Eligos, on the other hand, appeared unconcerned and even seemed to endorse the plan.

"Er, hang on," I interjected, wanting to establish something about my own (and, by extension, Seirina's) link to Iyrin. "Are you saying you can *control* the people you're linked to? Just when the hell were you planning on sharing *that* little detail?"

Eligos stood up and stepped back, clearly not wanting to get involved in something that didn't matter to him, while Seirina leant forward in her chair in interest.

Oh relax, it told me, apparently allowing Seirina to hear as well if her face was any guide. *I can only control someone if I have a bone from them. Taking a bone after death is different, so all I have with you two is a mental link to watch your lives.*

I looked over at Seirina and I could see my own relief mirrored on her face, both of us taking a deep breath in unison. Eligos stepped forwards again as he saw we'd satisfied ourselves with Iyrin's answer.

"Which bone is your preference?" he asked Iyrin.

It shrugged with an apparent lack of concern.

Anything, it replied. *A finger, toe, whatever.*

I winced at the thought of casually maiming anyone, even a sneaking, scuzzy little spy, then had a realisation.

"Um, hacking off a digit might be a bit noticeable if you're planning on sending him back into the Order as a double agent," I observed. "Even a toe might make him walk with a limp."

Eligos regarded me assessingly, clearly impressed that I had understood the plan and extrapolated the problem so swiftly.

"Interesting," he remarked, "and what would be your solution? The watcher requires a bone, so a bone must be provided."

I rubbed my chin, recalling a skiing trip I'd gone on several years ago.

"There're bones that can be taken with no lasting detriment to the body," I stated, wincing as I remembered landing on my ass. Vestigial it may be, but a broken coccyx still hurt like a bitch. "His tailbone. There're several small vertebrae in there, so you could take one and cause no obvious change to his appearance."

Iyrin nodded, since it had already exhibited its supreme lack of concern over *which* bone was used, and Eligos didn't seem to care much either. Iyrin hopped off the spy's chest and Eligos flipped him over.

His trousers were lowered enough to give access to the bottom of his spine, and Eligos laid a finger over his coccyx. Under his telekinetic power, a tiny vertebra erupted through the skin causing the spy to whimper in pain. Clearly Iyrin didn't have him *that* deeply asleep.

Iyrin grabbed the floating bone, holding it up on the end of its finger for a brief examination. It put that finger into its mouth, the long black tongue I had seen previously lashing out to wrap around it, and the vertebra disappeared into its mouth. No doubt to be relocated into its skeleton somewhere, or at least so I assumed.

Mmm, yummy, Iyrin relayed to me, making me scrunch up my face in disgust. Eligos turned away, apparently done, but I spoke up to stop him.

"Unless you plan on sending him off looking like he's been assaulted by the TSA with a rusty fence post and no lube," I remarked sarcastically, "which just *might* give people a clue that something's happened to him, you should probably heal that gaping hole you created."

Eligos stopped and took a deep breath, sighing out through his nose as he realised I had actually out-thought him but unable to deny the veracity of my conclusion. He turned back, hovered his hand over the guy's ass and the hole closed up (the new one, not the natural one).

Iyrin scuttled over to the terrarium, looking at Seirina who lifted it up so it could pass back through the glass into its 'room'. I was left to pull the poor violated bastard's trousers back up, then turn him over and refasten them.

As I finished, his eyes opened and he sat up, gazing around at all of us.

Chapter 28

"How the hell did I get in here, why the hell am I on the floor, and what the fuck are you all looking at me for?" he demanded belligerently, standing up and crossing his arms defensively. He was like a cornered animal, preparing to fight his way out.

There was a sensation like a building pressure coming from his direction as he gathered his magick, and then a pulse of some kind came from Iyrin. His expression immediately relaxed and his magick drained away.

"Excellent," remarked Eligos, walking around him and examining him up and down. "So the control is established and fully functional. I shall send him back out to the street where I found him, then we can discuss the information the watcher obtained from his mind."

So saying, he laid his hand on the spy's shoulder and they disappeared. Eligos popped back alone within moments and everyone relaxed, heading back to the seats we had been using during the meeting. Angie shuffled her chair closer to me and kept hold of my hand, an action that didn't go unnoticed by Seirina and the twins.

"Oh look," Gabby said, "isn't that sweet."

"She wants to keep him next to her," replied Izzy.

"It's nice to see they've finally got together."

"She did have some serious stuff to work through."

"True, and he did well to give her space."

"She did give him kind of a hard time last week."

"It's definitely understandable that he left the ball in her court."

"But nice love ultimately won out in the end."

All during the twins' usual back and forth conversation, Angie and I were looking at each other and trying not to laugh. I glanced over at Eligos and had to stop myself chuckling at the staggered disbelief on his face. When they finally ran out of steam, he took a dep breath and asked the same question as everyone else, although phrased in his unique style.

"Are the two of them consistent in this unusual conversational style?" he asked me, causing Angie to snort in amusement and Seirina to hide her grin behind her hand.

"You mean do they always do this?" I clarified, to which he simply nodded while his eyes remained widened in his consternation. "Yup. It takes a bit of getting used to, but it's kind of sweet once you do."

Eligos blinked a couple of times, then shook his head as though ridding himself of a gnat.

"Yes, well, 'cuteness' aside," he remarked with some asperity. "What were we able to ascertain from the mind of the operative?" This last comment was directed towards the terrarium, prompting Iyrin to climb back up its branch into view and sit down so as to be part of the conversation.

His name is Marcus, began Iyrin, still using me as its mouthpiece, *and he is thirty-seven years old. He has been working for the Order for the past sixteen years, since they approached him at university.* I thought Eligos would have hurried the watcher along to get to the relevant information, yet he sat patiently and listened.

Perhaps he felt even the guy's background might be relevant, so he was willing to let Iyrin take his time and lay everything out. Maybe that level of patience came more easily after several thousand years of living, who knows, but I had to force myself to breathe and relax. Eligos apparently noticed and actually inclined his head in approval of my efforts at forbearance.

He was studying Comparative Histories at York, heavily into the magickal module, also looking at the violence module, war and society, and power of persuasion. He had come from a family of magick users, so the Order had already been aware of him according to what they told him later, but his study selections had been what truly attracted their attention.

They had seen he was drawn towards the darker topics in his choices, so they had approached him with an offer to further his magickal education in certain directions. He had shown a significant aptitude and relish for torture, surveillance and information gathering, so naturally got placed in their special division, which they call the Stygian Blade.

The Blade's operatives specialise in the underhanded, devious side of magick, having to prove their allegiance to the Order above all else. To rise within the Blade, they also have to demonstrate the level of their abilities and show they are above average in power.

There are currently sixty-one Blade operatives, all of whom are significantly more capable than the regular Order members. When Gabriella and Isabella combine their abilities, they can attain a power level just shy of the weakest Blade agent. That revelation had all of the ladies looking at each other in shock and concern. Angelica squeezed my hand to pull me closer.

I shared their alarm, as what Iyrin was describing was a significant force of trained and powerful magick users, though I had something I wanted to clarify. Something that could make the difference between success and failure of this venture.

"How do they compare to Elrulin?" I asked intently. "And even more importantly, how do they compare to our forces? Also, are they all in one place or do they have a few in each location?" Eligos sat forwards at my questions, clearly recognising that I was focusing on the salient points with regard to our upcoming fight.

None of them are as powerful as him, Iyrin answered, causing me to sigh in relief. *In fact he's more capable than even the three most powerful Blade agents combined.*

"Like all tyrants, he fears someone will one day rise up to overthrow him," Eligos pronounced. "Therefore he eliminates anyone with that potential, only surrounding himself with weaker servants."

Iyrin nodded, confirming this was the pattern he had seen in Marcus' mind.

"And how are they spread out?" I asked again. "Are they all centralised at Bolton Castle, or are there separate cells at each location?"

There are apparently ten agents at each location around the UK in order to ensure they are familiar with the local area, Iyrin reported, at which both Eligos and I nodded in appreciation of the wisdom in that behaviour. *The last twenty-one have gone over to help set up the new headquarters and spread their influence in the States.*

"Hey, what about the other question?" Seirina asked, surprising me as she'd been quiet up to now. "How do these Blade bastards compare to us, power-wise?"

Iyrin turned its skull slowly, simply rotating its head like an owl.

Gavan, Eligos and I will be quite able to handle them, it said confidently. *You wouldn't be able to handle the telepaths, though you should be capable of dealing with most of the others. Without meeting the rest of the forces, I couldn't tell who might be able to assist with them.*

"My last question relates to finishing this fight," I stated, looking at both Iyrin and Eligos for the answer to this one. "How do *I* compare to Elrulin? Am I actually going to be able to do this, or is this all going to be for nothing?"

Iyrin very eloquently looked over and me and shrugged.

Without having been in contact with the Aaruan, it stated simply, *I couldn't say for certain. From what I saw in the Blade agent's mind, though, I would certainly say you have a reasonable chance.*

It looked over at Eligos, who was doing his whole 'tactical distance viewing' thing – what my mother used to refer to as a 'thousand mile stare'.

"I agree," Eligos reported, focusing back on the room. "Certainly he is older, though he has warped his abilities; however between your training, your energy stores and the power source Lucian gave you, you should have a good chance against him. His abilities are more familiar to him, though his execution has become twisted by his unnatural practices, which should help balance the equation."

The girls, on hearing that news, sighed in relief and looked approvingly at me; except for Angelica who moved her grip from holding my hand to hugging my whole arm. Up until that point, there had been no certainty we could truly come out on top of this fight so they were obviously relieved to get the reassurance.

While I was glad to get even some slight confirmation of my chances, it still would have been nice to get an 'oh yeah, you'll kick his ass without even breaking a sweat'. I guess I'd take what I could get, however, and at least they hadn't told me to run screaming from any confrontation. *That* might have been just a touch disheartening!

As I thought we were finished, I stretched and looked at Angie, considering how things might change now. Everyone else was also starting to relax, then Iyrin tapped on the glass to draw our attention back to itself and we all glanced over at the terrarium.

There were two other pieces of information I was able to glean from Marcus' *mind,* it said calmly. Something about the way it was focused on me caused the hairs on the back of my neck to start prickling.

"OK," I said slowly, on behalf of the group. "Do we need to hold our breath, maybe perform some ritual, or are you going to tell us? I, for one, am about ready to be done for the evening and think about other things."

At that point I squeezed Angie's hand, making her gasp softly and squeeze back. I also saw her cheeks colouring out of the corner of my eye, which didn't go unnoticed by the twins if their whispers and giggles were anything to go by.

Firstly, Iyrin stated primly, drawing our attention back to itself again, *the latest addition to the Stygian Blades only occurred in the last couple of weeks. It is an individual with whom I believe you're already familiar, Gavan: Dr Ciarán Heffernan.*

I felt a surge of anger that the slimy bastard had joined the Order, annoyance that he'd been capable enough to be accepted into the Blades, and elation that I'd finally have a reason to kick his ass. No way did I have to worry *he* was there under duress!

As I experienced the whirlwind of emotions Iyrin's pronouncement created, I heard it give a little sigh and realised what the sneaky little fucker had done. I knew it fed off of the emotions of those bonded to it, so it had deliberately kept back the juiciest morsels to create the biggest emotional surge for itself.

"Fine, that'll enable me to pay back a fair few debts owed," I remarked darkly. "I'm looking forward to seeing the son of a bitch's face when he finally realises how powerful I've become compared to him. I'm *really* going to enjoy this!"

You may have more to pay him back for than you think, given the last piece of information I obtained, observed Iyrin. Here we go, this was clearly the coup de grace it had been saving. *Heffernan's 'audition piece' for the Order was to bring them all the information he knew about you, Gavan.*

Once he had told them about your shop, he also gave them information on your family he had uncovered. He revealed to them you were estranged from your family, though you were still protective of them so it would be a way to hurt you.

He then volunteered to demonstrate his commitment to the Order as his way into the Stygian Blade, so he went and kidnapped your sister, bringing her back for Elrulin to feed on.

I heard my ears ringing and my entire vision went red.

Chapter 29

My eyesight slowly began to return and the tinnitus gradually faded, so I became aware of people calling my name. I saw the twins flat on the floor holding their heads, Seirina had disappeared behind her desk, Eligos was on one knee and bracing himself with his opposite arm, and the glass of the terrarium was spider-webbed with cracks with Iyrin hidden behind the foliage.

The only one still upright was Angelica, so even in my distress I was apparently able to tell her apart and protect her from myself. I noticed all of this in the abstract, though it didn't fully register at the time that I was the source of the problem.

"Kiss him!" Eligos ground out between clenched teeth. Angie stepped in front of me, put her hands on my face and kissed me deeply. My mind instantly shut out everything, focusing on her to the exclusion of all else under the direction of my baser caveman instincts.

She pulled away and I opened my eyes again, staring straight into her eyes and seeing the dilation of her pupils as she responded to her own primitive urges. I saw everyone getting back to their feet, which brought me back to my senses and made me realise what I'd done.

"Shit, I'm so sorry everyone," I apologised, reaching out to the twins to help them up. They grabbed my hand, pulling themselves up just enough to slump into their chair. Eligos groaned slightly as he pushed himself up using his own knee.

"Ugh," he groaned, "it's been a long time since I have been driven to my knees. Having felt that surge, I have reassessed your chances against Elrulin. If you can bring *that* level of power to bear on him, he will have little or no defence. The danger will be the risk of draining yourself, or harming others around you at the time. Also, how painful that level of emotion is to maintain."

As he finished speaking, something came thumping down the stairs and approached the study. The door was flung open, luckily not having been latched closed, as Paladin shouldered into it and came charging up to me in concern with Gauvain right above him.

I caught G, placing him on my shoulder, then knelt down to put my arms around Paladin's neck to reassure him.

"Hey, it's OK guys," I told them both reassuringly, ignoring the gasps of amazement at the huge dog that had suddenly appeared. As I leant back, I realised Paladin had filled out even more while he slept. He now resembled a good-sized lion, though still looking like a Jack Russell in the head and his colouring.

I sent them both a quick mental recap of what had occurred. They both quivered in fury at the thought of Ciarán's underhandedness but settled in silent support. Paladin pushed more energy through me into Seren, though not so fast as he did before. I cautioned him not to overtax himself then set the feeling aside.

"Um, this is Paladin," I introduced him to everyone, at which he wagged his tail almost hard enough to sweep my legs out from under me. "Lucian kinda gave him to me to help."

Eligos must have realised what I was talking about, since his eyes widened as he looked at my new friend.

"Stop changing the subject," he said, apparently still irritated by what I'd just done. "What the hell was that all about? I thought Iyrin mentioned you were estranged from your family?"

"There's a difference between not liking your sister and not caring when some greasy shithead feeds her to a vampiric soul eater!" No one smiled, so I guess they weren't *Die Hard* fans. Oh well, it takes all types. "I'm going to go and put a ward around my dad before the bastard gets ambitious again."

I teleported myself, Paladin and Gauvain to the garden of my father's bungalow and located him inside. He'd fallen asleep in his recliner with his poodle on his lap, so I was able to place the ward without disturbing him. Once I was satisfied, I went back to Seirina's.

"Done," I said as I popped back into the room. "Now I'd like a word with a certain underhanded skeleton. Iyrin, get out here!" I sent a surge down our link, at which the familiar rustling started up and its skull poked out of the greenery.

"I know exactly what you did, and I hope that little reaction gave you fucking indigestion, you prick!" I swore at it angrily, seeing Eligos nod at my analysis out of the corner of my eye. "There's some answers I want from you now, so you'd better 'fess up or I might just let my control slip again."

There's no need to threaten, it stated carefully. *I can appreciate your annoyance at my handling of the news; you're quite right, I went too far in my eagerness for your emotional response. I forgot to take your magick into account, or I never would have been so blunt.*

"Oh, so you're not sorry you pissed me off, only that you almost got hurt as a result!" I clarified, getting angrier. "I swear, considering you're called a 'watcher', you really have absolutely *no* idea how humans think do you?

"Leaving your rampant insensitivity aside, I want to clarify a couple of points about what you've done to Marcus. Will he remember what happened here? The last thing we need is for him to go back to the Order and report what we've done to him.

"That leads me on to my other concern: Do we know how much he's already told them about what he's seen so far? Do they know about the meetings we've had, especially who has participated? Are our new allies in danger?"

Eligos inclined his head towards me in approval again.

"All excellent questions," he remarked. "Ones that I was considering posing myself. So what is your response, watcher?"

Iyrin relayed its answers to me again and I passed on its responses to the room.

I removed the memory of everything from the time Eligos appeared in front of him, until the moment Eligos dropped him back on the street, it reassured us. *As far as his reporting goes, he prefers to gather as much information as possible before he informs his superiors. As such, he had made copious notes but nothing had been sent back. Those notes have now been destroyed, under my direction.*

"And how will you prevent him telling them, without controlling him so strongly they detect the difference in his demeanour?" Eligos enquired astutely.

I shan't need to, the watcher answered smugly. *I simply act as the voice of his conscience, although one which cannot be ignored as he seems to have done in the past with his own.*

"An elegant solution," replied Eligos. I was still pissed at the bony bastard but accepted its explanation. Creepily, it sounded as though it had done this before based on the confidence of the answers, though I decided not to go there if I wanted to sleep some time this decade.

Since everyone else seemed relieved, I shrugged and let it drop. Iyrin disappeared back into the depths of the terrarium, which drew my attention to the state of the glass. I walked over and put my hand on it, closing my eyes to focus on the structure of the material.

I already knew glass was the crystallised form of silica; plus I didn't need to alter anything, I only had to reform the structure. As soon as I reached out to the pane, I could tell how the repair could be done and accomplished it quickly.

I had toyed with the idea of leaving one big crack across the front to remind Iyrin of how much it had pissed me off, then thought better of it. I doubted it would even register it in the same way I would, and I didn't fancy irritating Seirina. She *would* notice the crack and would probably not appreciate the constant reminder.

Once I'd finished, I went back over to Angelica and Paladin and sat down in my chair. Angie took my hand, patting it reassuringly as if I were a skittish horse, while Paladin laid his head on my knee. He looked up at me adoringly as I rubbed his ear with my free hand. G climbed down my arm onto Paladin's back and started preening his neck hair.

"Right, I think I need to let the delegates know what we've discovered," I considered. There was general agreement from the room, so I got out my phone and wrote a text. I informed them that we had found out some new information about the Order that could affect our assault strategy.

"We can discuss it more when we meet up," I continued. "I think we've all had enough for one day. Maybe we should all consider getting some sleep." Yeah, funnily enough I don't think *anyone* was fooled by that. Even Eligos smirked right at me.

"Oh, shut up!" I said, which led to a burst of sniggering exactly like a bunch of six-year-olds when a ketchup bottle 'farts'. Angie patted my hand condescendingly.

"Isn't he cute when he gets flustered?" she asked, which led to more sniggering from the twins.

Eligos rolled his eyes and got up.

"Yes, well, as amusing as watching Gavan's embarrassment might be," he said dryly. "I believe I shall indeed retire. Notify me via Lucian when we are ready to gather prior to the assault." So saying he disappeared, leaving me alone with a dog, a bird and a gaggle of giggling girls.

"So, umm, yeah, well," I stated eloquently, to general hilarity from Gauvain. "I think I'll take Paladin outside before I settle him down for the night!" I then drew myself up and executed a dignified exit from the study. (OK, fine, I ran like a scared rabbit, shut up!) Paladin followed me, Gauvain riding on him like a jockey on a Grand National winner.

I went through the kitchen and outside, thinking of something important as I smelt some of Mrs Wilson's cooking.

"Paladin, are you hungry?" I asked, realising he hadn't eaten since I had given him form. The last thing I needed was a lion-sized dog with a terrier mentality getting the munchies in the middle of the night. I could end up missing a leg or more!

I'm a magickal construct, he told me, sounding significantly more mature and eloquent since he'd grown. *I actually don't require outside sustenance. My kind are linked to the energy of magick itself, which is why we often get used by others to provide them with a power boost.*

Mostly we get forced into the shape of something small like a battery, as you were told by the one who gave me to you. In fact, I may be the first in over a thousand years to be allowed a living form.

I stroked his head, my mind racing.

Was there a reason his kind were denied sentience? Were they too powerful to have independence? He certainly *seemed* friendly enough, coming running when he thought I was in trouble. He had also been providing me with energy, as Lucian had promised.

Then again, even regular dogs could turn nasty if they were mistreated. I would simply have to lavish him with the same love and attention I had always given my pets and hope he reciprocated. At least if he didn't eat, I wouldn't need to do pooper-scooper patrol!

With his exhibition of this newfound level of intelligence and self-awareness, I wondered why he had needed me to give him a name. Then I realised that if his species were usually denied sentience as he had said, they wouldn't bother with names.

He certainly seemed to be happy in his form, so I resolved not to treat him with the level of indifference he had described his forbears having experienced. I doubted I was capable of treating him like that now anyway, given his ability to communicate with me and my initial connection to him; I had thought of a pet, then got more than I bargained for, like a child getting a puppy for Christmas. For damned sure, I wouldn't be dropping Pal off at the local pound.

I chatted with Gauvain about Pal's arrival, and he happily confirmed his acceptance of this new addition to our family. I was glad there wouldn't be any friction: I had always believed that the strongest family was the one you chose anyway, not the one you were born into.

I heard the back door open and turned to see Angie step out into the garden. Her smile lifted my heart, something I sorely needed after what had happened earlier. She stepped over to me and I reached out to take her hand, pulling her close.

She lifted her face and my lips met hers almost without me thinking about it, my eyes closing as I lost myself to the sensation.

Chapter 30

I reached up to put my arms around her, and she suddenly jumped back as if stung. I opened my eyes, searching for a threat and had to stifle a laugh, seeing what the problem was.

I approve, Paladin told me, withdrawing his nose from Angie's groin where he had just inelegantly shoved it. Gauvain was laughing so hard in my head, I struggled to keep a straight face.

"Gah, what the hell?" Angie yelled at the same time. My composure broke and I snorted, bubbling into full blown laughter as she batted her hands at Paladin's head. His tail was wagging, smacking me across the backs of the legs, as he stared up at her.

"Oh gods, that's hysterical," I said when I could finally catch a breath. "Pal, what were you doing? I know you *look* like a dog, but you don't have to adopt *all* the doggy characteristics. Some things we can happily do without, like the cold nose to the groin."

Paladin wagged his tail even harder at my nickname for him, though he seemed completely unrepentant for disrupting our tender moment. Fortunately, Angie had seen the funny side of it and was chuckling along with me as I spoke to the hulking beast who had recently violated her most personal space.

You suggested this form, Pal answered, *I then incorporated everything about it into myself. Essentially I am a dog, though with a connection to magick which allows me to give you access to extra power.*

"Oh," I replied lamely, "I hadn't realised. I thought it would merely be the physical form and that the personality would be all you." Angie seemed a little confused, apparentlyly only hearing my side of the conversation, so I explained what Paladin had said.

Since we have been selectively bred specifically as power sources, my kind have little to no natural independence, Pal explained. *Therefore I had to fill in my personality from your suggestion when you gave me a living form. As I said, we are often pushed into the shape of a battery or a crystal, something that can be kept close to the one using us.*

I had a sudden thought that froze me on the spot. Elrulin had been with Lucian for years before he'd started using souls; had Lucian given *him* a 'battery'? I pulled out my phone and hit Lucian's number, explaining my concern to Angie, Pal and Gauvain as I did.

"Gavan, I wasn't expecting to hear from you," Lucian answered his phone jovially. "Eligos only just arrived back and was filling me in on the evening's festivities. What can I do for you?" I rushed to explain my concern.

"Did you ever give Elrulin one of these power supplementing entities when you were teaching him?" I asked bluntly, crossing my fingers and hoping.

"Ah, you've opened the bag and understand the power of it. Good," he replied, sounding unconcerned at my accusatory tone. "No, I never gave one to Elrulin. I might have, in the fullness of time, but he resorted to soul energy long before I would have considered giving him any kind of a boost."

"Thank gods for small mercies," I breathed. Then I had another thought. "By the way, how could you tell me to use this one up and discard him like some kind of disposable Duracell? He's a living being!"

I heard Lucian sigh on the other end of the phone.

"You gave it a living form, didn't you?" he asked in a long-suffering tone. "I *told* you to make it into a small portable item to keep in your pocket."

"Actually you told me that I *could* turn it into a battery or crystal to keep in my pocket for all you cared," I replied, thinking back to when he'd handed me the bag. "When I *opened* the bag, there was a pair of eyes in there! Of *course* that made me think of something alive, especially with the feel of the energy around them!

"How could you breed an entire race of beings simply to use them as slaves to provide you with energy? That's even worse than what you were doing in Aaru!" I was getting quite heated as I spoke, then suddenly realised I'd just unintentionally informed Angie of who and what he really was. I widened my eyes at her and put my finger to my lips, telling her silently not to say anything about it.

She nodded but I had a feeling that we'd be revisiting the subject later.

"Don't think you can judge me for things you don't fully understand!" he snapped at me. "Those things were energy clouds with no perceptible consciousness that could provide massive amounts of power with *no detriment to themselves*! *That's* why I started using them!"

"That's not my issue," I said, trying to sound more reasonable so as not to inflame things further. "It's the fact that you used them as slaves and then *discarded them* as if they were unimportant. Why not turn them back into their natural forms when you were done with them?"

I heard silence at the end of the phone. Lucian had apparently never considered that option. This was my point all along: He *still* didn't show any respect or consideration for other beings. OK, he was now using beings that didn't get hurt by it, but he continued to not see them as feeling entities.

"If you gave it life, then you're responsible for it," he informed me coldly. "I created magickal power sources, and that's what I provided you. The eyeballs merely gave the energy a focus to attach to until you decided on its form.

"If you'd *bothered* to assess them properly, you'd have found that they weren't from a living being. They were created *by me* as an anchor point. Don't snap at me because of your failure to fully assess what I gave you."

At that point he hung up on me and I sighed in resignation. Once again my naivety in magickal matters had caused problems, putting me at odds with Lucian once again. I really needed to find a way to stop sticking my foot in my mouth, though I still stood by my thought that he was treating these life forms poorly.

I put my phone away and acknowledged Angelica's enquiring look regarding my slip.

"Yes, OK, the Devil came from the same place as Elrulin and Isis," I confirmed. "That's why he found Elrulin when he was cast out and tried to help him. Please, keep that to yourself. He doesn't really want his origins spread around, and I agreed to respect that. It doesn't actually make any difference, anyway."

She nodded, and I breathed a sigh of relief and thanked her.

"Now, where were we?" I reached for her and she smiled, stepping willingly into my arms and kissing me again. My links with G and Pal hummed with their approval and happiness for my joy, and there was some tingling from my tie to Iyrin. I set those distractions aside, focusing on what mattered right now.

"So," Angelica said finally, after we broke apart to catch our breath. "How are we going to work this? I hope you don't think I've forgotten about your obligation." I furrowed my brow and tilted my head, not quite keeping up with her thought process.

"Several dozen roses and a Michelin starred restaurant, I believe was mentioned," she explained primly, and I threw my head back and howled with laughter, already giddy from the kissing. I thought back to that first drive as we escaped from Bolton Castle.

"I see, and does that have to be before or after you find out if it's bigger than an ant?" I asked her salaciously, making *her* burst out laughing this time and press up against me.

"Oh, even that first day I saw it was bigger than an ant!" she whispered saucily, reminding me of my mental XXX defence. My face instantly heated up, accompanied by more prominent changes further south.

"Uh huh, yeah, so…" I stammered. She laughed softly at my evident loss of footing. I may have flirted regularly with Summer but I always knew it was innocent, never a chance of going anywhere. This was so vastly different, I now felt about as sure of myself as a pimply-faced thirteen-year-old at his first co-ed dance.

"Hey, relax," she told me softly, kissing me lightly again. "We've got plenty of time to work things out. I know you're going to deal with Elrulin and the Order but we have a little time before things start. Let's just enjoy the next few days together. We can work out how to move forward once we're not planning a war."

I sighed in relief, accepting the logic of what she said and glad to put off deeper discussions for now. I pulled her into my arms and simply held her close. She rested her head on my shoulder and I sensed the relaxation spread through her body.

I savoured this brief moment of peace in the last few weeks of utter insanity. My life had changed so radically since that first day she'd walked into Dinas Affaraon, I had barely had a chance to catch my breath. Now I was expected to lead a magickal war!

A shudder ran through me as I considered everything I'd been through and what was yet to come. Angelica held me tighter and said nothing, lending me her strength and support in a way that went far beyond mere magick.

After a few minutes I loosened my grip and she leant away, looking at me in such a way that I swore she was seeing far beyond the surface, deep into my soul. I almost felt naked in the face of her gaze, though there was no embarrassment involved.

"You're a good man, Gavan," she told me sincerely. "I'm sorry I forgot that for a while. I'm not going anywhere and I'm not letting you get away again, so relax and enjoy it." She smiled cheekily and I beamed in response.

"Oh so I don't have a choice now, huh?" I joked.

She stepped back and swatted my arm.

"I think you kind of made your choice evident when you came charging in like Don Quixote," she said, not taken in for a moment.

I shrugged easily, freely admitting I'd made my feelings plain.

I took her hand and we walked back towards the house, Paladin falling in on my other side and Gauvain still perched on his back. Mrs Wilson opened the back door as we drew close, beaming at us again as she had when we came in together earlier.

The twins and Seirina were all at the kitchen table, so studiously *not* paying attention to us that they may as well have had a video camera pointed out of the window. Yeah, I was right with my first thought: My relationship was going to be scrutinised, analysed, dissected, discussed and reviewed at great length.

It might have only been the twins and Seirina right then, but I was fully aware Summer and Emily would gleefully jump on the bandwagon as soon as they got the chance. Sovereign and Aurora would probably pitch in too, once they learned of it.

I refer you back to my previous comments regarding the mysterious Sisterhood of Oestrogen, the Cult of the Double X Chromosomes. No man could stand against it and survive, unless he wanted to live without female companionship for the rest of his natural life.

"OK, let me hear it," I said, resigned to what was about to happen. "You've clearly all been watching, so let's get this over with." All three of them burst out laughing, then jumped up and started hugging Angie, me and each other.

I breathed again, glad I wasn't in for another round of dire sisterhood solidarity warnings, and watched as the happiness momentarily made everyone forget the worries of the upcoming fight.

Chapter 31

After a few minutes, I reached out to take Angelica's hand again and she reached back without even looking. As I closed my fingers around her hand, she faced me, smiling softly. The twins took Seirina's hand and stepped back, all three of them joining Mrs Wilson in staring at us.

"Aww, they're so cute," Gabriella said to the others.

"Aren't they just adorable?" Isabella chimed in.

"They look so right together, don't they?" added Mrs Wilson.

"It's been a long time since I felt such attraction and completeness between such a newly formed couple," Seirina stated.

"Oh wonderful, now there's four of them doing it!" I grumped, drawing a laugh as intended.

"*Men*, all the emotional sensitivity of a rock," Angie joked to the others, making me remember that the only other Y chromosomes in the room weren't human so I was vastly outnumbered.

"Yes, well," I fumbled, desperately trying (and epically failing) to regain some dignity. "I, for one, have had quite enough of this oestrogen soup, so I think I'll head up to bed before something important shrivels up and drops off!"

"Good idea," teased Angie. "Shrivelling is definitely *not* the desired reaction!" The others all laughed, making me feel like the sacrificial male at some witches' fertility rite. Not that I'd complain, there were worse fates I could think of!

"Fine," I said, aware I should quit while I was behind. "I'll see you in the morning, and we'll work out where and when I'm taking you, Seirina." The gentle reminder of her departure tomorrow calmed everyone down enough to start saying their 'goodnights', then Angie and I went up to my room together.

★

The next morning, after smiling my way through my shower and grinning while brushing my teeth, I strolled downstairs to the kitchen whistling Paul Simon's *You Can Call me Al*. (And no, I'm not giving you any more details about last night, you perverts. A gentleman doesn't kiss, or anything else, and tell. Use your damned imagination!)

I hadn't gone to Lucian's pyramid since I now had Paladin for energy and he was vastly more efficient, plus I didn't particularly relish running into the Devil after pissing him off the night before. Probably best to give him a few days to settle down.

I might have to teleport somewhere for a run later though, otherwise I'd go nuts without exercising again. I was sure G and Pal would appreciate getting out for a while too. Maybe I could take Angie with us and get Mrs Wilson to pack a picnic...

Musing away, I wandered into the kitchen for coffee and breakfast, stopping short as I saw four smiling faces staring at me expectantly.

"Someone sounds happy this morning," Gabby teased in a sing-song voice. Her voice was loaded with a couple of shipping containers full of innuendo.

"Looks it too, if that smile is anything to go by," Izzy joined in, matching her sister's tone. My face flushed brighter than a traffic signal, definitely not helped by the hand that rubbed over my ass and squeezed lightly as Angie edged past me into the room, kissing my cheek as she went.

"I should hope so," she told the assembled sisterhood, winking at them as she sat down. "I'm feeling rather good myself." There was general mirth at the obvious connotations and I resigned myself to being discussed like a prize stallion, with absolutely no recourse to object.

I walked over to Mrs Wilson who handed me two mugs with a beaming smile, then motioned me to sit down at the table. I handed one to Angie, filling her mug before my own, which certainly didn't go unnoticed by the rest.

"Oh, so *that's* how to get coffee from you is it?" Seirina joked, to the general hilarity of the room. I smiled beatifically back at her.

"Well, it's not the *only* way," I said. "But it's probably the most effective." I winked at her, setting the pot out of her reach for old time's sake. She mock scowled at me.

"Don't forget who you're dealing with, *boy*," she threatened me, her eyes glowing. Unlike when the twins and Angie had first arrived, this time her eyes glowed purple instead of green so I assumed she was using her enchantress abilities.

I smiled blithely at her and her eyes returned to normal, looking over at Angie. Something of significance passed between them in that glance, though I had no idea what it might be. Angelica apparently did, as her face broke into a bigger smile than I'd seen from her all morning. I assumed it was related to some unfathomable female secret and let it go, focusing instead on my coffee.

Mrs Wilson set a full breakfast plate in front of me and I set to with gusto, ignoring the inevitable teasing regarding the alacrity of my appetite. Man, it was as bad as a frat house in here. Whoever thought women weren't just as bawdy as men when they got together was sorely mistaken.

Once I'd eaten, I sat back with a sigh and sipped my coffee.

"Has Sovereign let you know where I'm taking you?" I asked Seirina and she shook her head, frantically trying to swallow her mouthful of toast.

"No," she managed to say finally, "but I've texted her. They're several hours behind us, don't forget, so it might be lunch time before we hear back."

"Oh yeah, that's true," I allowed. "In that case, I'm going to head out for a run. The garden's too small for a proper blow-out, and I'm sure Paladin would enjoy a good stretch. Anyone feel like joining me?"

Seirina shook her head again.

"I need to gather a few supplies to prepare for my trip," she said. "Clothes and a few magickal items."

I nodded in understanding, deciding *not* to voice the joke about women needing fourteen suitcases for a three-day trip. Not in a room with no other men there!

"We're more into yoga," Izzy told me.

"Running can get rather uncomfortable," Gabby explained, motioning to their joining.

I hadn't considered that aspect of their situation, though it certainly made sense.

There must be several things they couldn't do as a result of their circumstances, though the power increase they got from being together must allow them to do things others could only dream of.

I guess everyone adjusted to their own reality, though it was an interesting philosophical discussion. Did everyone want what they couldn't have simply because they couldn't have it, or were there some things we were genetically programmed to want?

Having magick now, I'd have to be careful about just obtaining anything I dreamed of. That way led to gluttony, greed, avarice, eventual unhappiness and darkness. Those with much often only wanted more, while those with little often learned to be content with their lot. An important lesson to remember, one that might have stopped Elrulin and even Lucian from ending up how they had.

I snapped myself out of my metaphysical musings and looked over at Angie, unable and completely not wanting to stop the smile that spread across my face as I gazed at her. She dimpled at me in return, making the twins sigh and whisper together. I raised an eyebrow at her.

"I'd love to c...join you," she said, obviously trying to avoid a phrasing violation with her answer, given the earlier conversation. I heard it in my head regardless, laughing and waggling my eyebrows in response.

"Could you pack us a lunch please, Mrs Wilson?" I requested, at which the twins practically melted.

"Oh, a romantic picnic." Gabby sighed.

"He's so sweet," Izzy agreed.

"Take your phone, in case I hear from Sovereign and need to get hold of you," Seirina advised, shaking her head indulgently, which I took as her tacit permission to breach the wards again. As an enchantress, hopefully she felt it was for a good cause!

I decided to change our destination and exercise plans: swimming was good exercise, and the availability of water gave us several interesting options. Gauvain would enjoy a change of scenery and prey, and Paladin would be able to run and swim to his heart's content.

I mentally informed the two of them of the plan and was gratified to hear their joyful acceptance. I left the ladies to their *kaffeeklatsch*, heading upstairs to put a few things into a bag. I included a couple of towels, a blanket, some sunblock and sunglasses. Then I did a quick Google search for pictures.

By the time I went back downstairs, accompanied by my giant hawk and steroidal Jack Russell, Mrs Wilson had an old-fashioned wicker basket packed with food and bottles of water. There was another round of "Aww's" from the twins, then Angie and I were finally able to escape.

She took my hand and Paladin leant against my leg, Gauvain firmly gripping my shoulder. I had the towel bag and Angie had the basket. I'd found a Scottish Isle called Harris on the internet. It apparently resembled a tropical island, had some of the best beaches in the UK, yet was far enough out of the way that the beaches were rarely occupied.

Since it was summer, it should be warm enough to be enjoyable. I recalled the picture I'd found online and took us there. The confusion on her face was priceless as she looked around, though it was soon replaced with delight as she took in the scenery.

"Going for a run, huh?" she asked jokingly, so I shrugged and tried to appear completely innocent (I failed dismally, but who cares?).

"I though a swim might make a nice change," I said guilelessly, laughing as she put her hands on her hips and tapped her foot.

"Oh really, and the fact that I don't have a bathing suit never crossed your mind?" she enquired primly, trying to act indignant but she was betrayed by the sparkle in her eye and the twitch of the corner of her mouth.

"Oh, I never thought!" I tried one last time to act innocent before dissolving completely into laughter. I undressed and ran into the clear water, spinning to admire her as she did the same. She swam towards me, her eyes blazing with her intent, so I swam to meet her.

Although we spent a very enjoyable morning on the beach and in the sea, I'm not sure just how much *swimming* we really did…

Chapter 32

I'd made sure to set an alarm on my phone, since I'd had a funny feeling we might lose track of time. We were relaxing on the blanket together after eating an early lunch (can't think *why* we were so hungry) when the alert went off.

I called Paladin from where he was sunning himself on a nearby rock after having run around and sniffed everything in the vicinity, and G returned as well since he'd been with him. The two of them were becoming fast friends; G had even shown Pal how to create a constant stream of energy through me into Seren.

It was slow enough not to tire him but potent enough to be useful in terms of increasing the store. I didn't bother telling him it was far more than I'd been able to collect on my morning pyramid trips; I just conveyed my thanks to them both.

Angie and I packed up, working together in comfortable silence with frequent brushes against each other. Then we gathered together and I took us back to the garden at Seirina's house. Mrs Wilson had the door open as we approached and I thanked her for the picnic.

"Glad you enjoyed it," she said. "I don't get much call to do that sort of thing anymore, ever since…" She trailed off and I knew she was thinking of what had happened to Seirina's husband. My resolve to make his murderer pay strengthened again and I stiffened. Angie rubbed my arm.

"Is Seirina ready to go, do you know?" I asked Mrs Wilson, and she shook her head.

"I don't think she's heard from America yet," she replied.

Her subtle reminder of why this fight was so important had highlighted to me that as much as I'd like to spend more time (maybe the next fifty or sixty years) fooling around with Angelica, this had to be the priority right now.

I looked apologetically at Angie and she kissed me lightly.

"We've got all the time in the world after this is over," she reassured me. She took the blanket bag from me and walked out into the hall, heading upstairs to put everything away. Paladin and Gauvain went with her while I went to the study, remembering to knock.

"Come," came Seirina's voice from inside, so I pushed the door open. I heard a chime as I went in and saw her pick up her mobile. "Oh, Gavan, you're back. Perfect timing," she said, picking up her phone.

"So I've been informed," I riffed, tilting my head. The twins, who were sitting by the desk, sniggered at my obvious joke though Serina merely snorted and shook her head.

"That was Sovereign," she informed me, ignoring my comment. "She's sent me a photo of where to meet her."

"Oh, great," I replied. "Let me know when you're ready and I'll pop you over there. Then you can all get on with...whatever it is you do."

She smiled a sort of knowing, secretive smile that looked kind of sinister, given that we were talking about making zombies.

"If you'll get my bags from the hall, I'll just say goodbye to Mrs Wilson," she informed me, getting up to walk to the kitchen. I decided *not* to complain about being treated as a porter, so I did as I was told.

A couple of minutes later, Seirina came back into the study. I got out of the love seat by the window and walked over to her bags, joining her as she arrived there. She reached out to take my hand, pulling out her phone with her other hand and calling up the photo she had been sent.

I examined it carefully, noting a couple of interesting bits of graffiti on the wall in the background, then made sure I had Seirina's bags close to me. I let G and Pal know I was going so Paladin could temporarily suspend his energy link, since trying to reach half way around the world wouldn't be a good idea. Then I transported Seirina and her luggage to the spot in the photograph.

As soon as we arrived, Sovereign stepped forward and greeted Seirina with a hug. They started walking toward a car idling nearby, leaving me standing with the bags. When I didn't move, Sovereign looked back at me, then at the bags, then at me, then at the car, then finally back at me.

I sighed and rolled my eyes, resigning myself to schlepping duties again, then took the bags over and put them in the back of the car. I refused to call it a 'trunk', and I know the word 'boot' confused the hell out of the Yanks, so I chose 'back' even in my head as a means of some kind of quiet rebellion.

I swept an extravagant bow to the ladies, finally drawing a snigger from Sovereign and a long-suffering sigh from Seirina.

"Good to see da boy ken do as he told," Sovereign joked, at which I crossed my arms and tilted my head. "Him still gat a fayah, doh!"

I sighed again. Gods protect me from women with a desire to poke the bear!

"Right then, I shall leave you ladies to your little crafting project," I teased, teleporting away with a smile as I saw them both round on me with fiery indignation on their faces. Oh, revenge was sweet, though I knew I'd probably pay for my momentary victory later.

I arrived back in the garden, deciding it was best not to pop back into the study in case anyone was in there. I went inside, managing to open the door myself for once as I saw Mrs Wilson was in the study cleaning.

My energy link with Paladin restarted, he and Gauvain sensing my return. I wondered where the twins and Angie were, though I didn't want to act too cloying or over-attached. We'd had an amazing night and a wonderful morning; I'm sure she probably needed some time to herself.

I went up to my room and lay down on the bed, crossing my ankles and putting my hands behind my head. I closed my eyes and considered what else I could do to assist our efforts, since I didn't want to spend the next few days just twiddling my thumbs.

I couldn't think of any magickal factions we hadn't already contacted, any large group of magick users who...

I snapped to sitting, startling Paladin who'd been about to climb up on to the bed to join me. There *was* another group of magick users, one which no one had mentioned and which I was uniquely positioned to contact.

I changed my t-shirt for a top with long sleeves, then stroked Gauvain where he was preening on his perch. Paladin caught my sense of excitement, though he didn't understand what it was about, and his tail started whipping the backs of my knees.

I told them where I was going, so they settled down again and Pal jumped onto the bed for a nap. He severed his link, though he sent a surge before he did so.

I hurried back down to the study and tapped Mrs Wilson on the shoulder as she was dusting the bookcases.

"Oh, Mr Maddox, I didn't hear you come in!" she said. I rushed to apologise.

"Sorry, Mrs Wilson," I replied. "I didn't mean to surprise you. I've dropped Seirina off in America and I wanted to let you know I have another errand to run. Hopefully, I shouldn't be gone too long. Do you know where Angie and the twins are?"

"They went back to the house Ms Crow let them use," she told me.

"Oh," I replied, and a little rush of disappointment swept through me. "I would have liked to say goodbye before they left. Did they say when they'd be back? And incidentally, how did they get through the wards?"

She patted my hand sympathetically.

"I'm sure she'll be back soon," she reassured me, not fooled for a moment about the real reason behind my questions. "You go and run your errand, leave the ladies to their ways. Best not to rush a woman before she's ready. Ms Crow made an adjustment to the wards before you left with her, so I can let people through the gate again."

I'd remember her advice; it sounded like one of those pearls older people occasionally throw out that young people usually ignore.

I said goodbye to Mrs Wilson and teleported away, arriving at the spot I'd remembered. I stepped out of the alley and hailed a cab, giving the driver the address I wanted. I could have gone straight there but I thought it might have been a touch rude to just pop in on magick users.

During the drive I utilised the same technique on myself Isis had used to aid my breathing right before I left Aaru, then simply sat back and enjoyed the ride. We soon arrived and I realised I had no cash, then breathed a sigh of relief that the cabbie had a card machine. I paid then stepped out, taking a deep breath and calming myself.

I walked up to the door and bowed to the monk there, smiling as his face lit up and he bowed deeply back.

"Is Gonpo here, please?" I asked politely, unsure if he spoke English but hoping that my interrogative tone and Gonpo's name would get my point across. The monk nodded enthusiastically, beckoning me into Tashi Lhunpo for the first time since I'd returned from Aaru.

I followed him through the monastery, seeing the peaceful gardens once again, until we reached the pathway behind the building. The monk pointed to the familiar hut and I thanked him with another smile and bow.

I strolled down the path and came to the door, so I knocked and stepped back. I remembered the last time I'd waited outside and knelt in a *seiza* style, as if I were in a dojo, to enjoy the evening. I'd forgotten about the time difference but was glad I'd arrived in time to witness a mountain sunset.

I could tell there was someone in the hut, though I hadn't spent enough time with Gonpo after getting my abilities to fully recognise the unique presence of his energy. I smiled at the thought of what he had done last time, keeping us waiting while he made the tea. With any luck, I might get some more this time.

I deliberately shielded myself from his detection, so that he wouldn't know it was me. I wanted to surprise him, after all the shocks he'd had for me. I breathed deep, enjoying the fresh air, and tried to meditate. My mind was spinning with everything currently going on, so I wasn't particularly successful, but I at least felt a little more relaxed.

After a while, I sensed someone approach the door and opened my eyes. I had a smile already on my face as the door swung inwards, which only widened as I saw the expession on the monk's face.

"Mr Maddox!" he exclaimed, his own face lighting up in pleasure to see me again. "Please, come in, come in!" I got up and removed my shoes, entering the hut and hugging Gonpo. "Tea?" he asked me.

"Oh, yes please," I said. "How have you been, my friend?" I enquired of him, to which he sighed happily.

"I now have no concerns other than caring for my yaks," he told me. "Since they mostly take care of themselves, my days are spent in relaxed meditation." I was happy for him, glad I'd enabled him to finally enjoy his retirement.

"So Ciarán hasn't been back to bother you?" I clarified, and he shook his head. I breathed a sigh of relief. "Good." I sipped my tea in silence for a while. While I wanted to get to the point of my visit, some things should never be rushed.

Monks and women both required some foreplay before going for the prize.

Chapter 33

After a while enjoying the peace and quiet together, I asked how Yeshe was doing. Gonpo happily chatted about his relative, telling me about a couple of nice engagements he'd had to take some groups around. Then I decided it was about time to get down to business.

"Gonpo, have you ever heard of the Order of the Nine Seals?" I asked him. I wasn't sure if I wanted him to say yes or no, since either would come with its own set of issues, but I needed to find out just where to start the conversation.

"Oh, yes," he assured me, looking the closest to annoyed I had yet seen from him. "Is that who you were working for?"

I rushed to clarify the situation.

"That's who sent the woman who hired me," I told him, "though I had no knowledge of them at the time. As I said last time, I was already dubious about them and wasn't planning on giving them the Veil even if I found it. Once everything happened as it did, I was even more certain.

"Since then I've had significant dealings with them, even rescuing the woman hired me from them after they were torturing her. I've now started gathering people together from many different magickal factions to try to destroy the Order."

I went on to give him more details about what I had been doing and the forces we'd gathered. Gonpo was nodding at various points during my recitation, his face clearing of the annoyance he'd shown when he thought I was actually an agent of the Order.

"I'm glad my feeling about you was right," he told me, smiling once again. "My reading of you was a decent man who didn't understand the full scope of what you were involved in. Now that you *do*, it's good to see you taking a stand."

"Thank you for understanding," I said, grateful he didn't hold me responsible for my ignorance. "So what dealings have you had with them?"

"Several of their members, years ago, arrived here having followed the same clues you did to try to find the Veil," Gonpo told me, his face clouding again as he remembered the monks' dealings with them.

"Since they didn't impress the current keeper at the time, they weren't even given the opportunity to even *try* to collect the Veil. The entire interaction with us was removed from their memory each time, then they were sent away with the thought that they hadn't found anything here."

That made sense, since even though I knew I was pretty smart, I doubted I was the first man to ever put the clues together. Still, Gonpo's comments did give me the opening I needed to move on to the main reason for my visit.

"I remembered you telling me last time that most of your monks had some degree of magickal ability," I said, taking a deep breath. "That's why I'm here. I was hoping that some of you might be willing and able to help us fight the Order.

"I want to remove the threat they pose to the magickal community, including this place, and any help we can get would make that goal easier to achieve. Even a few would be a benefit." As I spoke, Gonpo's face cleared as he understood the reason for my visit but he was shaking his head with a rueful smile even before I finished.

"I understand your desire," he told me, "and I applaud you for it. The Order is a blight on the magickal world and should certainly be destroyed to restore balance and freedom. Unfortunately, we of the monastery are peaceful and non-confrontational.

"Only the keeper would even consider affecting an outsider by tampering with their memories, though even then that was only because we were given the duty to guard Isis' Veil. Now that the responsibility for the Veil has passed to you, we are content to keep to ourselves. I am sorry, Mr Maddox, but we cannot grant your request."

Now it was my turn to start nodding midway through his answer, since I had expected something like this.

"I understand," I replied, "and appreciate you seeing me. I had to ask, since I couldn't expect others to put themselves at risk without trying all available options to get as much help as possible."

Gonpo nodded at my explanation, apparently understanding the position I was in.

We each had our responsibilities, though unfortunately this time they didn't coincide. Still, as reasonable men we could empathise with each other's opposing position without being at odds. Such a shame that most politicians couldn't act with the same level of maturity.

We said our goodbyes and I asked him to pass my best wishes on to Yeshe. I expressed the hope that next time I returned, I would be able to reassure him the Order was no longer a threat to the magickal world. He, in turn, wished me luck in our endeavours and promised that the monks would include us in their prayers.

I stepped outside, retrieved my shoes, and teleported myself back to the garden at Seirina's house. This time Mrs Wilson got to the door before I could, smiling at me indulgently as I snapped my fingers in mock frustration that she'd beaten me to it.

Pal came charging down the stairs to greet me while Gauvain merely said hello mentally, staying on his perch. I went down on one knee and hugged Pal around his neck as he tried to burrow his tongue through my head via my left ear as a hello.

"Well you needn't think *I'll* be throwing myself at you with quite that level of shamelessness," came a familiar voice, causing me to peer up through a haze of dog slobber. "I do have my pride, after all." Angelica's eyes were dancing with amusement at seeing me try to fend off a giant terrier intent on loving me to death.

"Ang – pbth Pal, get your tongue out of my mouth!" I sputtered as Paladin continued to say hello with the traditional alacrity of Jack Russells. He sat back, grinning at me, then bounced off to go back upstairs and no doubt claim the bed.

"Gah, dog spit," I complained good-naturedly, wiping my face as Mrs Wilson and Angelica laughed at my predicament. "Angie, I thought you'd gone back to the house Seirina leant you with the twins."

She shared an indulgent look with Mrs Wilson; a female look that no doubt communicated volumes regarding the idiocy, short-sightedness, and stupidity of men and the long suffering saintliness of the women who have to deal with them. Mrs Wilson simply nodded, commiserating with a pitying shake of her head.

"Hey, quit it!" I complained. "I realise I'm only a man, but I have feelings!" We all shared a laugh and I embraced Angie, happy that she was there.

"We've got a couple of days before the fighting starts," she said impishly. "I'm going to enjoy every minute I can. Besides, I want to give you plenty of reasons to stay safe and make it through this in one piece."

While I was ecstatic over the prospect of spending the next couple of days with her, a vague unease settled on my shoulders. I shook it off, hoping it was nothing, but it left a shadow in the back of my mind.

Elrulin already knew how she felt about me from his mental abuse during her captivity in his time vault. My feelings had also been made abundantly clear by me charging in to rescue her, with about as much planning as trying to wash the windows without bringing a bucket or sponge.

That meant Elrulin would know hurting Angie would be a prime way to attack me and shift my focus away from the fight. I also remembered what I'd seen through my accidental time viewing in Aaru.

I might have protected Summer as well as I could, but Angie was planning on joining the fight. I had no intention of letting her be on the front line, since her ability was telepathy so she would be of more use in interrogating anyone who surrendered or was captured.

I had no illusions she would stay out of it completely though. She had too much invested, too many reasons to want to fight back, to ever sit on the side lines and watch. I would simply have to do my damnedest to keep her out of harm's way.

For now, though, I fully intended to enjoy the next few days. I'd find out anywhere she'd always wanted to go and take her there. Anything she wanted to see, I'd show her (scenery, get your mind out of the gutter).

We could eat breakfast in Paris, lunch in New York, and dinner in Las Vegas. I'd treat these two days like my chance to make her happy. I refused to head to war with regrets over failing to show her how much she meant to me.

I kissed her deeply, holding her close until she was breathless. She gripped me just as tightly, clearly also desiring to squeeze as much out of the next couple of days as possible. We held each other, saying nothing but communicating our feelings in the most basic way.

I led her upstairs, sending Gauvain out of the window and Paladin downstairs once we reached the bedroom. I closed the door and the window and we didn't emerge until it was time for dinner.

★

Over the next two days, I did exactly what I'd planned. I didn't care that I was setting an impossible standard for myself to live up to. If we lived through this, I hoped Angie would be happy with a simple shopkeeper.

I caught myself, realising exactly what I'd been thinking. I was already considering the 'M' word when, to the best of my knowledge, we hadn't even used the 'L' word yet! What the hell was I thinking?

I was allowing my ten months in Aaru, spent fantasising about and idealising Angelica, to colour my perceptions. Yes, fine, she'd remembered my pornographic mental stream and enjoyed it. OK, so we both seemed to be wanting this.

Still, in Earth time we'd only known each other for a few weeks. We were still in the honeymoon phase, which explained the rush of endorphins every time I saw her, but that was a flighty premise on which to base a future.

I knew, on an intellectual level, that my poor history with relationships made me want to hang on to the first good thing I found. I had to keep my wits about me, and not let her feminine booby magick corrupt my focus.

Every man knew women were gifted with powers no male could comprehend, powers they used to ensnare us and weaken our free will. I had no problem with being a willing victim, but I had to focus on the upcoming battle and not allow myself to be distracted mid-fight.

Still, forty-eight hours with a beautiful woman who wanted to show me she cared was more than some people had in a lifetime. Finally, inevitably, a text arrived from Seirina informing us that she and Sovereign's team had completed their preparations.

It was time for the war to begin.

Chapter 34

Seirina's message said they wanted me there the following morning, New Orleans time, so I at least had one more night and morning with Angelica. I texted back to say I would be there as soon as they sent me a photo. I also messaged the other faction representatives to warn them we would be preparing the following day.

Since we'd already established an evening attack would be best, at least we wouldn't need to have everyone standing around for too long. That raised an interesting thought, though I'd need to wait until I was with Seirina and Sovereign to follow through with it.

Mrs Wilson kindly allowed me to commandeer her sacred territory to cook a special dinner for Angie that evening, which I served by candlelight in the dining room. I made stuffed mushrooms to start, and then beautiful steaks with home-made peppercorn sauce and thick cut chips (or fries, as the Yanks call them). I made a nice salad with dressing to go with that.

I finished off with my signature brownies with the salted caramel centre and topping served with ice cream, making sure to package some up for Seirina. I didn't want her finding out I'd made some and not saved her any, since that could definitely end badly for me.

I even managed to track down a really nice bottle of wine to go with the meal, thanks to being able to get anywhere in a blink. I still had to catch myself sometimes, since I tended to vacillate between hardly believing I could use magick now and becoming so blasé about it that it was laughable.

After we finished dinner, we adjourned upstairs and spent our final night of peace in each other's arms.

We woke feeling far too warm, due to the presence of a giant Jack Russell acting like a nuclear powered electric blanket on top of us. I heaved at Pal for several minutes, getting a series of groans and whining noises before he finally gave up and got off.

"Oh, thank God, I can breathe," joked Angie as the bed springs groaned from the release of canine compression. I laughed lightly, throwing off the covers and heading into the bathroom. Angie followed me, and we managed to share the space to get set for the day.

We were definitely becoming more comfortable around each other, something that amazed me given the rocky road we'd had. I only hoped the artificial situation we were in right now would translate into 'regular' life. A chill passed through me. I dismissed it, hoping it was just a draught from the window.

I was already fighting my own anxiety to allow myself to accept the good, occasionally having to suppress an extra surge now and then. I put the chill down to that, smiling at Angie and getting a soft, sweet, intimate smile in return.

I finished my morning ablutions and got dressed, then headed downstairs with Pal beside me and G on my shoulder.

So we are finally ready to begin, G stated. *I realise that you have been enjoying your sojourn with Angelica, however I must admit to a significant degree of boredom. I have sorely missed our morning exertions. I shall be pleased to engage in something more stimulating at last.*

I realised with a guilty twinge that in my infatuation with Angelica, I had been neglecting G and Pal. I could tell from our link G didn't resent me for it, but I felt awkward, nonetheless. Paladin was there for me regardless and had continued sending energy through me into Seren.

I apologised to Gauvain for my preoccupation and I sensed his amusement at my regretful attitude. I could tell that he was happy I'd found someone and he approved of my choice, he'd simply been bored with waiting for everyone to get their collective shit together.

I went into the kitchen to find Mrs Wilson happily setting breakfast on the table. I was about to sit down when there was a knock at the door.

My eyes snapped across to Mrs Wilson, before remembering she'd told me she could let people in now.

I followed as she bustled off down the hall, opening the door to reveal Gabby and Izzy.

"Hi Gavan," called Izzy brightly, waving as she saw me.

"You're looking well and happy," Gabby chimed in, smiling.

"He seems much more…centred than before," Izzy observed as they walked towards me, cocking her head away from her sister.

"Yes, almost an air of contentment," Gabby agreed, tilting her head the other way so it looked like a big invisible wedge had been stuck between them.

"I *wonder* what could have caused such a significant change?" Izzy remarked in a sly, sing-song manner.

"It must have been something *deeply satisfying*," Gabby answered, matching her twin's tone. I sighed dramatically, shaking my head yet refusing to rise to their teasing. My efforts at aloofness were derailed by a voice from the stairs.

"Oh, deeply satisfying would be a gross understatement," Angelica informed them as she descended the last few steps. The twins dissolved into giggles, joined by Angie. Even Gauvain laughed along with them in my head.

"I refuse to descend to your juvenile level," I stated, turning away and heading back into the kitchen. I needed coffee, stat! I heard lowered voices from the hall, followed by more sniggering, and hung my head in the knowledge that details of the last few days were being shared.

Mrs Wilson came back into the kitchen and patted my shoulder on her way to the stove to finish making breakfast.

"Oh, don't worry," she reassured me. "You're coming off well in the telling." I smirked inwardly and sipped my coffee, sighing as that first hit of caffeine touched my soul. The girls trailed in and sat down, all focusing on the coffee pot. I served everyone, accepting a plate of sausages and scrambled eggs from Mrs Wilson as I set the pot back down.

"So are you quite finished with my 'performance review'?" I asked teasingly, to be answered by another round of girlish giggles. I sighed indulgently, meeting Angie's smiling gaze.

"We got a text from Seirina," Gabby told us.

"Saying they were ready to get everyone together," Izzy added.

"They've apparently built a reasonable number of 'soldiers'."

"So now we can use them as our frontline force."

"It'll be good to finally get moving."

"Yes, it's been nice to have a bit of a holiday…"

"But it's starting to get a little boring just sitting around the house."

"It'll also be nice to get rid of the threat hanging over our heads."

"Then we can start to figure out what we want to do."

"Yes, we've never had a chance to get a real job on our own merits."

"We can't wait to have the opportunity to do something for ourselves."

"It'll take some thought to come up with some ideas."

"And we haven't exactly got any formal training or qualifications."

"The only thing we know much about is the magickal world."

"How about a job where you'll get paid, work with magickal items, have your independence, make new friends, and work somewhere that's heavily warded against aggression and danger?" I interjected, having considered this already. I felt somewhat responsible for them, so I wanted to at least offer them something.

Angie beamed at me, realising exactly what I was getting at and clearly approving. The twins, on the other hand, had identical furrows on their brows as they regarded me. A sense of satisfaction welled up in my chest at finally having the upper hand, even if only for a moment, in dealing with them. They had such an advantage because of their unique connection that it was hard to ever out-think them.

"That *sounds* fantastic," Izzy said cautiously.

"But we'd want to know exactly where and what before we agreed," Gabby observed. I quirked my eyebrow at Angelica, silently asking if she wanted to take it from here. She turned to the twins and put her hand on theirs where it rested on the table.

"I think he's offering you a job at his shop, Dinas Affaraon," she informed them kindly. They were obviously a little distressed by the idea that they might be cast out into the world with no support after this was all over.

It was hard enough for so-called 'normal' people out there, as I well knew; anyone who didn't fit neatly into a pre-conceived box was always at a disadvantage from the word go. I had an idea of how to develop my shop now that I was aware of the wider magickal world, and they would be a huge asset in achieving those aims.

As they realised I was serious, they looked at me with wide eyes that rapidly became watery with tears of happiness.

"Oh Gavan, could we really work for you?" Gabby whispered hopefully. Remarkably, Izzy didn't chip in for once but just stared at me, holding her breath.

"I would *love* to have you work in the shop," I told them. "I'm quite sure Summer would also be overjoyed to have you there to assist her. I've got expansion plans for the store that you'd be amazingly helpful for."

They promptly leapt up, barrelled around the table and flung their arms around my neck, kissing me on both cheeks simultaneously and hugging me tightly. The point where their necks fused was pressed against the front of my throat so firmly, I sounded like a dalek when I spoke.

"I take it that's a yes," I croaked out. "So could you please let your boss breathe?" They burst into laugh-crying, rushing over to Angie to hug her as well. Mrs Wilson nodded her approval at my suggestion.

The twins finally released Angie and went to sit back down, sniffling slightly as they calmed down. We all finished breakfast, then went into the study to talk about what would be happening later.

"OK," I started, "I'll be going to meet Seirina and Sovereign to bring them and Sovereign's team back, along with their undead army. We need to work out where we're going to gather everyone together.

"If each representative brings their team, we'll never have enough space here. We need somewhere big and open, not just so we're not all crushed together but also so that any portals I open don't run the risk of cutting people in half. Body parts flying around isn't exactly a good look, and killing our own soldiers probably isn't the best way to cement alliances."

The twins sniggered at my lame attempt at levity, while Angie shook her head and sighed tolerantly. I pulled out my phone and opened Google maps, zooming in on the Yorkshire moors.

That was the best location I could think of that would be away from people, have plenty of space, and not be associated with any of us so the

Order would have no reason to be watching it. Then I had a sudden realisation.

"Umm, how are we going to protect the vampires from the sun?" I asked worriedly. "If we're meeting in the afternoon, the vampires will turn into Roman candles when the sun hits them."

As long as they are out of direct sun, came Iyrin's voice in my mind, causing me to whip my head towards its terrarium, *they should be fine. Put up some sort of canopy for them. Four poles with a blanket stretched over them would do.*

It sounded fairly dismissive of my concern and its annoyance was palpable. Angie and I had been so wrapped up in each other that we hadn't even been in here in the last couple of days, leaving it on its own.

Still, at least we had a plan now.

Chapter 35

I asked Mrs Wilson for the largest, thickest blanket that she had and she dug out a woollen bed covering that looked to be made for a super-king bed. She also told me where I could find some bamboo garden canes. Those could all be magickally enlarged and strengthened to make a shaded area sizeable enough for all our more light-sensitive arrivals.

I switched the maps app to photo mode as I had before, finding the most isolated and inaccessible spot I could. I teleported there to ensure I knew where I would open the portals, setting up the pavilion while I was there.

The bamboo became strong pillars, sunk well into the ground, and the blanket became an awning to rival a Bedouin tent. I enhanced the protection it offered by including a magickal UV block in the wool. I then went back to the house and used some of Pal's energy to create shields for Angie and the twins.

I sent messages to all of the representatives, telling them to be ready with their forces, and to send a picture of where they wanted me to open a portal. Then we could all muster at the site I'd readied.

Finally it was time for lunch, though the excitement was getting to all of us now so we hardly felt like eating. Afterwards, we said goodbye to Mrs Wilson, the girls heading through the gateway I opened for them. Iyrin also went through to meet up with Eligos, having exited his leafy refuge as he had before.

I told them to keep the area to the left of the pavilion clear, so I could use it to open the portal for the voodoo team. They could figure out where to corral their zombies once they were here for themselves. I didn't see the need to start building pens, since the zombies should be under their control.

I had Gauvain and Paladin with me, as we had agreed they would stay with me now. I buckled on Muharar and teleported myself to the location of the photo Seirina had sent me. I could tell from the expressions that Sovereign hadn't warned her friends about my two 'colleagues', so I had to stop myself from laughing at their terror when they were faced with a Jack Russell the size of a lion and a hawk the size of an eagle.

I rushed to reassure everyone, though it was more Seirina's relaxed approach and greeting of my friends that seemed to settle the remaining doubters down. Meanwhile, I couldn't see any huge squad of undead warriors.

I sent a questioning look at Sovereign, and she turned to her fellow practitioners.

"Da boy t'inkin' we nat gat de promised fightas," she told them. I was expecting some annoyance at my lack of trust. What I *saw*, on the other hand, was amusement. They must have set this up, ready to have a laugh at my expense, and apparently I'd walked blithely into the exact position they'd wanted. This was no doubt the revenge for my earlier 'crafting' crack.

Sovereign raised her left hand and I jumped about a foot into the air as a sudden banging came from behind me. I spun around and realised what I had *thought* was a building was actually a huge shipping container. My mind flashed to an episode of *Grimm* and I realised they'd used the giant metal box to store their undead forces.

"Umm, did someone get the idea that I was an eighteen wheel truck this thing could fit on?" I asked, trying to think how I'd transport the damned thing to the Yorkshire moors. "Maybe you think I'm a container ship? Are you all planning on picking up a corner each and carrying it? And just how big a portal do you think I can open?"

The expressions of disdain at my histrionics became more pronounced as I went on. Sovereign finally looked over at Seirina.

"Him always dis *couyon*?" she asked, sounding like a kindergarten teacher speaking to a parent about a misbehaving child. Seirina laughed at me like a long-suffering relative observing said child having a tantrum. I was clearly making a *marvellous* first impression on the voodoo contingent.

"Gavan, we had to have somewhere out of sight to store the forces we were creating," Seirina explained patiently, making me feel like it was the most obvious thing in the world and I was an idiot for not understanding. "We'll open the container and make them walk through the portal when you open it."

OK, so maybe I *was* an idiot. It was kind of obvious when I thought about it.

"Fine, so how are we going to organise it?" I asked, trying to sound more reasonable and in control. "Will half of you go ahead to control the troops once they're through the gateway?" There were nods around the group. I doubted very much that the most powerful priest or priestess could control even one zombie from across the Atlantic, never mind a whole army, so it was the only way that made sense.

"Fine. I've picked out a nice, isolated spot in the Yorkshire moors," I told Seirina. "I've already set up some shade for the vampires. We can gather everyone together there before we head into the Edinburgh site."

She looked approving as I explained my preparations, even more so when I told her the twins and Angelica were already there and waiting. When I informed her Iyrin was also there, however, her expression shifted to near panic.

"You left them alone with *Iyrin*?" she almost shrieked, grabbing my arm tightly. "Are you nuts?! You know what that thing is like!"

I held my hands out placatingly.

"When it made its link to me," I explained calmingly, "I warned it that if it touched anyone I cared about, whether that was Gauvain, Angie, or anyone else, I'd make it my life's purpose to destroy it utterly.

"Since I've already made the twins an offer to work at Dinas Affaraon once this is all over, they now fall under that category. Plus, I'm actively monitoring via our bond, so it's fully aware I'm watching it."

Seirina took a deep breath and seemed slightly calmer after my reassurances, though she was understandably wary of the skeletal little bastard after knowing it for so long. I completely understood her caution and I had every intention of getting back to the girls as soon as possible, though I wasn't going to let on to Seirina.

I moved to the end of the container with Paladin, then Sovereign's team came closer. A couple of them still seemed concerned at being close to Pal, so I selected them in the half of the team that would head to England first.

We opened the doors and I peered into the dark interior. It was packed with bodies, all standing still, in various stages of decomposition. Some were simply skeletons, some looked almost fresh, and there was pretty much every stage in between.

It was like an episode of *Walking Dead* or one of the *Resident Evil* movies. Now it was my turn to be uncomfortable, even more so when they all turned in unison towards me and their eyes started glowing green.

I jumped slightly, edged away and turned towards Seirina and Sovereign. I noticed they both had glowing eyes as well, obviously controlling the bodies to freak me out. The whole group laughed again. I crossed my arms and huffed.

"Yeah, OK, you got me," I admitted reluctantly, then joined their laughter. "Hopefully, the members of the Order will be just as stunned to see that lot coming at them. Maybe it'll make most of them think twice about fighting, so we might be able to do this without too many casualties on either side. It should certainly make the ones who were coerced into being there surrender quickly."

I motioned the men and women who were going to head to England first to step to the entrance of the container. Once they were in place, I drew on Paladin's energy and opened a portal right in front of the doors.

I made sure it was wide enough that it extended beyond both sides of the metal box, so the undead warriors wouldn't be at risk of catching the rim and getting torn apart. I didn't want to waste the efforts made by the priests and Seirina over the last few days.

The advance team went through, spreading out once they arrived to prepare to receive the shipment. Then those left on this side raised their hands. The wash of power flowed into the container. The bodies inside all filed towards the portal, marching through without so much as a twitch which was understandable since they weren't actually alive.

"So where the hell did you find so many bodies?" I asked Seirina, wanting to break the uncomfortable spectacle of watching an undead army marching through the gateway. She glanced over at me, keeping the majority of her attention on the zombies.

"New Orleans has a huge number of vast graveyards," she told me. "That's one of the reasons voodoo practitioners like it here. The culture is also steeped in the occult, which again makes their practice more effective.

"Modern embalming techniques mean bodies last longer, so it's even easier to find suitable corpses. Those that are a bit too far gone fall into my sphere. The skeleton warriors are mine, the freshest are purely the voodoo work, then those in the middle are a bit of a mix."

I watched the parade of putrefaction proceed to penetrate the portal. I shook my head, wondering why my brain did things like that, then smiled as Gauvain snorted in my head.

Probably because you spent so long reading alone as a child, he observed. *As a result your vocabulary expanded and you learned to love linguistic linkages.* I chuckled to him as he followed my example.

The remaining few reanimated warriors finally made it through the gateway, then the rest of Sovereign's team promptly followed. Seirina was the last one, finally trailed by me with Gauvain still on my shoulder and Paladin beside me. As I approached the gateway, I took one final look around to make sure we hadn't forgotten anything, then stepped through into the Yorkshire afternoon.

I closed the portal once I was through, watching as the zombies were herded into a roughly circular group by the men and women Sovereign had gathered. Examining the size of the undead force they had created, I realised that I'd need to hold the gateway into the Edinburgh corridors for quite a while.

"Um, how fast can those things move?" I asked. "Are we talking a sixties moaning shamble, or can they actually move at a reasonable speed? Can we anticipate something more like *Resident Evil*, maybe even *28 Days Later*?"

"Why does everyone think movies are reliable?" Seirina asked Sovereign with a long-suffering sigh. I guessed this was something they got asked on a regular basis.

"Ain't no one gunna surrenda' if dey kin git away wit' bot' legs tied togedder!" one of the men in Sovereign's team called out, to general agreement from the rest of the voodoo contingent and amusement from Seirina.

"Just making sure," I stated, putting both thumbs up in approval. "That means they can actually *run* through the portal when I open it into Edinburgh. Otherwise they'd get picked off one at a time as they emerge."

They realised quite *why* I was asking, rather than just prurient curiosity, and calmed down as they understood I wasn't trying to disparage their contribution.

"Right, now that the largest force is here, I'll start arranging for the arrival of the rest of our allies. Time for the Avengers to assemble," I quipped, to general amusement.

Chapter 36

I opened a portal for the weres after the voodoo contingent were settled, since they were the next largest force. The forty-three, including Kazemde, came through in various stages of transformation. Kazemde himself was still fully human, probably electing to continue his liaison role until the fighting began.

There were those who were in full wolf form; some bipedal wolf men; six huge, shaggy bears; a few bipedal felines; and a couple of what looked like full-on panthers. The array of teeth and claws made me step back slightly. Kazemde and a few others appeared to smile in gratification at the effectiveness of their intimidation factor.

I knew on an intellectual level that they were on our side. Their appearance however, as I was certain they were all fully aware of, spoke directly to the more primal areas of my brain in the face of a huge group of predators.

Paladin stepped forwards defensively as he detected my anxiety, his hackles up and a snarl on his face. I put my hand on the ruff of his neck, reassuring him, and tried to calm my own reaction. To my surprise, many of the weres actually regarded Pal with their own degree of caution. I looked at Kazemde with a raised eyebrow and a head tilt.

"We can tell your dog is not a were," he explained, casting sideways glances at Pal. "A Jack Russell is a well-known breed, famous for their aggressive capabilities and used for hunting vermin. The only reason they are *usually* safe is their size makes them a threat to rodents but less so to people. Yours is approaching the size of a wolf, so the scaling up of that level of aggression and fighting ability causes some concern."

"Ahh," I said, understanding. My familiarity and mental connection had caused me to forget how others would see my friend. "He's not actually a dog, he's a being given to me by Lucian to support me with energy. I chose the form, not realising he would grow quite so far beyond the size of my initial imagining. He is, however, quite safe to be around. Unless, of course, you are daft enough to act aggressively towards me." Kazemde chuckled at my final comment, looking at me knowingly but obviously understanding.

The rest of the weres seemed to relax somewhat, though they all headed away to form their own group. They chose to be on the side of the pavilion away from the zombies. It was amusing but I couldn't blame them for their choice. I doubted the aroma of putrefaction was any more pleasant for them, plus their heightened sense of smell no doubt made our frontline 'cannon fodder' less than pleasant to be around.

I had already decided to bring the vampires last, to minimise the risk of them getting caught by the sun, so the Wiccans were the only others to come. Cheveyo had already told us that his people would help once we made it to America, but not before due to their power's attachment to their native soil. They *could* operate elsewhere, and with Paladin I would no doubt be able to bolster their energies. Still, they were more comfortable and confident at home. That, in itself, made them more powerful there.

I opened a gateway from the Wiccan's location, as per the photo they'd sent me, and they trooped through together. There were definitely more women, though there was a solid number of men who clearly didn't care that some viewed Wicca to be a traditionally 'female' discipline. I had already met several male Wiccans in my shop, so I had no such prejudices. As far as I was concerned, that idea was no different than the notion that women didn't belonged in the priesthood. Thankfully yet another idea that seemed to be disappearing these days, however slowly.

(To be honest I had never thought *any* system of belief or practice should be classified as gender specific, though humans tended to have all sorts of weird prejudices. As Isis had told me, we tended to try to put everything in a box, which I felt only served to weaken us by limiting our vision and scope. It was exactly that tendency that led to so much hatred and misery over the centuries. Whoa, that got deep and meaningful all of a sudden!)

I greeted Aurora, passing on my thanks to all of her friends and associates, and promised I'd come and talk to them once I finished getting everyone here. I had a couple of ideas on effective healing to show them, having learnt them on Aaru, though I wasn't sure how well they'd be able to use them since my methods had a magickal basis. Their powers were more rooted (cue flower power joke here) in the natural world, though it never hurt to offer.

Next I opened a portal from the vampires' location. Dominic had sent an image of the inside of a large room, something like a ballroom. I opened this end right at the entrance to the pavilion, so they could come through directly into the shelter I had created for them.

Once all nine of them were through, I heard Dominic call out that the portal could be dropped. I released the magick and as the opening winked out of existence, I saw the group observing my preparations approvingly. Dominic even raised a thumb in my direction briefly, though out of sight of the rest, no doubt to maintain their image of superiority and disdain for the rest of us.

Finally, I texted Lucian with a photo of our location and the fact that we were all together so he could let Eligos know, and a few moments later Eligos appeared. Iyrin cringed slightly at his appearance, which gave me a perverse pleasure to once again witness that there was at least one individual who could make it feel afraid.

Eligos, on the other hand, paid it no attention and instead focused on assessing our forces. He nodded to each of the representatives he had previously met, noting but not apparently offended by Aurora cringing slightly at his attention. She turned away and whispered to her colleagues, after which they all cast worried looks in his direction and edged away slightly.

I joined them as I had promised and tried to reassure them again, although I was only partially successful. They seemed to relax more once I mentioned my idea about including some of my magickal healing techniques, their interest eclipsing their earlier concerns.

As it turned out, there were a couple of their group who had some true magickal abilities in addition to their Wiccan techniques. I showed them the methods I had picked up and they caught on quickly.

They might not be as powerful as me but they'd certainly be able to heal some lesser wounds faster than before, now that I had upgraded their portfolio. I could tell I would be the one required to heal any major wounds – I just hoped I'd be able to get to anyone who needed that level of attention fast enough.

Meanwhile Eligos had moved over to the 'zombie herd' and was apparently praising Sovereign and her team, including Seirina. They all stood a little straighter, which was how I could tell he was congratulating them on their efforts. I smiled at this evidence of his leadership approach as a general, making sure his troops felt good about themselves and pleased to be noticed.

I caught his eye once he'd made his rounds, so he made his way over to me. He started complimenting me on gathering everyone together but I waved him off.

"I appreciate the sentiment," I told him with a slightly crooked, less than confident grin. "I'm aware of the responsibility I've taken on, and nothing you have to say will remove that. I wanted to ask how good your vision is of my proposed teleporting site into the Edinburgh tunnels. Will you be able to have another look before I go, to ensure there's no one there when I land?"

His eyebrows drew together and his lips pursed as I began my question, though the affront cleared from his face as I finished. Once he understood the direction my thought process was taking, he appreciated the validity of the concern.

"Of course," he reassured me. "A stealthy arrival is essential. Landing in the same spot as someone already there would be messy, noisy, and would alert the Order to your arrival before you are able to bring the rest of your forces in.

"I have selected an area that seems to be used for large meetings yet remains empty most of the time. I noted a schedule of some kind on the wall when I looked the first time, though I will certainly check it again before you go. It's only prudent, and I'm glad to see your caution has not abandoned you in the adrenaline rush of battle."

Try as I might, I still felt a rush of pride at Eligos' compliment. I turned it around and complimented *him* on his approach to everyone else, remarking on how they all seemed to perk up after he'd spoken to them and thanking him for his efforts. He, in turn, stood a little straighter himself, then laughed as he caught on to what I'd done.

We shared a chuckle at our mutual support efforts, then he went over to collect Iyrin. I found myself having to suppress thoughts of Iyrin not making it through the upcoming battle. The idea that my unwanted link might be severed for me was appealing but the little bastard *had* proved useful, at least occasionally. He'd brought Lucian to the party, at least, which had led to Paladin and Eligos becoming involved. He'd also been instrumental in the interrogation and subsequent use of the spy Eligos had captured.

Then again, even a stopped clock was right twice a day. Just because he'd been helpful a couple of times, he was still a self-confessed emotional leech of sorts. I wanted him out of my head so I could enjoy my relationship with Angie without having to struggle to suppress his 'feeding' all the time.

As I looked around, I remembered my vision in Aaru and realised this couldn't possibly be the war I'd 'seen'. There weren't enough people, certainly not enough non-humans, and nowhere near enough weapons. There was also no burning city in the background.

Eligos had been right in his comment: This was a mere skirmish, unimportant in the larger scheme of things, though a useful starting point on which to cut my teeth. I still worried about the upcoming battles, especially the thought of having to face an entity as powerful as Elrulin, but it was even more disturbing to realise bigger and nastier things were still to come.

I pushed away the thought, since I'd already managed to circumvent some of the things I'd 'seen'. I'd protected Dinas Affaraon against fire, I'd given Summer her warded Celtic knot necklace... I was determined to forge my *own* destiny, not just meekly accept whatever was thrown at me, no matter what Isis and Danu had told me!

Just then, I felt a hand on my arm and turned to see Angie looking at me. She touched the frown wrinkles between my eyebrows, smoothing them out and soothing me at the same time. I pulled her into my arms and held her, trying to tell her without words that I would protect her, and she squeezed me in return.

We stood for a moment, then I released her and she stepped back.

"You looked like you needed distracting," she told me, smiling impishly. "Remember, everyone here has their own reasons for fighting. You're not the cause of all this; you're merely the trigger for the response that's been building in the magickal community for years."

Gauvain shuffled on my shoulder and chipped in.

Indeed, he remarked, apparently including both Angie and me in his comments as she looked at him. *It is essential not to forget the implications of your actions. However, it is also wise not to dwell overmuch on things which are out of your control.*

Certain events may or may not occur, though trying to avoid a particular outcome may lead you inevitably exactly where you didn't want to go. Your actions to avoid one future may even create a far worse outcome than that which you were so desperate to avoid.

Wise advice. Now to try to get my brain to listen!

Chapter 37

I called the representatives together, other than Dominic, and we went to the opening of the light sanctuary so that he could participate as well. I informed them of what we had learned from Marcus, including the existence of the Stygian Blade and Ciarán's 'audition piece' for acceptance.

They were understandably concerned regarding the existence of a group of more advanced magick users within the Order, though somewhat reassured to hear we'd only have ten to face at Edinburgh. I kept a much tighter grip on my emotions when I mentioned my sister's fate, though I could tell everyone still felt my power building and they were glad when Angie took my hand to calm me.

I moved on, much to their collective relief, next ensuring everyone was familiar with the details of our assault plan. Kazemde assured me the weres had no problem allowing for surrender from individuals, though they would hold such people in one group until they had been screened.

The vampires, all of whom could naturally hear our discussion due to their enhanced hearing and the fact that there was only so much room in the tent, were less enthused. Still, they seemed mollified when I assured them they could be the executioners for any who were scanned and found to be lying in a last-ditch attempt to save their own asses.

I used Google maps again and saw the Princes Street Gardens would make a perfect location for the Wiccans to set up a field hospital for any wounded. It was open ground, right next to the castle, and green with plant-life. Also, since we'd be making our assault late in the day, hopefully there wouldn't be so many people around.

Aurora made the suggestion for her coven to go there first with me, since they had a technique they used to gently 'encourage' people to avoid an area they wanted to later use for a ritual. Hopefully that would enable them to clear the gardens by the time we commenced our attack. I agreed, using the satellite photo to take her and her group there straight away.

When we arrived I was glad she'd made the suggestion, since the gardens were full of tourists and locals enjoying the late afternoon sun. The Wiccans set to work discretely, moving around the periphery and doing something at various points. I left them to it, transporting myself back to the staging area on the moors.

The rest of the Wiccans would be transported to the gardens about half an hour before I made my entry so they could join forces with Aurora's coven to prepare the area for their use. The rest of the delegates went back to each of their teams to update them on the information I'd given them, while I went to talk to Eligos.

He was apparently meditating, though he opened his eyes the moment I headed in his direction. I asked him to check on his chosen transport area in the underground warren below Edinburgh Castle. He unexpectedly reached out and put his hand on my wrist.

I was shocked to find myself taken along as a passenger, almost like watching a virtual reality video, as he sent his mind into the tunnels beneath the Scottish fortress. I felt dizzy as we shot across the countryside, racing north at the speed of thought (which, from what I could tell, was a hell of a lot faster than light!). I was definitely glad my stomach wasn't along for the ride, otherwise Eligos might have ended up wearing my lunch!

He slowed as we reached Edinburgh Castle, allowing me to appreciate the true scope and enormity of the complex. There was no way in hell we would have any chance of gaining access to the *grounds,* even with ten times the number of troops we had, if we came at this in a conventional way. Thank the gods for magick, or we'd have had to give up before we started.

Eligos agreed with me mentally, which made me suddenly remember how closely we were connected right then. I could feel his amusement at my distraction and sudden 're-alertness'. He carried us down, through the courtyard, into the Order tunnels.

I could tell they were set up in much the same way as those under Bolton Castle – an identikit office standard of boring, no doubt set up by the same magickal method in each case. It probably made it easier, since the method wouldn't have to be altered at all, plus it meant visitors from other sites would immediately know their way around.

The meeting room I had seen under Bolton was the same here, which was the area Eligos had selected. I would have agreed, except for one essential point: it wasn't empty. There were tables laden with food and drinks, streamers draped across the ceiling, and a huge banner on one wall which read 'Happy Birthday Alison'.

Given the closeness of our mental connection, I could sense that Eligo was stunned, especially as he had evidently checked the room schedule I could see posted on the wall. The party wasn't listed, which *I* could easily understand, so he had naturally considered the room to be unused during this time.

What is this human need to celebrate becoming older? he demanded. *Yours is such a short-lived species, yet you glorify your aging in a way that is truly incomprehensible to me. I have witnessed these festivities over the millennia yet have never appreciated the reason for them. Often, fun is even made of the aging process at the expense of the celebrant! So why do these events continue to hold such significance?*

I initially had to control my hilarity at his confusion. As he explained further, I began to feel sorry for him. As an immortal, and a lone entity as far as I knew, he couldn't understand the human need to form connections with others during our brief stay on the mortal plane.

It's not about *the ageing,* I told him patiently. I tried to keep my sympathy for his ignorance out of my tone, since I knew he wouldn't appreciate it nor understand the reason for it. *We aren't celebrating getting older. Indeed, that's why most people don't bother with birthdays past a certain point, especially if we're on our own.*

The celebration is on the part of those who care about us. When we celebrate someone's birthday, we are celebrating the birth of someone we are glad to have in our lives. We poke fun at getting older as a way of gently teasing our friends to make them laugh and thumb our noses at mortality. I concluded.

I can understand what you've said on an intellectual level, he replied carefully. *Yet why do you seem to enjoy surprises so much? Clearly, this event has been omitted from the schedule in order to perpetrate a deception against the intended target, this 'Alison' named on the banner.*

Actually, I answered, *many people* hate *surprises. They make us feel out of control and unprepared, often causing anxiety and distress. Something like this, however, causes a spike in adrenaline when the surprise is revealed. That intensifies the emotions, so hopefully the person receiving the shock feels the joy and love of those around more acutely.*

I felt what I could only interpret as a mental shrug or head shake. The understanding wasn't necessary, though could be an interesting discussion for a later date, but the end result was the same: We needed a new teleportation site.

I brought my memory of the Bolton site up and showed it to Eligos. He took us to the floor below, where there was a slightly smaller room that would do for our purposes next to a library. I hadn't seen that in my wandering, probably because that had been the floor where the fog had been swirling in the corridor.

As we checked this one was actually empty, we heard a couple of people in the hall discussing the upcoming party.

"How come we're doing this so late?" came one voice.

"The night shift wanted to be involved," replied the other. "Everyone loves Alison. She brings in the best buns and cakes for everyone else. She always makes sure to save some for the night shift, too, and she bakes cookies every Tuesday."

"Tell me about it," replied the first voice with a chuckle. "I must have put on ten pounds since she's been here!" The voices moved away and Eligos turned his attention back to me.

This is excellent information, he told me. I knew immediately what he was referring to, and it wasn't the news of Alison's exemplary baking.

I know, I agreed. *If Alison is so popular, to the extent that both the day and night shift want to celebrate with her, hopefully everyone from the whole site will be in one place. We'll only have one place to attack and we won't have to worry about being ambushed as we make our way through the corridors.*

They'll also be unable to start wiping computers or destroying documents, so we should get some good, usable intel when we search after the fighting. We might not even have to fight at all, if the wall of zombies at each door intimidates them enough!

I scanned around the new teleport site carefully, committing the room to memory, then notified Eligos that I was ready. In a split second, we were back in our bodies on the moors and I staggered slightly at the sudden relocation when Eligos released my wrist.

Angelica grabbed me, apparently having come over when she saw us standing together and not moving. She scowled accusingly at Eligos at my apparent weakness, though I rushed to reassure her and explain what had happened.

"That's all well and good," she replied after I had told her what we'd done. "He still could have been more subtle and gentle with the return journey!" She was bristling with indignance, obviously determined to fight my cause and tell Eligos off. He sighed and apologised, so I nodded in acceptance while struggling to keep a straight face.

Eligos walked away and I swept Angie up in a hug and spun her around.

"My fearless protector," I said as we spun, laughing as she squealed when we twirled. I kissed her as I set her down, making her laugh as she slapped my chest gently.

"Of course," she told me. "You're just a man. It's now my job to watch over you and stop you from doing anything too stupid. You're merely the brawn. I, quite clearly, am the brains and beauty in this equation. Learn your place, accept my guidance, and we should get along fine."

I could tell she'd definitely been getting hints from Seirina and the twins, though I had no problem with her analysis of our respective roles. I roared with laughter as she laid out our positions, deciding to remember it to tease her about later.

Beauty yes, I absolutely agreed, she had me beat. Brawn, no problem, I certainly was physically and magickally stronger. *Brains?!* Oh, now we needed to have a discussion. I might cede her the *common sense* card, but pure intellect I took pride in.

Still, I decided we could have a long, drawn out, vigorous 'discussion' later. We may even need to revisit the 'discussion' multiple times until I could get my point across and obtain her 'agreement'. Last time we'd 'discussed' anything, she'd seemed more interested in praying than agreeing!

I swiftly moved on in my mind, preparing to open the portal rather than my trousers. I called the delegates together again, informing them of the new information Eligos and I had discovered. They were all pleased to hear everyone would be in one place, though Kazemde brought up an important consideration.

"We need to find a way to prevent them from using their mobile phones, too," he observed, to the agreement of the group. "We don't want them notifying the other sites, especially the headquarters. Nor do we want them accessing their computers through their web browsers and deleting their servers remotely."

"Excellent point," I said, praising his foresight. "Any ideas?" I had one of my own that involved creating a temporal bubble around the room. That would however, as I had experienced during my lesson from Lucian and my subsequent practice, take energy and time which might allow someone the opportunity to do something or make a call before I finished.

"Could you not make a signal-suppressing shield around the room?" suggested Dominic to my surprise. He usually seemed so aloof, so hearing him engage was something of a shock.

"I probably could," I allowed carefully, "though I've never done it before and I wouldn't want to get it wrong when it's this important." No one had any better ideas, so I tried a couple of times to create a suppression field around us.

It was easier than I had thought, especially once I remembered Danu's advice about thinking of what I wanted to achieve and letting the magick do the rest, rather than trying to create a specific 'spell'. I was able to create a bubble around the entire group gathered on the moors without any significant energy expenditure. The annoyed expressions of several of them at being cut off in the middle of their phone calls told me it was effective.

We had a plan, now to execute it.

Chapter 38

I gathered the Wiccans together first, advising them it was time for them to join their colleagues. I designated a portal area and told them to keep it clear, then teleported myself to the Princes Street Gardens where I'd left Aurora and her coven.

Whatever method they used, it seemed to be remarkably effective since the last few straggling tourists were departing as I arrived. One of the coven caught sight of me and hurried to let Aurora know I was there.

"Oh, hi Gavan," Aurora call as she jogged over. "So what do you think?" I expressed my congratulations and admiration for their work, the entire group beaming as I did.

"It's time," I told them simply, at which the expressions changed to apprehension and determination in equal measures. I stepped away and opened a portal from the moors, beckoning the Wiccans still there once it was ready. They all trooped through, many exclaiming in pleasure at the sight of the gardens as they arrived. One of the men was a vocal exception, however.

"Humph," he grunted, "I don't see what's so wonderful! Plants should be left alone to grow naturally, not forced where they didn't want to be. Bloody humans, always buggering about with everything until nothing's the way it should be!" I could see his point, though this was apparently an old and tired refrain of his if the response was any indication.

"Oh, for the love of the Goddess!" complained one of the women near him. "Why don't you give that tune a rest! We all know how you feel, you spout off ad nauseam every chance you get. Just be thankful there's some greenery left!"

I turned away and covered my smirk, since the speaker looked to be all of about nineteen yet harangued the complainer with all the authority of a family matriarch. One of the older women sighed, shook her head and walked over to me.

"She's wasting her time," she commented to me under her breath. "Seb's been like that ever since I've known him. Good job he's actually a decent Wiccan, or we'd have booted his ass years ago. His problem is that he's always cared about the plants more than people.

"Anyway," she continued, handing me a bag. "We made these in preparation. They're called scapulars, and they're protective charms. Not as powerful as your wards, I'm sure, but might help in a pinch. Hand them out when you get back." She hunched her shoulders as if embarrassed and hurried away, so I called my thanks after her, including everyone in my gratitude for their forethought.

"I hope we won't need to call on your healing abilities, but I'm glad you're all here nevertheless." I told them. Then I said good bye and transported back to the moors.

Eligos had already departed with Iyrin when I got back, or so Angie informed me. I thanked her, then asked everyone to get ready for our assault, handing the bag of scapulars to the twins to distribute. I took a few deep breaths as I tried to calm my battle jitters, which currently felt like that image of the breeding ball from *Anaconda 2* roiling around in my midsection.

My brain was fast-forwarding through every permutation of screw-up it could come up with, which *really* wasn't helping. I tried to calm myself by remembering what Iyrin told me (yes, OK, the little bony git had some redeeming aspects. There I said it!) about how my anxiety was just my heightened perception of possible outcomes.

Angie squeezed my hand in reassurance, so I gripped back in thanks and told my mind to shut the hell up. While Paladin merely leant his weight against my hip in silent support, Gauvain rubbed his face against mine and tried to balance my pessimistic view.

You cannot assume the responsibility for the outcome of this endeavour entirely on your own shoulders, G told me gently. *While I accept that you did begin this resistance movement, everyone here has their own reasons for fighting. They merely needed a focus to bring them together. Plus your awakening, and knowledge of Elrulin, have created a unique opportunity.*

He was clearly including Angelica in our conversation, as she was agreeing with his comments.

"Oh, well, if you're going to team up against me," I remarked, only slightly sarcastically. "I suppose I have no choice other than to accept, and bow to, your superior wisdom." The pair of them developed almost identical airs of self-satisfied superiority, which was the thing that lifted me out of my neurotic spiral and put a smile back on my face.

Since it was the height of summer, it would still be daylight when I opened the portal. I couldn't quite figure out how to get the vampires safely through, so I went over to talk to Dominic. When I mentioned my concern, several of the other vampires turned away and I swore I could see their shoulders shaking.

I got a sneaking suspicion, and a particular snippet from Bram Stoker's *Dracula* popped into my head. In it, Stoker remarks that vampires are not instantly incinerated by the sun, especially the older ones. In fact they can even move around in sunlight, though their powers are reduced.

"You're fine in the sun, aren't you?" I asked with a sigh. "I didn't even need to put up this damned tent, did I?" One of them lost it at that and I saw the tears of laughter running down her face.

"Oh wow," she said, her shoulders still shaking. "It never gets old when people believe all the hype about us. As if we'd have been able to live this long when a wind-blown curtain, a splash of special water or two crossed sticks could destroy us."

The rest of them were laughing now, even Dominic, so I grabbed the blanket as if to rip it down. The sudden change in their demeanour told me that although they could tolerate a little sun, standing out in the blazing summer daylight still wouldn't be their first choice.

"OK, so you *will* at least be able to walk to the portal when I open it then," I concluded, to which they nodded, apparently relieved I hadn't actually pulled the tent apart.

As I turned away, my phone rang. My mind immediately went to Summer, so I grabbed it and answered without even checking the number. Then came some of the words that everyone dreads to hear…

"Hello, this is a call to tell you that seven hundred pounds has been charged to your Amazon Prime account…"

"I don't even *have* a Prime account," I interrupted loudly, drawing stares from all around the group. "So why don't you go fuck yourself in the ass with a barbed wire baseball bat and jump in a shark tank?!" Funnily enough, the caller hung up only a few seconds into my tirade, so I was denied the satisfaction of hearing their response.

I blocked the number on my phone, then looked around to see the amused expressions on the assembled faces.

"I fucking hate scam callers!" I stormed, at which there was a flurry of agreement.

"Always at the worst possible time!"

"Oh, tell me about it."

"Bastards."

"Nice imagery on the come-back!"

"Maybe we should go after the scammers once we're done with the Order?"

"They're definitely annoying enough to have been set up by demons or something!" There was general agreement at this last comment.

It was nice to see that even though this was a disparate group from different locations around the world, there were some things that could unite people outside of evil organisations. Though scam callers might actually fall under that category, thinking about it.

The call did have one benefit: it reminded me to put my phone on vibrate so it wouldn't ring at an inconvenient moment during our assault. I saw others realise the same thing, so there was a sudden flurry of mobile phones being pulled out of pockets and either switched off or put on silent or vibrate.

I took several deep breaths to try to calm myself again, though my irritation with the call folded into my anger at the Order. I realised it could be dangerous, both for myself and the Order members, since in this state I would take stupid risks and be less likely to listen to attempts at surrender.

G was aware of my agitation and tried to help me settle.

I fail to see why you allow this incident to unsettle you to such a degree, he observed calmly. *This is an annoyance, though not one that has caused you any serious inconvenience.*

Since he hadn't followed my thought process, I tried to explain.

"It's not the phone call itself," I told him, so annoyed that I spoke aloud rather than mentally as we usually would. "It's the fact that these assholes prey on vulnerable people, like the elderly who might be confused and worried, and take their money. They steal from them, often more than just the amount they first mention, and scare them with tales of disastrous outcomes.

"So not only do they take money, but they also cause anxiety and can cause serious problems. Not only financial, though those can be significant, but the stress can lead to health issues too!" This conversation, far from helping me calm down, was actually getting me worked up even more.

Angelica came over and took my hand, pulling gently to get me to look at her. Then she kissed me softly. My brain immediately shut up and focused on the important consideration.

"Better?" she asked calmly. I could feel Gauvain's amusement that something so simple could completely divert my thought processes.

Thank you, he told her in relief. *I was achieving little in my attempts. To be honest, I believe I may even have led to a deterioration in his mental state. You may have just acquired a full-time position as his mental stability facilitator!* he joked finally, making Angie laugh.

"I don't think I have the strength for that," she riposted, nudging my ribs with her elbow as she leant into my side. "Besides, certain things lose their effectiveness if they're used too often."

"Oh, absolutely," I agreed. "Daily use of those methods would probably lead to a decrease in effectiveness within a couple of centuries!" Both of them chuckled at my sarcasm, though Angie's cheeks acquired a rosy tint at the intimation of my enduring interest in her.

So now that you are calmed sufficiently to think clearly again, G said, projecting his thoughts to Angie as well (I could tell because she looked at him when he started 'talking'). *You have clarified the issue regarding the vampires accessing the portal, so should we not be making our final preparations to begin the assault?*

Angie nodded, standing up straight and bracing herself. I agreed and waved to attract everyone's attention.

"Get ready," I called out, loud enough to be heard around the various groups.

"It's time."

Chapter 39

There was an immediate change to the previous light social feeling that had gradually pervaded the gathering. Everyone was reminded of why we were here, what was potentially at stake, and what we were about to do.

Smiles were exchanged for game faces. Some of the weres who had originally shown up in human form underwent total or partial transformations; I saw flashes of red eyes and white fangs from the depths of the vampire tent; and the zombies seemed more active as they no doubt received the transmitted agitation of their…handlers? Puppet masters? I'd have to check with Sovereign or Seirina on that one.

The twins joined Angie and me, determination almost radiating from their eyes.

"I know you're all eager to have your revenge," I said to them and Angie. "Still, combat isn't where you'll be of the most use. Remember, we need you to help with the screening of anyone who surrenders. Then to help us locate and access any useful information after the fight.

"I want you to hang back once the fighting gets heavy. Until then, stick with me *cariad*." The endearment slipped out without my thinking about it, something I'd remembered from my early years. It was what my father had called my mother in his more tender, expressive moments. I'd looked it up and it was the Welsh word for 'love', often used to mean 'dear' or 'sweetheart'.

Angie tilted her head at the unfamiliar word, no doubt wondering what I'd said, so I murmured, "Later," to her. I cursed inwardly, thinking of all the situations and lives that had been ruined by that one simple word, and I pulled her to me.

"It means 'sweetheart'," I told her quietly. "Just stay safe, *please.*" The last word came out as both spoken and a mental entreaty, at which she touched my cheek in a gentle caress. I closed my eyes and took a deep breath, centring myself as if I were about to enter a martial arts tournament.

I snapped my eyes open, ready to kick ass and chew bubble gum – and most definitely being all outta gum. Angie and the twins stepped to my left, taking up position just behind me so as to be out of my way, and Paladin took up station on my right. I drew Muharar with a flourish.

"It's time to start reclaiming our world!" I shouted, raising my sword above my head to try to fire up the troops. "It's time we stopped living in fear of those sons of bitches in the Order. Time to reclaim our rights of freedom and peace!"

The roars that greeted my impromptu speech told me everyone was ready to go. It may have been a touch cheesy but it worked, and I fully intended to use every tool at my disposal to see this thing through. I sent a brief mental message to both Eligos and Iyrin to inform them we were about to begin, to enable them to coordinate the attacks.

I made sure the designated portal site was clear, then teleported to Edinburgh, first popping into the gardens to inform Aurora and her team that we were beginning our assault. I went into the Order stronghold, picturing the new room I had located with Eligos. It was mercifully still empty, so I wasted no time opening a portal from the moors to start bringing in the teams.

To my surprise, since I'd planned on bringing the zombies first, the vampires were actually the first through. I raised an eyebrow at Dominic questioningly and he shrugged dismissively.

"We don't *follow*, we *lead*," he informed me, to the agreement of his cadre. I forced myself not to roll my eyes, instead turning back to the portal. With the vamps having rushed through, I was totally unsurprised to see Kazemde leading the weres through next.

"Let me guess," I said with a sigh. "Anywhere the vampires go, the weres are unafraid to go as well?" There was a resounding confirmation, though some grumbled in irritation at a "you men 'follow like good little doggies'" comment from somewhere amongst the vampires.

Fortunately, so hostilities couldn't derail our assault even before it began, Dominic snarled at his group followed by ordering them to shut up and focus. Kazemde nodded stiffly in his direction, and the weres grouped themselves on the other side of the room from the bloodsuckers.

Angie and the twins came through with Paladin, followed by Seirina and Sovereign who then turned back expectantly. I could see the revenant horde moving towards the portal, but then they abruptly ran into something as they tried to come through.

I could see them pressing up against the opening, yet it didn't let them pass. I knew it wasn't my portal, since I'd used exactly the same method to bring them over from New Orleans. I reached through and gripped the wrist of one of the less mouldy and disgusting ones, then tried to pull it across the threshold.

It was like trying to push a ball into a tub of over-concentrated jelly. The surface gave and stretched a little but wouldn't allow the zombie passage. I released my grip and reached out with my magickal senses, trying to discover what was going on. I was aware that time was rushing on with its ever-present alacrity, so we needed to sort this quickly.

I discovered a ward against our dead forces, preventing their passage. It *didn't* block vampires, since they were *un*dead, likely because there were vampiric Order members, so this must have been set up specifically to keep zombies out of the site.

Why would there be something like that, unless someone had informed the Order of where we were planning to attack and the state of our forces? I looked at the vampires and weres, all of whom were equally puzzled from what I could see – though it is kind of hard to interpret the expression of a three thousand pound bear!

I probed mentally at the ward, testing to see how hard it would be to break. It seemed fairly rudimentary, so I drew my sword again and simply slashed down the centre of the gateway. The ward separated like curtains and the zombies poured through, followed by the rest of the obeahs.

I should have known it was too easy.

The air around the zombies flashed a rainbow of colours, highlighting the links from the voodoo practitioners and Seirina, then those links were severed and we were left staring at a pile of corpses. Simultaneously, an alarm klaxon went off, completely scuppering any chance of a surprise attack.

"Oh, well that's just fucking great!" I swore as the bodies crumpled to the floor, shouting both because I was pissed off and to be heard over the wailing alarms.

"Someone must have betrayed us to the Order!" yelled Seirina. "All that time and effort, wasted! When I find out who…" Her face promised eons of pain for whichever misguided soul had revealed our plans. I refused to allow the opportunity to slip by us, however.

"I know, but we don't have time to think about it right now," I interrupted. "We're here, and it just means we'll have a real fight on our hands instead of the walkover it might otherwise have been."

At that, the vampires and weres seemed to perk up.

They'd seemed resigned to the potential ease of surrounding a party with zombies and the Order members being terrified into surrender. Now they'd actually get to fight. Dominic and Kazemde almost had a Looney Tunes moment of getting stuck together in the door, though at the last moment Dominic held back and allowed the Egyptian through first.

"You'll need the head start," he promised, smiling evilly. "We'll still get more than you!" That reminded me of my friendly wager with Seirina, which would have also been derailed by the zombie plan (though she'd have no doubt claimed all the members here as hers since she'd helped create the zombies. Typical female cheating!)

I remembered to cast my cell-phone dampening field before doing anything else, threw Seirina a fierce grin that she returned, and joined the rush out of the room. I curved around Kazemde and Dominic, both of whom had stopped to try to figure out where to go.

"Follow me!" I crowed, heading straight for the stairs with Paladin only half a step behind me. I was glad the layout was the same as the Bolton Castle site, since I remembered my trek through there. I'd also made sure to plot the route up to the party when I'd been linked to Eligos for our little remote reconnaissance.

Everyone barrelled after me, not caring about noise since our surprise attack was no more. Still, they say no plan ever survives first contact with the enemy. I just hoped that meant plan B would actually work. Time to try some shock and awe!

In that vein, I actually blew the door and part of the wall into the hallway when I reached the top of the stairs. It helped me express my anger, looked intimidating, plus helped enlarge the opening so our forces could pour onto this level more easily than filing through the previous opening.

Since the fight was happening in confined quarters, Gauvain and I had previously agreed this wasn't the best location for him to join the fight. He stayed in his claw on my wrist, though I felt him join with me to keep an eye on the battle and watch my back as best he could. He also kept in contact with Pal, to act as a sort of coordinator for us.

We all charged along the corridor, heading for the double doors on the opposite side half-way down. Those were the first entry point to the main meeting room where the birthday party was being held.

Before we got even a third of the way there, the doors were yanked open and Order members streamed into the hall. Some also came around the corner farther down, doubtless having used another door. I could see that tables had been moved to allow use of the nearest door, which was obviously why it had taken them longer to get it open.

For a moment, both groups stopped and simply stared at each other. Then someone behind me snarled, one of the weres or possibly one of the vampires, and the freeze-frame shattered.

Both groups roared and charged at each other, fangs and claws out, weapons aloft. A couple of the vampires, plus several weres, leapt over the first few rows of Order members to land in amongst the oncoming horde. They knocked over several Order members each, then jumped to their feet and proceeded to tear into the surrounding creatures.

The rest of us charged straight ahead. I watched Paladin crash headlong into a troll and grab it by the thigh, shaking his head exactly like a regular Jack Russell with a rat. Due to Pal's enhanced size, the troll was flung around like a rag doll until I heard a snap and the screaming stopped as the monster's neck broke.

The rest of us, on both sides, had stopped in amazement to witness the unrestrained display of savagery. I took the moment to try and give them the opportunity to surrender if they wanted.

"We're here to destroy the Order and its leader," I shouted into the stunned silence. "Anyone who is here under duress, of whatever kind, if you surrender and are found to be telling the truth you won't be harmed. If you fight, you'll be shown no mercy."

The Order members looked at each other and I noticed a few trying to sidle back into the party room. After a few more moments, the rest regarded us us with sneers of disdain. They no doubt didn't rate our chances, thinking they had us outnumbered now that our zombies had been disabled.

With a combined roar, we renewed our attack determined to show them precisely what we were capable of.

Chapter 40

Paladin stayed by my side this time, defending my left, though I noticed most were shying away from him after his earlier display. It gave me greater freedom to move and I made full use of it, laying about with my feet, my sword, and my magick.

At one point I tried to cast a taserball at the same time as I swung Muharar. The two actions combined and I found myself swinging a bar of lightning. I immediately began focusing my magick along the blade, rapidly switching between flames, electricity, and even plasma to see if I could create a lightsaber (it didn't quite work that way, but it was worth a try).

My anger started spilling out into a variety of colourful epithets directed at the creatures I was facing. A troll got called "a smelly, green, hippo-ass-faced shit stain". A female vampire prompted me to borrow from Ryan Reynolds and refer to her as both a "horse-humping bitch" and a "cock-juggling thunder-cunt".

A werewolf I stabbed just before he could drive his claws through Pal's neck became a "troll-sucking vampire-fondler", and a spell slinger whose fireball glanced off my wards before it could hit me square in the face was a "goat-fellating back alley camel's anal whore".

Some of my allies, close enough to hear me, started laughing and attempting to come up with their own choice appellations. Soon it degenerated into a competition not only of who could kill the most, but also who could create the best insults.

We started shouting out random point scores for particularly creative endeavours, either physical (the vampires and weres were way ahead on those) or vocal (I flatter myself that no one else came close to matching me there).

The Order members seemed to find our humour intimidating, and a few more of them turned back to the meeting room to join those who wanted to surrender. My wards and the scapulars seemed to keep our forces safe, for the most part.

One of the bears fell to a troll who swung a huge, spike-encrusted club. A couple of wolves were consumed when they got caught in the union of three separate fireballs which created a sudden conflagration around them. They were gone in seconds, before I even had a chance to try to quell the flames.

Several of the human Order members fell to their knees and stared adoringly at Seirina as her eyes shone brightly with her enchantress powers. Those were rapidly dispatched by some of the obeahs with her, others of whom were still trying to raise some of the fresh corpses. The ward against zombies still seemed to be in effect, however, so their efforts were met with a slight twitch at best before the corpses fell still again.

"Forget it," I told them eventually, stepping back from the fight for a moment. "They clearly knew we were going to use zombies and managed to prevent their successful entry. It's not your fault. Take out your frustrations on those bastards who ruined your efforts."

They drew blades and rushed into the fray. I joined them once more, my magick and blade claiming limbs and lives as I went. Paladin leapt into the thick of them like a ratting terrier in a barn, terrifying to behold in his ferocity.

The Order members were forced back, their ranks thinning as they went, until we finally managed to have them fully contained within the party room. At that point, the battle became yet more surreal, as party streamers and balloons wrapped around weapons while food and drink turned into artillery barrages.

There were frosting face slams, wiener-waving warriors, sausage roll slingers, and cupcake cannonades. Sodas were shot-putted and the floor became as treacherous as an ice rink.

A chill abruptly ran down my back. I turned and my heart stood still. An Order member in a black leather jacket had managed to get behind Angelica and was about to stab her.

I didn't even think, I simply threw out my hand and shouted, "Stop!". Somehow I managed to instantaneously create a time bubble around the man with the knife, so he seemed to be moving slower than frozen molasses.

I reached out and pulled Angelica to safety, then set my own blade in the guy's way before releasing the field. His eyes widened as his lunge thrust him onto my sword, deliberately set low to catch him right in between his legs. His momentum carried him forwards, Muharar sinking into the bottom of his pelvis and flipping him over to crash head-first into a table.

My shout and the subsequent crash drew attention from everyone nearby. Those who had seen what I'd done whispered to those who hadn't witnessed it for themselves. The fact that I'd used an ability they'd only ever seen from Elrulin (or Atma as they knew him) – and even then only as a room he'd set up as his torture area – seemed to make them realise what was arrayed against them.

I yanked Muharar out of my victim's lower body, wiped it off fastidiously on his upturned ass, then sheathed it with a flourish. I formed a ball of intense flame in my left hand, heating it up until people started sweating and stepping away from me. I surrounded my right fist with enough electricity that it started arcing out as if I was holding a lightning bolt.

Everyone, allies and enemies alike, backed away from me and the fighting soon wound down. Order members formed groups, some moving away from others as they tried to identify themselves as the 'under duress' contingent. I eased back on the energy I was feeding into my hands, much to the relief of those around me.

"OK, now that everyone has gotten *that* out of their system," I remarked, looking around the room. "We now enter the scanning portion of our evening. You have two choices: Allow one of us to scan you voluntarily, and we can do this without pain or lasting trauma. Alternatively, you can fight, and *I'll* be the one to scan you. I promise you, you will *not* enjoy it, and I'll be extremely thorough.

"If, unlikely but possible, you are able to resist even me," I continued ominously, "I will call someone who will be able to slice through your defences like a hot knife through butter." The shuffling spoke volumes, though there were still some angry and defiant gazes cast my way.

I turned to the twins and Angie, motioning them forwards to begin scanning. Several members obviously recognised the twins, narrowing their eyes at the turn-coats. Others seemed to realise their presence, and my trust in them, confirmed my earlier comment about sparing those who were there under duress or were truly repentant.

It was in that moment, when I thought we were past the worst of the danger, that it happened. Another member in a black leather jacket cast a ball of green light at Angie. I was expecting it to bounce off her wards; instead it continued directly through and surrounded her entire head with an emerald glow.

She raised up onto her tiptoes, her head thrown back. The glow seemed to be absorbed into her head, at which point she collapsed to the floor in a heap. I dropped to my knees beside her and saw her face actually lost the tension that had been there constantly since we had escaped from Bolton Castle.

Even in her most relaxed moments over the last few days (many of which were directly due to my 'input'), there had still been a trace of tightness around her eyes. That had finally disappeared, which was wonderful to see but left me wondering how and why it had gone.

I left her where she was, since she seemed to be alive and safe for now, and straightened up. I turned towards the Order member, drawing my sword as I did so, and saw the fear erupt on various faces. Energy radiated off of me, much as it had when I had stood in Seirina's doorway several days ago, and clearly it was as visible as then, if not more so.

Even my own allies were backing off, similar to the way they'd shied away from Paladin earlier. I used the space to stalk ominously towards the offending person. I reached out with my magick and lifted the son-of-a-bitch to the tips of his toes, surrounding him with a field that held him so tightly he could barely breathe, let alone move.

I closed in. The other Order members backed away from him as if he'd been stricken with some contagious disease. My rage built and I had to hold myself back from ending his life too quickly. I wanted him to suffer.

I knew the field I had around him would hold everything together and stop pieces falling away, so I decided to just start slicing. My first swing, however, deliberately impacted with the flat of my blade: a full-on golf swing into his fun-zone, which made everyone else wince and grimace while he gagged, wanting to throw up.

He was prevented by my magickal 'stasis field', instead forced to internalise and endure his agony, exactly as I planned. I began driving Muharar into the tenderest and most sensitive areas of his body, or simply slicing through sections completely.

By holding the parts together, he was unable to bleed out and the severed nerves were still held exactly where they were before. I made sure to start with hands and feet, then work inwards in case the nerves couldn't transmit once they were severed no matter how closely together the ends were held.

I was swearing at him, using amalgamations of various insulting epithets as I progressed. I started with the obvious "motherfucker", drawing it out to make a slice with each syllable, then progressing on to more imaginative creations.

Some of those I'd either used or heard during the earlier fighting were recycled now, plus more as I proceeded to slice ever finer. His arms and legs were reduced to bologna, then I repeated the golf swing to his balls.

I then sliced off his genitals completely, proceeding to work my way up his body in narrow increments. I knew that once I cut through either his heart or brain it was probably all over, so I tried to draw out his pain as much as I could.

Finally pretty much all that was left was his ribcage and his head, off of which I had already sliced or gouged every part of his face. I crushed him until I heard his bones cracking, then swung Muharar as hard as I could, an overhead slice that cut vertically straight down through the shit-stain who had dared attack the woman I loved.

I finally released the field holding him, watching as he turned into a pile of mince and blood. I turned away, noting the terror on other Order members' faces and severe consternation on my allies'.

"Remind me to never piss you off," murmured Dominic, appearing awed by the level of violence I had displayed. I ignored him, motioning the twins to get on with scanning the rest with a perfunctory jerk of my head.

I knelt down by Angie again, stroking her cheek softly. She sighed deeply then opened her eyes. I closed mine briefly to breathe a sigh of relief. She sat up, furrowing her brow as she looked around at her surroundings, so I took her hand. To my dismay, she pulled back from me with wide eyes.

"Hey, it's OK," I reassured her. "It's me, Gavan."

"Gavan? Gavan who?" she asked, and my heart stopped.

Chapter 41

"Gavan *Maddox*," I told her, desperately hoping against hope and reason that it would all come flooding back to her.

"Oh," she replied, sounding like she recognised my name. My heart started beating again, only to falter once more at her next words. "Now I recognise you from your photo in our record. I was reading your file only a couple of days ago. I was going to pay you a visit to offer you a commission to locate an artefact for us. What are you doing here?"

"Umm, you came to see me," I reminded her. "About a month ago, at my shop Dinas Affaraon. You asked me to find the Veil of Isis." I was beginning to have a sneaking suspicion of what had been done to her, though I couldn't understand why her wards hadn't stopped the spell.

I had seen fireballs and blades turned away by the defences I had set up around her, yet this had hit her as if they didn't even exist. Still, if her memories *had* been erased back to before she met me, that meant her memories of being tortured were gone as well. No *wonder* the tension had finally faded from her expression.

"You've been hit by a spell that erased your memories," I informed her, wondering exactly how to catch her up on what she had forgotten. Or to be more accurate, what she had had forcibly ripped from her.

My rage at the recently deceased (dissected and deconstructed) Order member rose again and must have shown on my face. Angie scrambled away from me, slipping on the mixture of spilled food and drink.

"Hey, hey." I held my hands out to try to calm her down. "I won't hurt you, I'm not mad at you. I'm angry at the person who stole your memories."

She eased herself up into a nearby chair, still looking somewhat askance at me.

I found a cup of lemonade that had somehow survived the chaos and handed it to her. "Have a drink, breathe, and take a moment to steady yourself. I'll be back in a minute." I straightened up and turned toward the Order members, feeling the anger contort my features again.

The only ones who didn't cower were a group of eight men and women; all of whom were wearing matching black leather jackets with a knife embroidered on the left lapel. Seeing the emblem made me realise who they were, and why the two who had been in similar jackets had seemed more capable during the fighting.

"The Stygian Blade, I presume," I said to them, seeing the surprise at my knowledge of their group – a fact which was made evident by their widened eyes. "Yes, I know who you are. One of your number just attacked the w…One of my friends." I changed what I had been about to say since I didn't think this was the right time for Angie to hear me profess my love, in view of her current state. She couldn't remember me, so hearing me say *that* would definitely freak her out.

"Since I'm fully aware that those of you in the Blade have to strive to gain acceptance," I continued, pacing carefully toward them. After all, it *would* kind of ruin my dramatic speech if I slipped and went ass over tit. "I am fully aware none of *you* are here under duress. Therefore, I have absolutely no need to scan your minds."

So saying I reached out to them and closed my fist, imagining each of their hearts as I did so. I watched with a perverse pleasure as their faces turned red and purple, their eyes bugged out and their hands clawed at chests and collars as they desperately fought to live.

I kept staring as the light flickered and was extinguished from each pair of eyes, finally releasing my grip only after the last one went limp. Once I let go of their hearts, the force keeping them upright was gone and they crumpled into a heap together.

"Hey, you promised *we* could be the executioners," Dominic protested, while most of the rest of my allies were regarding me with fear at my actions. I shrugged at him.

"You wouldn't have wanted them," I replied. "They were rotten to the core. They'd have made you sick to your stomach, and probably tasted utterly rancid. There's plenty left, anyway." I turned my gaze on the rest of the Order members. "We'll scan them and hand you any that don't deserve freedom."

The rest of the vampires grinned savagely, drooling in excitement and anticipation. The twins stepped forwards, ready to begin, then looked over at me. I pointed to one of the Order members at random.

"Start with that one," I told them, seeing that I had indicated a youngish woman with skin almost as dark as Sovereign's. "If you're satisfied, she can go. If not, the vampires can have her. If she resists, call me over and I'll try."

I turned away and walked back towards Angie, wanting to try to jog her memory again. I was in two minds about it though, since I wanted her back with me but didn't want her to have to recall her torture again.

I knew her heart, she'd shown it to me over the last few days, and I could always help her get to know me all over again. It could allow her to go on without the mental trauma Elrulin had inflicted on her, so in that moment I made a decision.

"The file I read said you had no magick," she told me as I drew closer to her. I smiled as I felt her reaching out to my mind, probably as she had that first day in my shop, though this time I gently held her back as I had after my return from Tibet.

"As I said, you came to see me about a month ago asking me to find the Veil," I replied. "I succeeded, which eventually led us here. I'll catch you up on the important bits later but for now, all you need to know is that your boss was unhappy with the result.

"He held you captive, I rescued you and the twins, and now we're taking the fight to the Order. This is the Edinburgh site, and we've just finished the fight. We're going to scan those who are left, freeing any who were coerced and making sure the rest can't cause problems ever again."

"The twins?" she asked, looking around. When she saw Gabby and Izzy, she started and grabbed the edge of the table next to her. "They're Atma's personal attack dogs!"

"No, they were blackmailed into serving him, the same as you!" I rushed to explain, realising quite how much would need to be gone over again. "Their brother's life was threatened by 'Atma'. We wouldn't have even escaped if it weren't for them." (I didn't say I could have simply teleported us out. I thought the story of their assistance might help her trust them again.)

"You and they have spent a lot of time together over the last few weeks," I continued. "You grew to trust each other and became friends." She was still looking at me sideways, unsure about the believability of my statement, but her tension lessened somewhat. The twins, in between scans, glanced over at her and smiled.

I could tell Angelica was still confused and uncertain, which was understandable given that her recent memories seemed to be gone. She was going to need time to adjust, relearn what she'd forgotten.

I was starting to get a headache trying to anticipate how she was going to react. "Look, just give it some time. I'm going to help the twins finish scanning the rest of the members in here, then we need to search for any information on the new American site."

I pushed myself up to my feet. I looked down at her for a moment, feeling the loss of what we had, then turned away sadly.

I stepped over to the twins, putting a hand on their shoulder as they finished their scan of one of the men. They smiled at this one and he breathed a sigh of relief, though I could see the vampires feeding on two others who had apparently not been so innocent in their actions or intent.

"So what exactly did they hit her with?" I asked, hoping they knew of both the spell itself and how to counteract it. Maybe I could tweak it so I could choose what memories to restore for her. Then I could leave out the torture she had suffered and restore the good stuff (myself included, naturally). "She seems to think it's back before she ever came to see me at my shop."

"Oh," said Gabby. "So *that's* what it was."

"Maybe they thought she'd stop fighting if they did that," replied Izzy.

"Interesting idea, and definitely a novel method of attack."

"Yes, very inventive."

"We've only ever seen it used by healers before."

"Yes, it's very effective for traumatic experiences."

"Girls, please," I interjected, getting an idea of the magick Angie had been subjected to. "I need to know if there's a way to reverse it?"

"Ooh, we've never known anyone to try that," Izzy replied, getting in ahead of Gabby this time.

"No, we haven't."

"Not many people want to remember trauma once it's been erased."

"No, they don't."

"Though they do say that something lost…"

"Can always be found again if you look hard enough."

I was reminded of my words to the magick user at my shop after I stripped her of her power. Maybe there *was* a chance, even if the twins didn't seem to know exactly how.

"Well, that's something we can consider later," I said, getting back to the matter at hand. "How's the scanning going?"

"A bit slower than expected, with only the two of us."

"Yes, a third scanner would definitely have helped."

"We could probably finish quicker if you pitched in."

"It would certainly speed up the process."

"OK, I get it, I'm on it," I cut them off, rolling my eyes at their badgering tone. I turned to the remaining assembled Order members, picking out the one who looked the most obstinate. I stepped over to her and placed my right palm on her forehead, in order (pun intended) to speed the process of accessing her mind.

She was disciplined, though her defences were nothing like those of the Stygian Blade operative Eligos had captured. I fleetingly regretted not saving the ones from here to interrogate, then I reasoned that Iyrin and Eligos would have their own contingents to question. Besides, the fuckers had it coming for attacking my girl!

It took us about half an hour to scan the rest of the group. There were a solid number who had been coerced in some way and were overjoyed to be free. Many of those promised to join us once they had checked on their families and gotten them to safety, so our forces were actually increasing.

The vampires were almost struggling by the time we handed them the last genuinely nasty piece of work, they had gorged themselves so much, then I faced the half dozen I had set aside as falling in between. They hadn't been coerced but were instead more misguided, having been lied to or raised by the Order, knowing no other truth.

For them, I had come up with an idea that the twin's comment from earlier had crystallised for me. Something I'd done once and now planned to repeat.

"You six are not evil," I said, "But your allegiance is still to the Order. As such, you're a risk to us. I can't simply release you as you are, but I don't want to kill you. You deserve a chance to turn your lives around.

"Therefore, I'm going to remove your potential threat." With those words, I reached into their minds, as I had done to an Order member once before, and removed their magickal abilities. "As Gabby and Izzy reminded me, what is lost can be found again. If you decide to change your ways, come find me. I can help."

I turned away from their stricken faces, not wanting to witness the loss etched on their expressions. It had been necessary, otherwise we'd have had to kill them too. Danu was right, damn her. The battle had to be properly finished.

"Time to see what useful information we can find in this shit hole," I remarked.

Chapter 42

I turned to see Angelica regarding me with a look of horror. Since she couldn't remember the discussions we had been having about our plans of attack, and since her motivation had been significantly affected with the loss of her torture memories, it was kind of understandable. Still, it was painful to see her afraid of me.

"We released as many as we could," I explained patiently. "The rest *had* to be killed to stop them from joining up with the others still in the Order and fighting us again."

"Oh, I agree," she said cautiously. "I've seen enough in my time to know there're plenty of members whose best contribution to the world would be to leave it." *That* sounded like the Angie I knew; so why did she still appear to be terrified of me?

"OK, I can definitely go along with that sentiment," I remarked. "So what's the problem?" I couldn't understand it; I'd been as merciful as possible, and she said she understood why we'd killed the rest.

Even that had been relatively painless, since vampires had a natural anaesthetic and euphoric in their saliva according to the literature. That was why some humans apparently became addicted to being fed on, ending up as familiars or even thralls.

"But the way you dealt with those last few," she continued, her anxiety showing again. "Stripping away their powers…"

Suddenly I understood. To a magick user, someone who had had the power their whole life (unlike me), that must be the worst fate of all. Worse even than death, like being unmade.

"They weren't inherently evil in their thoughts," I rushed to explain. "They didn't know anything else, so they were simply misguided. They deserved a chance to change but we couldn't leave them as a risk. Taking their power was the only way to eliminate the threat while still giving them the potential for redemption."

"But how were you even able to do it?" she asked, seeming slightly less fearful and more interested at this point. "How did you discover it was even possible?" By this time most of our force were listening in, clearly just as interested in my answer. From what I could gather, they'd never seen it done nor even knew it was feasible.

"There was a girl sent to my shop to try and break the wards I'd set up," I told them, remembering the young magick user. "She'd been on guard outside the prison level when I went to Bolton Castle on my rescue mission.

"I knocked her out without realising she was a girl, since I couldn't see her face or body shape in that damned robe and hood. Elrulin must have been pissed at her for failing to stop me, so he sent her after I'd killed the first group of mundanes he sent to burn my shop.

"When she failed, I didn't want to kill her but I didn't want her as a continued threat. I went into her mind to see if I could do anything, which is when I discovered how to remover her magick. My hope was that Elrulin would regard what I'd done as a worse punishment than anything he could devise and just let her go."

"So it was an attempt at *mercy*?" Lilian, the female vampire who had commented on my misunderstanding of the myths back on the moors, looked incredulous. "Shit, with friends like you…"

"Yeah, well, I guess my sensibilities don't have only two settings: bite and don't bite!" I rounded on her angrily. "The world isn't black and white; there are shades of grey."

"Yeah," commented some joker behind me. "About fifty, from what I hear!" There were a few sniggers and even I had to clamp my lips together to control a giggle.

"We just have to ensure we're on the lighter end of the scale," I remarked, once I had control of my humour. "That's why I left them the chance to regain their abilities."

The twins looked supremely unconcerned and even Angie seemed happier about the situation.

"Now that we've got that straightened out," I stated, ready to be done with this and get out. "Where abouts are the records likely to be stored?"

"The archives in Bolton are stored near the prisoner cells," Gabby told us.

"That's how we got rid of the information on our brother," Izzy chipped in.

"Yes, we stopped in on our way to you."

"It was quite convenient, really."

"Yes, it was."

"The set-up should be the same here."

"It certainly should."

It was interesting to note how they seemed to speak more to me as a pair, compared to how they used to. It has previously been a conversation between themselves that progressed their side of a discussion. I hoped it indicated them coming out of their shells and trusting others more now; and it was wonderful to see.

"I spent some time in the Bolton archives when I was finding out about my assignments," Angelica volunteered. Hopefully it was a sign of her still wanting to fight against the Order; after all, she still remembered what Elrulin had done to force her to work for him, even if she didn't recall his more recent atrocity against her.

"Great," I said to the three of them. "You three take the archives. Seirina, you and Sovereign take the obeahs and go with them. Kazemde, you and your weres take the next three floors. You're the largest group, you can cover the most ground.

"Dominic, you and your vampires come with me. We'll start at the top and work our way down. If you see anything that looks useful, whether it's ancient texts or modern files, grab it. We'll take it all and go through it later." I directed my last comment to everyone and got acknowledgments all around.

"Once we're done, we'll burn everything else. We leave nothing for them to come back to." Everyone headed off in their respective directions, Angie leaving without a backward glance. I watched her go, an emptiness echoing in my chest at the loss of what we had been only a few hours ago.

To my surprise, Dominic stepped up beside me and put his hand on my shoulder. He said nothing but squeezed firmly, enough to let me know he understood. I realised he must have lived several human lifetimes already, probably having loved and lost long before I was ever born.

"Enough of this maudlin crap," one of the other male vampires said behind me. "She's not dead. You can just seduce her again, and this time you already know what she likes. Insider knowledge, and all that."

Dominic smiled and nodded, squeezing my shoulder once more and then letting go. I sniffed inelegantly, squared my shoulders and turned to the small group behind me.

"Yeah, but I still don't know how she feels about marmite!" They looked at each other, shrugging, probably having been turned long before marmite was created. I needed a much younger audience for my pop culture references.

"Never mind, let's get on with this. Oh, that reminds me…" I reached out with my magick and dropped the mobile phone suppressing field so that the different groups could keep in contact. I then sent a quick text to Seirina, Kazemde, the twins, and – completely automatically – Angelica. I told them the field was down and to notify me if they found anything they needed help with.

The vampires and I walked out of the meeting room and went to the nearest offices. Without needing to speak, we split into pairs and each pair took an office. We ransacked the filing cabinets, desks, and drawers. We banged on the walls, searching for any secret compartments and generally tore each room apart.

Any useful looking files went into bags we took from the wastepaper baskets, any older texts going on top. As we worked, my phone chimed with a text alert. I pulled it out to see a message from the twins, asking me to meet them down in the cells area.

I left Dominic and the others working on the offices and went towards the stairs. Paladin, who had been laying in the hall to keep out of the way while we searched, jumped up and followed me.

We jogged down the stairs, hearing the sounds of offices being ransacked as we passed each floor. I smiled in the certainty that anything useful would be found, if the noise was anything to go by. I reached the bottom, Paladin bouncing alongside me with his tail wagging as if this was simply a fun day out in the park.

I shook my head in amusement at his innocent enjoyment, then pulled open the door to head to the cells. As expected, the corridor was a carbon copy of the Bolton Castle site. I followed it, noting the same huge metal door I had seen at the other location.

I walked through, glancing around with interest since I had been unconscious when I was carried into the cells by Stheno. There was a desk where a guard could sit, with monitors no doubt showing the cells and the corridor outside the doors.

I smiled in satisfaction that my suspicions of being watched at Bolton had been proven correct. Although with Stheno out cold after my taserball defence, there wouldn't have been anyone there to watch the monitors while Angie and I had been talking.

I walked past the desk, hearing voices but not stopping to check the screens. Why bother, when I was about to walk in there anyway? I stepped through the door into the cell area to see Gabby and Izzy standing there, talking to someone in one of the cells.

I could tell by the complex engravings on the bars that this was the magick suppressing cell, the local version of the one in which I had woken up. Now I understood why they'd called me down here, but I wasn't sure how to break open something specifically designed to resist magick.

"Just to check before I do this," I said, struck by an incongruous thought. "Can you tell me who you are and why the Order had you locked up?" The individual spun toward me, her cloak falling off as she turned, and I caught my breath.

She was stunningly beautiful. Her hair was so blonde it was almost white, falling almost to her waist, with subtle waves along its length. Her eyes were so light they seemed colourless and almost glowed, though as she turned slightly I could detect that they were a delicate shade of grey. Her skin was as smooth, unlined and white as an alabaster doll.

When her hair moved as she rotated to face me, I caught sight of something that made my blood run cold and my brain shift into high gear. Her ears were tapered to a point. I knew I would have to be extremely careful in dealing with her, since all the literature I had seen was rife with the perils of dealing with her kind.

She was some kind of Fae.

Chapter 43

I blessed all the time I'd spent reading about the magickal world before my 'awakening'. Although almost everything I knew came from books – other than my last few weeks of practical experience – I at least had some basic awareness.

Still, not everything in books could be trusted and there was a lot of contradictory information. Some said they were descended from the Tuatha de Danaan, which would mean Danu was the ultimate Fae.

There were legends telling of high-borns and low-borns, others stating they were more equal. There were beneficent legends of helpful encounters, alongside legends of child abductions and changelings.

Stories of Fae beings falling in love with humans, against stories of taking humans as hostages and playthings. The time-shifts between their realms and ours were also highly disputed – at least that was something I had experience with, having been to Aaru.

"I see," I said, trying to stall for time to allow my brain to catch up with the situation. "So was it just because you're one of the Fae, or was there a more specific and personal reason for the Order to lock you away my lady?" I thought being polite was probably the best way to start, since most of the legends did mention their touchiness and readiness to take insult.

"Meaning no disrespect or offence, I need to be sure I'm not about to release someone whose first thought would be to kill me and then move on to my friends and allies," I continued.

The Fae turned fully to regard me, her face remaining expressionless as she examined me.

Tearing my gaze away from her face with a real effort, I noticed her body. Her form was far less voluptuous than I had expected. She was built more like an athlete, wiry and slim with strength evident in her limbs. There was only a slight fullness to her chest to indicate her femininity.

She was dressed in brown knee-high boots, dark green form-fitting trousers, a matching blouse with long sleeves and a cord at the base of her neck, and a jerkin that matched her boots. I could see she wasn't wearing the cuffs I had woken up in, so it didn't seem as though they were planning on moving her anywhere. She was simply being held there. But why?

"My name is Alcina," she said, and a thrill ran through me at the sound of her voice. I had been expecting something high-pitched, light and tinkling (OK, I knew she wasn't Tinkerbell, but she was still a fairy).

Instead her voice was low and musical. It possessed a vibrancy that seemed to resonate through my entire being. I saw images of sunlit glades in leafy forests, while simultaneously understanding the carnal pleasures that could be had in such a place.

She seemed to embody total purity and utter debasement in the same moment with a single tone. Listening to just those few words, I could imagine her being kept here for the sole purpose of hearing her speak.

I stared for a moment, then mentally shook myself to clear my head. I now understood even more about the perils of the Fae. Merely hearing them speak would distract most people, allowing the Fae even greater freedom to direct things in their favour.

I recommend finding some way to protect yourself if you plan to have an extended conversation, came Gauvain's voice in my head. *The seductive nature of her voice appeals to your baser instincts. I suggest focusing on something that has already claimed and fulfilled your attention: your feelings for Angelica. Fortunately, my differing origins seem to afford me some degree of immunity.*

Genius, bud, I replied. *Thanks. I'll give it my best shot.* As I filled my head with thoughts and memories of the last couple of days with Angie, mind cleared of Alcina's influence and I could think clearly again.

"I see," I said out loud to her, looking over at the twins and seeing them appearing lost in the magickal constructs caused by the Fae's voice.

"Would you mind turning down the beauty of your voice? I'm afraid your full appeal is too much for our simple human brains to handle."

She smiled at first, then tilted her head and narrowed her eyes as she looked at me.

"You say that," she said, her voice modulating to a more human timbre, "and yet you seem able to hear me and yet manage to retain your senses. Impressive."

"Oh, it was a very close run thing," I admitted without any shame. "However a friend gave me some advice that helped me regain my equilibrium."

She stared levelly at me, apparently not fully believing my explanation. After all, all she could see was Paladin.

"Anyway, why did the Order lock you up Alcina?" I repeated, still wanting to be sure of who she was before I let her out.

"I was sent by my queen from the Summer Court as a liaison," she told me, which of course made my mind immediately think back to Angelica's first visit to my shop. "My queen was curious about the Order, given their magickal interests. She instructed me to find out what their aims were, to see whether they would be worthy allies."

The thought of the Order having access to the knowledge and power of the Fae made my skin crawl. I seriously hoped she hadn't agreed to help them, though her presence in the cell made me think it was unlikely.

"And your assessment?" I asked, quietly holding my breath.

"I will simply say they did not particularly impress us," she replied impassively. I released my breath quietly but she seemed to notice anyway, the corner of her mouth lifting ever so slightly. I spread my hands open in admission of her perception.

"So do you have any ideas on how I can open this cell for you?" I enquired. Given she was Fae, she was probably significantly older than me and therefore would have far greater experience. Maybe she'd seen this sort of warding before.

"You would require either the key..." At this point I couldn't help myself, I rolled my eyes at the basic level of explanation she seemed to think I needed. "Ahem, yes, well, I suppose that was a little obvious. The alternative would something that could cut through the lock without being affected by the warding runes."

I considered what would be required for that. As I mused, I noticed that not only did the casing for the lock have runes on it, even the deadbolt itself was carved. Still, if the bolt could be cut it would definitely be the easiest way to release her.

I saw her eye fall to my waist and realised she was looking at my sword (the metal one, perverts. Keep your minds out of the gutter).

"I can tell your weapon has magick in its construction," she said, at which I fought to keep the smirk off my face. "Even in this cell, I am aware it is no ordinary blade."

"Thank you," I said. She tilted her head ever so slightly. "As I wasn't around when blacksmiths were common, I had to make my own sword. Since I needed it quickly, I had to use magick.

"I watched the man who made my ring," I told her, holding Seren up for her to see. "He incorporated multiple protections, since it was to house and protect my heart-stone." Her eyebrows rose and her eyes widened in the first obvious expression I had seen on her face.

"I incorporated what I'd learnt into my forging, so my weapon would only be usable by me and would resist magick." She nodded, tilting her head to one side and her lips pursing.

"And what did you name your blade?" she enquired.

"Muharar," I said, pronouncing it as 'mu-HA-re-ron', which was what Google translate said was the correct way. I'd checked after Kazemde had remarked on my pronunciation. "It means 'liberator'." Her eyes widened again, this time accompanied by a raised eyebrow.

"You didn't name it something more aggressive?" she remarked. "I was under the impression that humans liked to have scary, impressive names for their weaponry."

I smiled this time, thinking back to my struggle to find the right name.

"I agree," I allowed, choosing not to argue her veiled disparagement of human attitudes. "However once I'd made the sword, I thought about *why* I was standing against the Order. I'm not doing this to take their place, I want to free the magickal community from the threat the Order poses." Alcina crossed her arms and drew her head back, apparently impressed, despite her clearly jaded impression of humans.

"A noble and worthwhile endeavour," she observed. "I was unaware such selflessness still existed among humankind. I believed it had faded when knights and their code of honour disappeared."

I told you I obtained my personality characteristics from your admiration of those beliefs! Gauvain chimed in. I saw Alcina look around the area, so G had obviously projected his thoughts to her too. *Actually, no, I didn't,* he replied, picking up the thought from my mind. *She must be able to hear me anyway. Maybe the Fae's ability to speak to animals is not just a myth.*

"So it *was* the dog I heard earlier," she remarked, looking at him. "Is he your familiar?"

"No," I replied. She tilted her head again, so I tried to explain. "Paladin is a friend who supports me by providing me with extra energy. My familiar or, as I prefer to call him, my friend, is Gauvain. He was staying in his claw during the battle to avoid being in the way. I think you can come out now, buddy."

Gauvain responded with alacrity, bursting out joyously into full form and landing on my shoulder. For the first time Alcina stepped back within her cell, one hand pressed against her chest.

"I had no idea animals in this realm had those kinds of abilities," she said, stunned.

"They don't," I replied simply. "He isn't exactly what you might call 'local'. Still, that's beside the point. Shall we see if the protection in my sword is sufficient to release you, or would you like to stand around discussing comparative zoology?"

She smiled, acknowledging my point, and gestured to the door of her cell as if ceding me the floor at a talent show. I drew my blade with a flourish, G fluttering his wings to keep his balance as I did so.

I approached the bars cautiously, touching Muharar against them gingerly to see what would happen. There was a slight spark, like the static charge you might get walking through a deep carpet then touching a radiator, but nothing more. Maybe this could work.

I held the sword out and aligned it with the narrow gap between the door and the frame of Alcina's cell. I slid it in (oh, be quiet you perverts!) and rested the edge down onto the deadbolt.

I reached for the energy stored in Seren, along with pulling through my link with Paladin, and focused it into Muharar as fire. I heated it up as much as possible, hoping it might weaken the lock and make it easier to cut through.

I raised the sword to the limit of the doorway, held it for a moment, then slammed it down with all my strength. There was a shower of sparks and it felt like I was back in the amusement arcade on the pier, during my summer holiday when I was twelve.

Did you ever play that game where you had to hold onto the two metal grips while the electrical current was increased? It was exactly like that, only about a dozen times stronger. Even though the hilt was wood and wrapped in leather, the charge made me feel as though the sword was trying to writhe out of my grip.

It felt like a lifetime but was probably only a couple of seconds as the blade passed through the bolt, then it was over. I dropped to one knee, panting, then pushed myself up using Muharar like a cane.

I heard a creak and looked up, just in time to see the door swing wide and Alcina step through.

Chapter 44

I stepped back, still not a hundred percent sure I'd done the right thing by releasing a Fae. The twins had headed to the archives once Alcina had transferred her attention to me and then modulated her voice, so it was only the four of us here now (Alcina, Paladin, Gauvain and I).

"Liberator, in truth. You are most kind," Alcina said as she stopped in front of us, glancing at Muharar. I noted that she neither thanked me directly – which would have meant she owed me her gratitude – nor did she even acknowledge that I had done her a favour or service, which would have indicated she was in my debt.

"Kindness and generosity are important," I replied, thinking fast to respond in kind while still trying to ensure I made her aware *I* knew she needed to balance the scales between us. I could tell I was going to get a headache if I had to interact with the Fae on a regular basis. "There isn't enough in the world of either, and too many take them for granted when they are bestowed."

Alcina smiled slightly, nodding once slowly in appreciation of my adroit manoeuvring. There was no way for her to avoid admitting the position she was in, so she didn't even try. Having a Fae in my debt could definitely be useful, though I needed to be careful how I handled things.

"Before you go back to your realm to report to your queen," I continued carefully. "I would be interested to know precisely who you are. Our legends often tell of Fae princes and princesses acting as ambassadors, while other tales tell of only lower creatures being sent to interact with humans.

"While I can see you are no lower spriggan or sprite, I would be interested to know who I have liberated." Her face cleared of the annoyance it had shown when I mentioned lower creatures, though she hesitated before responding to my question. I merely waited, fully aware of the contempt the Fae had for humans who showed a lack of patience and decorum from my reading.

"You are correct in that high-borns are generally trusted with the most delicate missions," she stated finally, almost seeming reluctant to explain this to me. I guess saving her life, or at least her liberty, was paying off already. "I am not, however, royalty. My uncle is the Summer Queen's advisor."

"Oh, the true power behind the throne," I observed. She drew her head back at my remark but this time I knew I was right. "Please don't insult my intelligence by pretending you don't know how things work.

"Though a queen may make the final decisions and have the authority and power, her conclusions are based on the *way* the information is presented to her. The Medicis, Machiavelli and the Borgias were all advisors and spin doctors rather than royalty, yet no one can deny they changed the course of events in their lifetimes."

"You are indeed more perceptive than I appreciated at first," she allowed. "However, I shall not be revealing the inner workings of my queen's council without gaining her approval first."

"That's fair," I answered, keen to know more but not wanting to alienate her by pushing too hard. "Have you learnt anything about the Order that might help us in the meantime?"

"Only that you have those among your allies who are communicating with them," she informed me. I had already deduced as much from the oh-so-convenient anti-zombie wards that had disrupted our initial plan. "I overheard my watchers discussing the tip they had received. They seemed convinced your numbers were too small without your 'supplementation', so they could go ahead with their party."

Now I understood why there hadn't been lookouts posted. Someone among our allies had informed someone in the Order about the zombies, though hadn't told them what other forces we'd gathered. It was almost as though they were hedging their bets: trying to come out on top, no matter which side prevailed.

"Intriguing," I observed. "Though I must admit, I already had my suspicions when we encountered the ward. Still, it's nice to have confirmation." I made sure to follow her example, not thanking her directly. I said goodbye, wishing her well and expressing my hope to see her again, then left to go to the archives.

I turned back just before I left the cell area to get one final glimpse of her. Unfortunately she had already gone, only a fading spark of her portal remaining. Her face seemed to glow in my memory, full of mystery and promise, until I thought of Angelica's face again and the Fae faded almost into insignificance. I knew I'd be seeing Alcina again, however.

My chest tightened again as I recalled the memory wipe Angelica had been subjected to. I was torn between wanting her back the way she'd been so we could continue our relationship, and being glad her trauma had been wiped away.

I thought back to what the twins had told me, about how the technique was used by healers, and abruptly realised why Angie's wards hadn't stopped the spell. If it was a *healing* type of mojo, rather than an outright attack, the wards weren't set up to block it.

I had wanted to make sure the Wiccans could heal any of us if we were hurt, so I had only blocked attacks in my creation of our defences. The Blade operative must have exploited that loophole, like an underhanded doctor using a medication to do more harm than good. I would have to bear that in mind in the future: Some people could turn even the best of intentions to foul purpose.

I found the ladies by following the noise. The twins were tearing through the papers in the archives, throwing anything useless on the floor. It would make a great start for burning the place but wasn't exactly neat. Angelica, on the other hand, was hanging back somewhat. Clearly she wasn't fully comfortable with what was going on just yet.

It was understandable. Although she knew about Elrulin's coercion, she wasn't aware of all his recent atrocities. While the twins were going to town, I stepped over to Angie and tried to explain.

"I know you were forced to work for the Order," I told her. "You came to my shop and sent me to find the Veil of Isis, though it didn't quite work out the way your boss wanted. I was the one who ended up gaining power from the Veil. Then your boss went bananas. He held you and tortured you to find out about me, so I went to rescue you.

"Gabriella and Isabella saved us both when I got captured too. Then Seirina, who initially told me about Bolton Castle, helped us gather a group of people who all had reasons to fight the Order."

She apparently appreciated my explanation, though she obviously didn't have the same degree of drive without the memory of her mental trauma. I also wasn't sure how to restart our relationship. I certainly wasn't planning on redoing the whole 'XXX defence' idea, especially since she couldn't simply wander into my mind whenever she felt like it any more.

"I *will* say I am extremely grateful to you," I continued, which made her tilt her head and raise her eyebrows. "Without you coming to see me and sending me after the Veil, I'd still be sitting in my little shop *dreaming* of unlocking my abilities."

Finally I got a smile from her, recognising that I was genuinely thankful. She looked over with a secretive little grin, appearing to come to a decision.

"I have to admit something," she told me shyly. "I actually volunteered to be the one to see you after I saw your photo in the file. I was wondering about your abilities when I saw them earlier, since the information the Order has on you says you're merely a shopkeeper with no magickal powers." She flushed deep pink as she told me, though my spirits leapt at the thought.

So I hadn't been imagining it when she came to the shop. She really *had* been interested! All of a sudden, the world seemed a brighter place again. As long as the underlying attraction was there, I could still have hope. That made my mind up: I wasn't going to risk bringing her traumatic memories back now; I would simply allow things to develop naturally again.

I left her musing on her photographic lusting (hopefully) and went to join the twins. They'd almost finished ripping through the files, so I wanted to see if they'd discovered anything useful. They pulled out the folders from the last drawer as I reached them, flicking through them and dropping the lot to the floor.

"Nothing!" complained Gabby bitterly.

"Waste of time," agreed Izzy.

"The information on the American site must be at the headquarters in Bolton."

"I'm sure Elrulin wouldn't want it anywhere else."

"No, he'd want it under his control."

"He wouldn't trust anyone else with something that sensitive."

"He always did play everything close to the vest."

"We'll have to see what we find when we get into his private files."

"We'll also have to get rid of all of his blackmail materials," I chimed in, snapping them out of their insular back-and-forth. They looked approvingly at me, Angie stepping over and nodding as well. Then she frowned.

"Umm, quick question," she asked, raising a finger. "Who's Elrulin?"

"Oh, sorry, I forgot to mention that part," I said, realising once again how much we'd need to explain. "While we were being held in the Bolton cells, I was questioned by your boss. He's taken over the body of one of the Order vampires and he bit me, which got him past my defences.

"While we were linked, I saw some of *his* memories too. One of which was him being cast out of Isis' home dimension. I heard his true name in that memory, 'Elrulin'. That's why he wanted the Veil in the first place: He wanted to try to use it to get home."

She blinked a few times at the revelations, a fierce smile stealing over her lips at the possibilities the information provided. It was wonderful to see the excitement in her face, this time without the overtones of the mental trauma that had coloured her eagerness after our escape.

"There's more we need to catch you up on," I continued, wanting to wrap this up so we could get out of here. "That can wait for later though. For now, let's get everyone back to the moors. I'll burn everything here, then we can meet up with the teams from the other sites. After that, we can work out how and when to go after the Bolton Castle site."

I didn't mention Alcina's tip about our double agent, since I wasn't quite sure what to do about it myself. So far I'd only come up with one idea: scan everyone to identify who had betrayed us and why.

I texted everyone to meet where we'd come in, then headed up the stairs with my little posse. After conferring with Seirina and Sovereign, we decided to leave the corpses here for cremation with the remains of the Order's site.

I opened a portal and sent everyone back to our initial gathering site, Paladin and Gauvain going with Angelica, then popped over to the gardens. I informed the Wiccans that we were done, opening a portal for them to join the rest. I returned to the tunnels, teleporting directly to the archives and flinging a few fireballs around to get things going.

I went up the stairs, propping the doors open on each floor to ensure the fire would spread. I ended by going back to the corpses, bathing them in a stream of flames fuelled by the energy from Seren. I knew bones wouldn't be consumed by a normal building fire, so I wanted to make certain the bodies were properly reduced to ash.

I considered they deserved that level of respect, since their eternal peace had been disrupted for our needs. Once I was done, I teleported back to the moors.

Time to root out a traitor.

Chapter 45

I arrived back to see much more mixing than before the assault. People were recounting their battle experiences, congratulating each other on a particularly fine showing, and generally acting more like a cohesive force.

That was definitely about to change.

"Can I have everyone's attention for a minute?" I yelled, to be greeted with absolutely nothing. They were far too busy talking amongst themselves to hear me. I thought about the best way to get their attention, then launched an exploding fireball into the air. I also focused my magick on my vocal cords to amplify the volume.

"Yo, shut it for a minute!" I called, my enhanced voice ringing out across the plateau. "First off, I want to thank you all for participating. You did amazingly well and I was glad we had so few casualties.

"To those who joined us after the fight, welcome. We're glad for any help we can get. We should also thank the Wiccans who, along with healing some of your wounds since you returned, also helped protect many of us with their scapulars."

There were cheers all around and Aurora's group, who had been looking a little left out, braced up at the attention and beamed as many favoured them with grateful grins and thumbs up. I noticed Eligos reappear at the back of the crowd with Iyrin, surprised to realise he hadn't been in contact before now.

I motioned to the side with my eyes and he nodded, apparently prepared to wait to deliver their reports until I was finished.

"However," I continued, my jovial manner disappearing, "we have a serious issue to deal with. Someone informed the Order we would be using zombies. That's why the ward prevented their entry initially, then disabled them and set off the alarm once I managed to bring them through."

There was an angry buzz to replace the previous happy undertone as everyone started looking around, trying to assess who it might have been. I noticed the vampires were all at the mouth of their tent and many angry glances were being sent their way.

People were starting to separate into their factions again, each casting glances at the others. It seemed as though the weres and the vampires were the favourite suspects for the rest, likely due to the various legends surrounding them.

"I have no intention of allowing this to destroy the trust we've built up by fighting side by side," I announced, keen to nip this in the bud before it devolved into a real-life witch hunt. "I'm going to personally scan everyone to find out who it was, then the representative of each faction will join me to interrogate them and pronounce judgement."

There was a hum of agreement, people looking around and nodding at the plan, so it seemed I was on the right track so far. Now to see if I could make it work.

"To make it fair, and prevent any group from appearing to be targeted, I'll scan one from each. Then go around again and again until everyone's been scanned. Obviously as all the members of a group are finished, that group falls out of the rotation."

People seemed relieved I was trying to be fair and democratic in my method. I even noticed Eligos indicating his approval in the background, though he soon turned his attention back to the crowd. Dominic actually volunteered to go first, which surprised many if the expressions were to be believed.

"Since most of you seem to think vampires are inherently evil and untrustworthy," he remarked, stepping to the very edge of the tent opening, "I suggest you start with me. None of us will resist you. Indeed, anyone who resists should immediately be treated with the highest suspicion."

He looked around everyone as he spoke, smiling at the surprise on their faces caused by his willingness to be scanned. I took the opportunity to add to his comment, deciding to warn them what was in store if they decided to resist.

"Agreed, and thanks for getting the ball rolling Dominic," I stated. "Just so everyone is aware, anyone who *does* decide to resist me, we have Iyrin the watcher who will take over." I pointed to the skeletal figure where it crouched next to Eligos. I noted several shudders at its appearance, deciding to build on the mystery of who and what it was.

"It is a being unlike anything you've likely encountered. It can slip into your mind, past the strongest defences, with ridiculous ease. It can even take control of you if it wishes. I've seen it happen and trust me, you *really* don't want to go there," I finished emphatically, grinning as those closest to it edged away.

"So," I continued, clapping my hands once. "Let's get started." I walked over to Dominic, raising my right hand to place it on his forehead and inclining my head to silently ask his consent. He acquiesced and closed his eyes so I laid my hand on his brow. I was interested to note that he wasn't as cold as I had expected.

His mind was not as different as I had anticipated, though to be truthful I wasn't quite sure what I *had* expected. I could feel the strange, almost hypnotic attraction they could clearly focus on their victims; though Dominic was keeping it damped down.

I skimmed through his memories from the last few weeks, ever since our first meeting, and he was clear of any underhandedness – at least with the Order. I didn't go rooting into the rest of his activities, given what he was.

The rest of the faction liaisons went next, all of whom were cleared. As a show of good faith, I asked Eligos to read me and report on my honesty to our assembled allies. He did so smoothly and painlessly, reported my good intentions to general relief.

I continued, night falling and the vampires emerging from their tent as I worked. Once they had been cleared they offered their assistance to speed things along, as did the twins and Angelica, and I accepted. Eligos also joined in, as he no more wished to be here drawing things out than he had wanted to hang around Seirina's house between meetings.

With so many telepaths, we quickly worked our way through those gathered. The two largest groups, the weres and the Wiccans, were soon the only ones with members still unscanned. Neither wanted the vampires anywhere near their minds, a decision I respected as they all had history, so the vampires went to sit down and wait with those who had been cleared.

I was starting to doubt whether we would find the culprit, even to the point of considering Alcina might have misled me for some reason. But if that was the case, how would the Order have known to put up wards against zombies? And why in Edinburgh?

I was getting a headache from all the scanning but just sighed and turned to the next person. I smiled when I recognised the Wiccan who had handed me the bag of scapulars, surprised to note that she had her shoulder hunched up with tension practically radiating from them.

"Don't worry," I reassured her. "It doesn't hurt and it'll be over before you know it."

"That's not it," she replied, sounding like she was about to cry. "You don't need to scan me. I was the one who told someone what we were doing." She finished on a whisper, barely loud enough for me to hear, and a chill ran down my arms.

The traitor was a *Wiccan*?! Moreover, one who'd helped protect everyone with the scapulars they'd made for us? Why?! What possible reason could she have had? Regardless, I needed to handle this openly and fairly, as I'd promised. I wasn't looking forward to Aurora's reaction when she found out!

I called the faction liaisons over, seeing everyone else reacting with interest since they knew it meant the traitor had been identified. I took the Wiccan into the tent previously used by the vampires, since that would afford us some privacy while we conducted our interrogation.

As we walked, I saw a younger woman detach herself from the rest of the Wiccans who had yet to be scanned and follow us. She stopped by the mouth of the tent, stepping aside to let the faction leaders enter. I created a ball of light so we could see, by which I noticed Aurora's expression harden as she walked in and noticed who was here.

"*Fiona*?!" she asked, aghast. "It was *you*? But why? What could possibly have made you…"

"My niece," Fiona interrupted miserably, motioning towards the young woman in the doorway. "She was taken by the Order and made to work for them. I thought if she gave them some useful information, it might make them trust her more so she might then be able to escape.

"I only told her about the zombies, since I thought the rest of you would be enough to defeat the Order members who would actually fight. That way, she'd be free too. I was trying to make sure she'd get away whichever way the fight turned out."

My heart went out to her, immediately understanding the crappy choice she'd had to make. This was why it was essential to take the Order down: They corrupted innocent people just by association, perverting their best intentions and turning them against their allies.

I knew my own thoughts on what should happen now but I looked to the others, since I had promised our assembled allies that each faction would be involved in the administration of justice. Besides, her actions *had* led to the death of three weres I knew of for certain, though I couldn't remember anyone else dying.

"Many of us had relatives taken by the Order," Aurora stormed, taking the lead as the one who had brought Fiona in to this and the liaison of her faction. "If you'd only kept quiet, the zombies could have made this an entirely bloodless enterprise.

"Instead you forced our allies to fight, causing several to die in the attempt! How *could* you have been so selfish, putting one person's freedom above everyone else's safety? Both in and out of the Order?"

"The three that died were of my kind," Kazemde added, stepping forwards. "We all came, knowing we might die in the battle but willing to try because of the worthiness of the cause. That doesn't mean we wouldn't have preferred to be taking everyone home alive and well! I do not say you murdered them, but you are certainly at least partially responsible for their deaths."

Aurora's and Kazemde's impassioned words changed my mind on the right way to proceed. I had thought she should be merely reprimanded but allowed to continue with us, since her intentions were based in love.

That didn't excuse the end result, any more than a mother getting in a car to collect her child, driving drunk and ending up causing an accident. Love was no excuse for hurting others out of simple carelessness and lack of forethought.

"We've heard all we need to from you, Fiona," I told her. "Go and join your niece. We need to confer over how best to proceed from here. You shall have our decision shortly."

She looked around tearfully one last time, then left the tent.

"So what do we do with her?" I asked.

Chapter 46

Dominic looked supremely unconcerned at this point, seemingly happy he and his vampires were cleared. Sovereign seemed politely engaged, though far less invested than Aurora and Kazemde. Seirina and I weren't far behind them, given the effort we'd put into this whole affair.

"Well now that we've been cleared," Dominic remarked impatiently. "Can you send us home? Call us when you're ready to go after the Bolton Castle site."

"Well that'll be either tomorrow morning or tomorrow evening at the latest," I told him. "We don't want to give them a chance to find out there's a problem and start preparing for us, so the sooner the better."

He shrugged unconcernedly.

"Whatever. We need a chance to digest our meal," he said, reminding me of the amount of blood they'd consumed from the Order members we'd condemned.

"Fine," I answered impatiently, wanting to get back to sorting out the mess with Fiona. "I'll create a portal for you. Just be ready when we call you."

He rolled his eyes and sighed.

"OK, OK," he huffed. I walked him out and opened a portal for him. He beckoned his compatriots, leading them through, after which I collapsed the gateway and went back to the tent.

Fiona didn't even look at me as I passed her, her gaze fixed firmly on the ground with tears streaming down her face and dripping off her nose and chin. Her niece had her arm around Fiona's shoulders but everyone else was keeping their distance, casting angry glances in her direction.

Aurora and Kazemde looked at me as I entered, their faces set and their minds clearly made up. Seirina had her arms crossed and merely looked accepting of their decision. Sovereign had her chin lowered, seeming deep in thought with a sorrowful expression at the outcome of their discussion. Eligos, meanwhile, looked approving at the conclusion they'd reached.

I paused, suspicious of exactly where they'd come down on the punishment scale but almost afraid to find out.

"So do I *want* to know your verdict?" I asked carefully. "Although the verdict isn't really in doubt, is it? It's the sentencing that's in question."

"We cannot allow this to go unpunished," Kazemde said softly, his deep voice carrying around the tent easily. "She caused the death of three people who came to help free us all from the threat of the Order. If she had only had faith in our plan, we could have accomplished our mission without any of us getting hurt.

"She betrayed us to our enemy, causing the death of our allies. If we don't make a hard example of her, more may think to act in the same way causing further unnecessary injuries or fatalities."

"The only thing to do is take her life in recompense for those she ended," continued Aurora. "At least that may give the families of those we lost some sense of closure and justice."

"Can we really afford to lose *more* allies?" I asked, wanting to make sure they'd thought this through fully. To my surprise, Eligos spoke up.

"One person more or less will not tip the scales," he observed calmly. "To ignore her actions would condone them and send the message that any may act against the rest if they choose, as long as it is in their own best interest. That way leads to chaos and the collapse of your forces."

Much as it pained me, I had to agree. We couldn't have everyone doing their own thing, otherwise we'd never get anywhere. We had to work together and trust each other. Plus, she *was* responsible for the deaths.

If we hadn't lost the zombies, the Order members would have been surrounded without any of us getting hurt. Plus, if she hadn't told them we were coming in the first place, we could have had them all focused on their party and in one place.

"I have to agree," I said sadly. "Much as I may not like it, it's the same as our fight against the Order: a short-term hardship for a long-term gain. Now we need to let everyone know and carry out the sentence. But how?"

"She knows she was wrong," Aurora replied. "She's already been torturing herself over this, I don't think we need to add to that. We need something swift and painless." To my relief, everyone seemed to be in agreement. I wasn't sure I could have condoned something long and drawn out.

"So who does it?" I asked. I looked around the tent to see everyone looking at me, suddenly realising what that meant. "Hey, wait a minute, just hang on there! Why does it have to be me? Shouldn't we like, I don't know, draw straws or something?!"

Much to my dismay, nobody looked away or flinched. Eligos spoke up again, and my heart sank as he stated the reason it had to be me.

"You are the *de facto* leader of this whole enterprise," he observed, to the agreement of everyone else. "As such, that makes you the supreme commander of this army. That means all matters of justice and punishment are your ultimate responsibility."

Well, shit.

"But if I'm the head honcho," I blurted, seeing a glimmer of hope, "doesn't that mean I can delegate all the unpleasant tasks?" I knew I wasn't going to win this as soon as everyone else started shaking their heads.

"You need to set a precedent," Eligos informed me. "Only an army that is together for an extended period can have an established judicial system. This force will *hopefully*," he stared meaningfully at me at this point, "not be together long enough to require one."

"Dude, you suck!" I exclaimed, at which everyone else fought to keep a straight face as befitted the occasion. "Fine, I'll do it. But you're all gonna stand right there with me as I pronounce sentence."

"That's fair," allowed Seirina, and the rest nodded in agreement. I sighed in relief that I wouldn't be left standing in front of everyone on my own. Now I had to figure out *how* to actually carry out the sentence.

The best idea I came up with was to draw out all of her energy. That should make it feel like simply falling asleep to her, and I could store the energy in Seren which could then benefit our fight in the future. In that way, she could still contribute in a positive way with her sacrifice. I told the rest of them about my idea and they all approved. Even Eligos looked impressed.

"Your idea once again demonstrates your desire to work for the best interests of everyone," he observed, to the general agreement of the group. I was grateful for their support, since I really wasn't looking forward to being an executioner.

Paladin and Gauvain provided reassurance with their silent presence, and I was comforted to know I had them with me regardless. I felt another pang at the loss of Angelica's support, since I really could have used it right about now.

"Well, standing around in here isn't going to make this any easier," I said, deciding to get this done. It was like anything else unpleasant: The sooner it was done the better, just like the old Band-Aid removal advice.

I turned to walk out, hoping that everyone would follow me, and headed to an open area. I raised a small area by about a foot, so that everyone would be able to see, and stepped up onto it. I turned to face the assembled groups, relieved to see those from the tent had actually followed me as promised.

As we had no torches, I created several orbs of light, as I had in the tent, and set them in the air around us. Then I gestured to Fiona to step forward, pointing to the spot right in front of the dais I'd created. I noticed her genuine distress and had to harden my heart, reminding myself that saving one life couldn't justify the loss of three – especially if those three hadn't needed to be lost.

"We have discovered who leaked our plans and why," I announced to the crowd, magickally enhancing my voice as I had before. "Fiona here told her niece. Her niece, as many of you may be familiar with from your own experiences, had been taken away by the Order and then coerced to work for them.

"Fiona was hoping that by passing the Oder information on our plans, her niece would gain their trust. Then, under less scrutiny, find an opportunity to escape if we failed." At this, there was a general dissatisfied grumbling at Fiona's lack of faith in our chances.

"The alternative," I called out, my enhanced voice rising above the swelling voices and quieting them down again. "The alternative was for our attack to be successful. Her niece would not fight when I offered the chance as I had planned, then would be scanned and found to have been coerced.

"Unfortunately, successful as our attack was, we lost three valiant weres who gave their lives to destroy the Order and free those enslaved by them." Again, angry grumbling arose all around. "Had Fiona simply kept faith, not informing her niece of anything, the young lady would still have had the chance to stand aside.

"The zombie plan could have gone off without the loss of life on either side from fighting. Then only the hardcore members would have been dealt with after scanning." Now I addressed Fiona directly, but I kept my voice enhanced so everyone could hear.

"We have discussed your case and come to a decision. Although your motive was love, your actions were selfish. You showed consideration for only *one* life, while the rest of us were trying to save *multiple* lives.

"Your selfishness directly led to increased risk for those of us participating in the direct assault, while you were safe outside, merely waiting to offer aid to anyone who was injured. You may have assisted in the creation of the scapulars, but they did not prevent the loss of life.

"The families of the weres who died have an absolute right and expectation of justice. We do not want the rest of your family to be the victims of a blood feud or vendetta, as a result of your sole actions.

"Therefore we, reluctantly but necessarily, sentence you to death." Fiona nodded numbly, while her niece sobbed and threw her arms around her aunt's neck. The weres thankfully appeared satisfied, murmuring amongst themselves.

That gave me hope that, however unpleasant these proceedings might be, the families of those lost would be appeased and we wouldn't be left with a were versus Wiccan feud.

"How will you do it?" came the tremulous voice of Fiona's niece.

"I will take her life energy," I replied. "It will be stored, able to benefit us in our ongoing fight against the Order, so even in death Fiona will continue to support us." There was widespread approval at this, to judge from the expressions I could see. Even Fiona looked less distressed at the thought of being able to provide restitution in such a manner.

"How are you any different from the leader of the Order, taking her energy like that?!" stormed Fiona's niece at me. I had thought about this myself and was glad to have the chance to explain my thought process to everyone, so this didn't fester in others' minds.

"I will only be taking her energy," I explained. "Her soul will be untouched, free to move on to the afterlife and watch over you."

At my clarification, Fiona actually smiled in relief and laid her hand on her niece's shoulder.

"I accept the judgement," she said calmly, "and thank you for your explanation and consideration. I wish to express my sorrow to the weres for my actions, most especially for the distress they caused, and ask that they convey my heartfelt apologies to the families of those lost."

She stepped forwards and knelt in front of me. I laid my hand on her head, then transferred her energy in one rush into Seren. Since my right hand was on her head, her niece saw the wings of Isis flare brightly at the rush of power into the stone.

She gasped, putting her hands over her mouth as she understood the significance of the symbol. As a Wiccan she already worshiped Isis, so hopefully the thought of her aunt's energy being associated with the goddess would give her some comfort.

I lowered Fiona's body to the ground gently, then motioned to the other Wiccans to collect it. They could take it and perform any rites they chose for their member. Hopefully Fiona's niece could then take her aunt's place in the coven, so keeping them at full strength.

Glad to be done with this unpleasant duty, I turned away and walked out of the lit area. I sat down on the ground, Gauvain leaning against my face on one side and Paladin lying down on the other to lend their ongoing support.

Chapter 47

I rested my head in my hands, my elbows propped on my knees, and closed my eyes with a sigh. I sensed someone coming up behind me but I was so lost in my own thoughts, I completely ignored them and let G or Pal deal with warning them off.

That was why I was so surprised to feel a hand on my shoulder. I startled hard enough to make Gauvain wobble as I straightened up. I looked up to see Gabby and Izzy, my heart sinking when it wasn't Angie.

"Sorry, we didn't mean to scare you," started Izzy.

"But you looked like you needed a friend," added Gabby.

"You did what you had to do."

"And did it despite not wanting to."

"We could see you didn't enjoy it."

"But you were as gentle and merciful as you could be."

"And you sent a message, both as a leader and a team mate, that there is a line that cannot be crossed without consequence," came a different voice from behind me. I turned to see Eligos approaching, so I patted the twins' hand in thanks and told them I'd catch up with them later.

"You did what was required, performing your duty with decisiveness and consideration for both the accused and her victims," Eligos continued. "I have rarely seen someone step up to a leadership role so effectively. You will do well."

"Thank you," I replied, appreciating the extensive history his opinion was based upon. "Speaking of things going well, I hope everything went

OK with your and Iyrin's assaults?" I lifted my tone at the end to indicate the question, giving him the chance to fill me in on their reports.

"The attacks were flawless," he said, with no small dose of self-satisfaction showing through. I had already noted his arrogance in military matters, no doubt well deserved from his experience, but after what had just happened, it seemed somewhat insensitive. I let it slide as I didn't particularly want to start an argument just then.

"Any useful intel?" I prompted. "Any coerced members now willing to join us?" He shrugged, at which I got a bad feeling. "You *did* give them an opportunity to surrender, right?"

"We weren't quite as fortunate as you," he temporised, at which my sense of foreboding increased. "Not every site was having a birthday party with everyone in attendance."

"Are you telling me," I clarified, standing up and crossing my arms as my irritation increased, "that you ignored my instructions and killed everyone?!"

"It was the simplest, safest, and most expedient method," he informed me, as if that were sufficient reason to kill innocent people. "There were some who stood aside and didn't resist, so those were spared and then scanned. The truly innocent were released, though none seemed inclined to join us. I will admit, I did not appeal to them with the impassioned speech I am sure you employed at Edinburgh."

"At least you paid *some* attention to my directions," I told him, still annoyed that he'd mostly done his own thing. "I'd have thought, as a legendary general, you'd have a better appreciation of the chain of command. We established that *I* am the leader of this undertaking, making me the supreme commander. That means *I* make the decisions, you follow my orders.

"I realise that's an unusual situation for you, but you yourself agreed to me being in charge. It's too late now to address the people, since we can't exactly resurrect those you've killed. Did you at least get names or contact details for those you *did* spare?"

I didn't even have to hear his answer; his face told me all I needed to know. He was already bored with my apparent preoccupation with these mere humans (I'm interpreting here). He clearly just wanted to get this whole thing done so he could be finished with his debt to Lucian.

"Fine," I allowed with a sigh. "Did you find any useful intelligence from their archives?" To my relief, he pulled two flash drives out of his pocket and handed them to me.

"Downloads from each site, including personnel files," he told me. "I have not gone through them, though I believe they include information on who was coerced as well as contact details." This last was delivered in a particularly pointed tone, though I refused to congratulate him for information when he'd been so callous about lives.

"Fine," I said. "I'll go through it in the morning and see if there's anything we can use. Be ready for the assault on Bolton Castle, with your forces, tomorrow evening." He nodded shortly and disappeared, much to my relief. Then I detected a vibration in my link with Iyrin.

Now that he has gone, it said in my mind, *there is something important you need to know.* I looked over, finding it unerringly in the shadows by following the feel of our link. I advised it to wait until everyone else had been sent home, to which it agreed.

I stepped back up onto the dais and informed everyone we'd be mounting our Bolton Castle assault the following evening. I then created portals for each group to head back to their various homes, sending each on their way with my thanks for their help and advice to get some rest.

I informed Sovereign and her obeahs of my actions with the corpses before they left, and they thanked me for dealing with the issue. Since we would have Eligos' forces for the Bolton Castle fight, we wouldn't need them to create more zombies.

Once everyone was sent on their way, I collapsed the dais and reduced the tent back to the blanket and garden canes it had started as. Then with those in hand, I took Seirina, Iyrin, the twins, Angelica, G and Paladin back to Seirina's house.

The twins and Seirina had apparently spoken to Angie at various points since her memory was wiped, so she was at least caught up on what was going on with the fight against the Order. She had initially been a little skittish around the twins, as she had been when they first helped us escape.

Their willingness to let her scan them if she wished, along with the explanations from Seirina and them, had at least reassured her over their trustworthiness again. It also meant she understood she was staying in the safehouse Seirina had provided, so she wasn't worried about coming with us.

Upon our return, Mrs Wilson made a huge fuss over us. She was so relieved to see us all back safely, she hugged each of us in turn – except for Iyrin, obviously. Then she bustled off into the kitchen to make tea, showing her true Yorkshire roots.

We finally made it into the study, whereupon our little skeletal associate climbed up the base of the terrarium and entered directly through the glass. It climbed up the branch to observe us during the conversation. I almost laughed as I noticed Angelica trying to edge away.

I tapped her shoulder, smothering my grin as she jumped. I motioned to one of the chairs by Seirina's desk, so she sat down. She cast another nervous glance at the enclosure with its creepy occupant, so I cleared my throat to draw her attention.

"I'll fill you in later," I told her, motioning towards Iyrin with my eyes. Then I turned to it and ceded it the floor (or branch). "For now, I believe you have something you wanted to share with us Iyrin?"

Well yes, it began, sounding coy. *Still, nothing in life comes for free. We already have our uneasy alliance, so I will provide this now in anticipation of a favour to be repaid at a later date. Keeping within the bounds of our existing agreement, of course.* It tilted its head in that birdlike way it had, waiting for my response.

I sighed heavily and rolled my eyes. I should have expected the creepy little bastard would do something like this, though it wasn't like I had much of a choice. We needed whatever intel it had discovered, so I just raised my hand in acquiescence and motioned for it to proceed.

I didn't want to reveal this in front of Eligos, given his association with Lucian, it told us, using me as its mouthpiece as it had done before. *When I was reading one of the Stygian Blade operatives, I found that she'd been seconded to Bolton Castle around thirty years ago.*

While she was there, she saw Lucian arrive and go into Elrulin's office. He was in there about two hours, then he left.

I was stunned at the revelation. Lucian had told me he and Elrulin had parted ways after Elrulin consumed his first soul and took over the person's body.

"Are you *absolutely certain* of what you saw?" I asked. "Could she have been lying somehow? Showing you a fabricated memory? I don't fancy accusing Lucian and ending up in another fight for no reason, thanks."

When I saw the memory, I delved into it as deeply and intricately as I could, it replied, clearly having anticipated my reaction and proceeded accordingly. *It was a genuine memory, no sign of magickal tampering in any way.*

It abruptly withdrew from my mind and, its bombshell dropped, Iyrin gave another bird-like head tilt before turning and disappearing back into the leafy depths of its refuge.

My head was spinning with the potential overlapping levels of self-interest I was now dealing with. How many lies had I been told? Or had each individual merely told me their slant on the truth, phrasing it to show them in the best light possible?

One thing I knew for certain was Lucian had lied to me about his association with Elrulin. Now I had to wonder what other lies I had been fed. What was the real relationship between Lucian and Eligos? Why had Eligos agreed to help us? How did Iyrin know Lucian, and what was their real dynamic?

My mind flashed back to Alcina's warning of treachery: she had said *those*, not someone, so she had apparently been aware of more than just Fiona.

Seirina and the twins seemed almost as stunned as I was. Angelica merely looked puzzled at our distress. One more thing we'd have to catch her up on.

"Well that wasn't something I expected to hear," Seirina said thoughtfully. "Still, we know so little about Mr B...Given that he admits to being the Devil himself, should we really be surprised at any underhandedness or treachery from him?"

She raised an interesting point, one which I'd been considering myself. Some of his attitudes, such as his blasé approach to Paladin's kind, had already given me cause to doubt his so-called reformation.

"I agree," I replied thoughtfully, "but I don't think we should rush to cut ourselves off from him and his help. We need Eligos and his forces for Bolton and the American site."

Seirina nodded, the twins and Angie joining in. I could see we were going to have a busy day tomorrow, between the two flash drives, catching Angelica up on the situation, and then the attack in the evening. I could also do with checking in with Summer, make sure everything was OK at the shop.

"I think we all need to get some sleep," I said. "We can discuss this more in the morning, preferably with coffee in hand." I scrubbed my face with my hands, the stress of the day catching up with me.

There was general agreement, everyone getting up to head to their rooms. I felt another pang as Angelica headed to one of the guest rooms, rather than joining me as she had the last couple of days.

Life was looking set to change all over again.

Epilogue

I sat on the bed and tried to process how much my world had changed in less than twenty-four hours. My head was quite literally buzzing, to the extent of tinnitus ringing in my left ear. I decided to grab a shower, maybe try to get rid of the dirty feeling brought on by becoming a cold-blooded executioner.

Did you really think you deserved to be happy with a woman like Angelica? I spun to look at Gauvain, only to see he was already snuggled down on his perch with his beak buried in his chest feathers. Pal was curled up on the floor, breathing heavily enough to make the bed covers ruffle where they hung near him.

That's right, dickhead, came the internal voice again. *Just because you've kept busy recently, doesn't change who you really are. You're still the same neurotic, insecure asshole you've always been. The guy who was too useless to set up a decent ward to protect the woman he loves.*

Oh, fuck off, I told myself, recognising the taunting tone of my inner anxiety. I didn't need to hear myself recounting my failures, they were engraved on my memory. I stepped into the shower, desperately trying to scrub myself clean but knowing the stains were on my conscience and my soul.

Finished, I went and sat back on the bed and tried to work out quite what to do next. Would the flash drives give us any information on the Order's American site? Would Angelica's memory be retrievable? Could we recreate our relationship?

I lay back, staring at the ceiling as my mind continued to spin. I finally drifted off, my worries seamlessly slipping into my subconscious to continue taunting me in my dreams.

GAVAN MADDOX WILL RETURN IN

THE ROCK OF
BANISHED SOULS

Acknowledgements

As ever, there are a number of people I need to thank here. Firstly, my wife Melanie for her ongoing support. Without her, I'd probably still be trying to figure out my first book. She also is my long-suffering assistant when it comes to going through the voluminous edits I get sent.

That leads me to Keidi Keating and her team, who struggle through my atrocious grammar and punctuation to knock my story into an acceptable form.

Thirdly, to Tammy and Larry for putting up with my horrendous first draft and suggesting how to turn it into a more coherent story.

Lastly, to all of you my readers. Thank you for sticking with me and Gavan through our adventures. Don't worry, there's more to come…

www.ingramcontent.com/pod-product-compliance
Lightning Source LLC
Chambersburg PA
CBHW020817260626
47169CB00003B/711